Rhyme Reason and Repartee

on Life, Romance & Religion

Bob and Stef,
I hope you will
enjoy reading and pondering some
of Uncle Jim's prose and poetry!
Merry Christmas
2022
with love,
Mom B.

James E Foy

ISBN: 9798352078617
Imprint: Independently published

DEDICATION

To Nancy Lee Foy, the mother of our children.

To our amazing daughters:
Jenni Hetrick, Wendi Green, Debbi Coder

CONTENTS

ACKNOWLEDGMENTS

Nancy, Jenni, Wendi, & Debbi
who challenged me over the years to write.

Gatlin Kate James cover design.

Cover Illustration by Atenais.

Greg Mann sheet music pages design.

Holly Virden whose consultations and instructions were so helpful.

Sherry Remy, Karon Hawkins, Wendi Green, Cooper Green
who advised me on the music.

David Nicholas, Bob Plunk, Connie Ferch Blood and
other friends who encouraged me.

My brother and six sisters all of whom challenged and
cheered me on to produce this book.

James E Foy

FOREWARD

Light is both visible and invisible.

We see light and do not see light. There are unseen light waves.
We see *through* ubiquitous light but do not usually focus *on* light as discernible. We see rays, or beams, of light thrusting through clouds; yet if that light beam shines directly in our eye, it will blind us temporarily or permanently. We are warned: Don't stare at the sun, even in an eclipse.

We see because of light, and in the absence of light cannot see.
Light is one, a unity; and light is a spectrum: a multiplicity of bands and colors, aka God's rainbow.

Light is described as both particle and wave. Light is a mixture of both electricity and magnetism that can travel in a vacuum.
Light from the sun enables all growth and energy. No light, no life.

A prism refracts white (or clear) light into all the colors that exit in pure or blended form. The prism doesn't create the colors, it reveals the colors. All of us have a prism through which we see everything: a worldview. We should be wise in developing our worldview. Live in the light, enjoy the light, be true to the Light.

Rhyme Reason & Repartee sheds light on the experiences, beauty, and facets of life, romance, and religion. That's where we all live. Some of these poems you may wish to read over and over again at certain events or occurrences.

James E Foy

INTRODUCTION

Fun and profitable. This book will stimulate enjoyment and thought in areas of Life in general, Romance, and Religion. All vigorous topics. I love Life; am a Romantic; and take Religion seriously. That opens many wavelengths for heady Repartee. I trust we will find harmony, laughter, and common ideas as you read. Let's begin, however, with this stipulation: It's understood that everything I write will be said with my slant to it. Similarly, everything you read will be heard with your slant to it. We may look through a different prism. Where we do not find harmony, I trust we will skip discord, and instead, employ consideration of the other point of view, openness to the possibility that the other view has value, and then perhaps to discussion of the reasons each of us has our view. There's sufficient material herein to expose ideas that rouse differing opinions, emotions, and reasons. Isn't that one purpose to read a book? What *are* the foundations for our thoughts, beliefs, and pursuits in regard to Life in general, Romance, and   Religion?

Nothing herein is a claim that I've achieved any level of complacency, but rather, what I've written is a prayer, a goal, to be a person who is more loving, understanding, more giving and forgiving in my own life even as I make the same appeal to others.

The fact that many of my thoughts are put in RHYME does not diminish the seriousness of thoughts expressed. There is REASONing behind each page of this book which I hope will be discovered and fairly contemplated. Perhaps the ideas expressed could stimulate conversation — REPARTEE. Perhaps even some new ways of thinking will be introduced. Some new whys or a different approach to certain aspects of life. Maybe a fresh enjoyment: fun together with profitability. I trust it will be beautiful to you, like light through a prism.

Here is one Example of a thought refracted through a prism:

Love has a *Spectrum*.
The *Beauty* of Love: Love is the beat of the heart, the breath of the soul,
the joy of the mind.
The *Vulnerability* of Love: The breaking of the heart, the vacuum
in the soul, the wounding of the mind.
The *Complexity* of Love: Convolutes the heart, bewilders the soul,
frustrates the mind.
The *Reciprocation* of Love: Expands the heart, overflows the soul,
enchants the mind.

There is a child's love of a parent, a parent's love for a child, love between friends, love between a pet and owner, God's love for us and our love for God, patriotic love of Country, and romantic love all highlighted in these pages.

There are items herein that thinkers ponder. Others that children enjoy. You'll find personal perspective and information in this book because we all have similar experiences and circumstances in our lives. Therefore, I believe we can enjoy and benefit from real-life happenings of other people. If we know each other, you might be in this book incognito, not in an obvious way. Most of my writings come from interactions and observations of real people. Some coincidental combination of you and others could be herein. My hope is that you will be caught up in this book to the point that you want to share it with others for their enjoyment of the Rhyme Reason & Repartee.

SECTIONS of this Book
Getting Started: sets the stage
On Life in general
On Romance
On Religion
Music:
eight (8) original songs
with melody, lyrics, chords

SECTION ONE

1 GETTING STARTED

UNBIASED EYE
Our Slanted View is Innate

Though noble the effort, valiant the try,
No one can see with an unbiased eye.
Though listening intently to words that are said,
There's no ascertaining the other man's head.

Though wearing their shoes and walking their street,
No one can feel that man's steps in his feet.
Though wisdom, experience, and insight can start,
No one plumbs fully intents of that heart.

Everyone's soul hosts their core point of view.
Everyone's mind has lists they eschew.
Everyone's mouth speaks forth from their past.
Everyone's judging has verdicts precast.

Whenever our eyes see the very same view
There's no guarantee I see as do you.
Our total experiences, varied and vast,
Create different frames in which views are cast.

It's not that it's bad, yet, for everyone's good,
Let's recognize *why* we use the word "should".
Our biases color all that we see,
All that we read. Found easily in me.

No one can hold a neutral position.
And changing one's mind – a rare transition.
Let us therefore be cautious, slower to wrath,
And quicker to seek the meek, humble path.

What's thought to be clear can be an illusion,
And, wrongly construed, tends to delusion.
Make this the resolve that's here driven home:
It's better to pass than to cast the false stone.

Yet, Reality reigns, factual Truth is enthroned.
Let's seek the Wisdom that keeps our minds honed.
Wisdom Eternal as our beacon of Light.
Trust the Ultimate Standard, not just deepen the night.

What's this?

DO YOU KNOW what you are seeing?
A WHY KNOT?
WHY NOT enjoy this book?

Shy Poet

People May Not Be What They Seem

Do you know that there are people not adept at social graces?
People quite uncomfortable among a bunch of faces?
Could be friends; could be strangers; or be those you see at church.
Could be someone thought unfriendly, or set smugly on a perch.

Do you know that these are people who in fact are interesting
if drawn in conversation about several serious things.
Common folks who think their true experiences in life
Would bore most any others, so they seldom risk a try.

They might be thought as snobs who feel too high to interact.
They might be thought eccentric, or some esoteric quack.
Might be thought a dullard: can't put two thoughts together.
It's likely a shy poet craving birds of feather.

Typically, the thought of groups is not their game or comfort zone.
Usually, they're less distressed connecting one on one.
Normally, when found alone with someone beyond trivial,
 The stuck-up oaf can be revealed as someone quite convivial.

You extroverts have all the couth – all of the advantage.
So confident you work a room. Could you expand your forage?
Would you employ your empathy — give introverts a chance?
When music plays, and they're alone, risk snagging one to dance.

No Easy Way

You cannot adventure unless you pursue the unknown.
You will not find boldness unless you push on alone.
You won't reach new heights unless you climb past your exhaustion.
You cannot find love until you risk finding rejection.

A Mimic or Sage

Don't Put It Off

Much unsung poetry, never yet writ,
Awaits the poet imagining it.
It's there in the ether, in quiet, unlipped,
Never composed in score or in script.

So many conquests of life still unmet.
So many goals not yet even set.
Perhaps there are promises yet to be kept.
Perhaps tears of empathy yet to be wept.

Too many "Love Yous" have never been said.
Too many "Sorrys" choked back and left dead.
Too many hugs unbirthed from arms spread.
Too many prayers unkneeled at the bed.

Expressions of gratitude not given space.
Actions of courtesy lost without trace.
Withholding forgiveness just to save face.
Won't risk getting hurt by extending real grace.

Then comes a sickness or advancing age.
We realize that time may be short on life's stage.
Played too long the mimic and too late the sage
Till no time remains to an Everest engage.

Heed to the message in this little verse
Since life can only get better or worse.
Now! say, be, and do what must be traversed
To attain to the plaudit and not to the curse.

Establishing Perspective

Let's reason together. Seeing a rainbow is dependent upon one's point of view in relation to rain & sun. If one doesn't see the rainbow, that does not prove the bow doesn't exist, nor does it prove that those who claim to see a rainbow are in error. It may demonstrate that one is viewing from a different perspective — some may not see the rainbow because from their position it cannot be seen.

Of course, if one is color blind, you do not see the colorful rainbow. That's not a fault, it's an unfortunate reality. But one's not seeing reality as it *is* does not make reality an illusion to those who see it in full color.

Seeing a mirage is a real vision. But the mirage is not real. Experiencing an actual vision does not make the vision actually true. One cannot drink from a Mirage to quench their thirst. One can tell us how beautiful is the mirage, but don't expect us to put on our swim suits. If one genuinely believes the mirage itself is reality and true, then they have a serious issue. It's called delusion. If one enjoys the illusion, enjoy; but other folks should not pretend they believe that delusion. Other folks who truly want the best for you will seek to enable you to distinguish between a true lake and a seeming-lake caused by glimmering heat waves. Meanwhile, don't try to compel others to drink from, or swim in, one's imagination — even if there are others who do see the same mirage. It is seeable because there is a rational cause for it. Rational people know a mirage is a mirage. The reality of the cause does not make the mirage a reality.

Reflections are also interesting. There is truth and fiction involved. The object is real while, simultaneously, the reflection is surreal. That's why magicians easily fool people using mirrors. They make things credibly seem to appear and disappear. One can enjoy the trick, but don't try to pull rabbits from thin air for the meal today, though it might be a successful diet plan. Many people are fooled today by tricksters.

Rhyme Reason and Repartee probably contains views that you agree with and you dispute. That's expected. It also may create interest or curiosity. We can both be in a quest for truth and reality, yet not be in the respective places to both see the rainbow at the same time or with the same intensity.

Seeing at all is totally dependent on the light. Sight requires light. Where we stand in relationship to light impacts our sight. If one is in the light, they'll see this allegory, and appreciate or respect other points of view. This respect is a good starting place

Nothing that I write should be taken to mean that I think I've reached some kind of advanced state or notable achievement in life. Anything that could be understood, or rather misunderstood, to sound like that should be taken as a prayer or as a desire rather than as an alleged accomplishment. I'm a pilgrim on a journey with some understanding of what the journey is intended to look like because I've read those who've gone before me, and I've watched wise folks within my field of vision. Moreover, I've read intently the Manual, the Bible. One judge of the validity of my viewpoint is the results produced in my own children and in the family in which I grew up – my parents and siblings. Examine the fruit hanging on the family tree. Not perfect, but not discards. We have chosen repentance, forgiveness, and overcoming rather than defeat. Most are attractive, delicious, and nutritious fruit.

I hope I've learned in life both from correct decisions and from mistakes. I've written about the good choices and the mistakes with their lessons, and about my understanding of the goals. It is said in humor that people want wisdom to not make mistakes, but such wisdom comes from someone making mistakes.

Be willing to:

Try again.
Take a reasonable risk.
Consider a change.
Listen to counsel but think for yourself.
Follow the good example.
Start — take a step.
Put in consistent effort sufficient to
enable achieving the goal.

CONFESSION

There was a time I felt so very strong,
To always seek the right and shun the wrong.
I thought that I could walk among the best,
And come out near the top of any test.
But now with wiser eyes I see the frailty of this man,
Know it's only by the strength of God if I should stand.
And only by His grace could I get through,
So, humbly, Lord, I lift my voice to you.

> In every way I need You, this one thing I know,
> Please help me, keep me, show me how to go.
> In every way I need You, this one thing I know,
> Lord, guide me, teach me, living here below.

There was a time I felt so very wise,
Living seemed so simple in my eyes.
I even knew how other folks should live,
With good advice and insights I could give.
But now I understand the limitations of my mind,
And answer to a different point of view more kind.
And when I realize that I was wrong,
To humbly ask forgiveness in this song.

> In every way I need You, this one thing I know,
> Lord, help me, keep me, show me what to do.
> In every way I need You, this one thing I know,
> Forgive me, guide me, on the path with You.

(music for this song is in the Music section)

7

SOME FIND THE MAGIC

It has been said, and worth saying again,
    "This life is about what you make it."
There are people that know, who swear you can go
    In this life, wherever you take it.

There are folks just as fine, who whimper and whine,
    Who trudge through life moaning and crying,
Who don't see the good or the joy that they could,
    Being busy degrading, maligning.

There are folks in this city who could ask for pity,
    Who could justify anger and hate;
But instead, they find joy helping others employ
    The tools that will overcome fate.

Yes, some go through life reinforcing the strife,
    Fixed on seeking and wailing the tragic.
In this city I find a much wiser kind
    Who search out, and pass on, the magic.

INVEST — *in Life*
ENDURE — *in Faith*
REJOICE — *in Hope*
FORGIVE — *in Grace*
COMMIT — *in Love*
TRUST – *in Truth*
LIVE – *in Honor*

You're My Inspiration

I hope you don't fret when you connect the dots.
I hope you don't mind that you inspired my thoughts.
That by thinking back or by dreaming ahead,
The words that I wrote from the thoughts in my head
Were compelled, or inspired, by concepts of you.
Winsome daydreams, unfounded, yet somehow thought true.
I hope you find pleasure in the power you've got
To enthrall my mind and capture my thoughts.
And force me so meekly to put down in words
More than I otherwise could, perhaps should.

There is truth basic in all Fantasy.
There is something mystic in Reality.

How does one measure the depth those two reach?
When you've stood at the surf of some beautiful beach,
Did you stick in your toe to test the water?
Let's each risk a toe in this innocent barter.
If we discover the water is fine and warm,
We'll wade up to the knee without alarm.
We may or may not get into the swim.
That larger decision's not made on a whim.
Now, since we've imagined to this extent,
Why not bring to an end bewilderment?

I insert for you this miniature song
To inspire us as we go along:

Come take my arm and walk with me.
Walk and see what we shall see.
We need but walk a little while
To catch the meaning of your smile.

A longer walk, we both concur,
To grasp the context of our words.
One can't discover in a day

The biases in things we say.

Walk long enough to sit a spell
And see if laughter suits us well.
Longer still to make mistakes
Then see the form forgiveness takes.

We must walk on, further still,
To know the bent of both our wills:
Hurtful or considerate,
Compromise or obstinate.

Around that bend into the shade
A child is selling lemonade.
We'll see how each of us responds
To help a working child along.

In some small park, you'll sit a swing.
Jump out. Almost a childish thing.
Oh, to be a child again
And do such things that mem'ries spin.

Walk past the little country chapel:
Discuss the garden and the apple,
And why we each so need a savior,
How he impacts our own behavior.

We're nearly back to where we started.
Serious insights were imparted.
I guess we went a country mile
But never did outpace your smile.

I felt your hand slip down my arm
And clasp my hand without alarm.
Felt comfortable. And I must say
I somehow feel it still, today.

Along the way two hearts revealed
What now is by two souls concealed.
And should this good walk be our last,
How precious was the time we passed.

But if we never share the trail
Would we find our tales to tell?
We'll never know the why or when,
Or mysteries that might have been.

But if we gift a day or three
To delve the complex you and me,
At least we'll know within our plight
Steps to avoid or of delight.

Well, my little song is sung
But its import not yet done.

Regardless how the outcome is decided,
We'll have memories of when our lives collided.
Whether time together is broad or is slim,
We'll both fondly remember that walk back when.

In a real sense, we'll be walking together
as you read Rhyme Reason and Repartee.
That reality inspired my book.

One Unique Day

There is a day, a specific date, that can be seen as the highlight of your life regardless of how young or old you are. It's an ordinary day and an extraordinary day. Here are clues to help identify that day. 1. What was the best day of your life? 2. When did you come closest to death?

People will search their past for special days to relive the best day of their life. Maybe going through old photographs or discussing memories with friends and family. But finding the best day of a life is not difficult.

People tell stories about close calls with death — "I came so close to death!" "I was never so near dying as that day." Perhaps referring to an accident or serious illness.

Consider a different point of view. A view that generates gratitude and awareness. 1. *Today*, this very day, is the best day of your life. You reached this date alive. Be thankful. Celebrate.

2. *Today* is the closest you've ever been to death. Be aware. Be prepared. Don't procrastinate.

In such a positive-and-negative reality, *today* is a truly momentous, significant day in your life. Live it well, wisely, and timely.

That doesn't mean be dour or gloomy. Laughter is both medicinal and fun. A high spirit raises awareness and alertness. Have your coffee, ice cream, vitamins and apple cider vinegar. See your family. Exercise. Talk to God, listen to God. Make plans. Enjoy and use well this day. It's the best day of your life, and it's the closest you've ever been to your last day. Live as if there's no tomorrow — (*pause*) here on earth.

Acknowledgment: I realize there are exceptions. There are people literally praying to die today because their condition is dire. I understand that; I empathize with that reality and do not mean to hurt anyone with what I said above. My comments here go to those not caught in such a difficult situation. If you are hurting, may you experience God's presence.

SECTION TWO

2 RRR ON LIFE

DECISIONS

He was a wise old man who liked to whittle in his yard.
If you stopped to talk a spell, he would listen hard.
He'd tell old-fashioned stories while he carved a wooden top.
The kids liked most his riddles, and learned to call him Pops.

The kids would bring him puzzlers. Pops always worked them out.
They tried and tried to stump him. Pops was smart without a doubt.
Pops sharpened knives, would fix your bike, adjust your roller skates,
If you'd listen to his stories starting, "When I was your age..."

One day the leader of the boys just happened on some luck.
The night before, with wind and hail, a vicious storm had struck.
There before him on the ground, tossed down by the wind,
Was a naked baby bird, mouth open, stretching up to him.

He took the baby bird in hand and looked to find its nest.
But then a riddle hit him. This riddle was the best.
He got his friends together and shared with them his thoughts.
This riddle was impossible. This time they would stump Pops.

He said, "I'll take this baby bird, and hold it in my fist.
Behind my back where Pops can't see, I'll handle it like this.

I'll ask old Pops if baby birds could fall, as this one did,
From way up in a tree top, and hit the ground, and live.

"If Pops should say the bird would die, I'll show this bird alive.
But if he says the bird would live, I'll squeeze, and it will die.
No matter what he answers, we've got him this time sure."
The boys ran off to find old Pops, with that tiny bird.

They found him in his garden. The leader said, "Pops, hey.
We've got a question for you. We'll stump you sure today.
Behind my back I'm holding a baby bird I found.
It fell out of its bird nest about twelve feet to the ground.

"Would falling kill a naked bird, or could the bird survive.
In my hand I've got it. Is it dead, or is it live?"
The boys grinned at each other, they knew Pops couldn't win.
The leader kind of giggled as he looked at Pops again.

Pops took his time, looked at the boys, and studied every face.
The boys could feel their hearts beat. A quiet gripped the place.
Pops scrutinized the leader, his eyes pierced him clear through,
Pops said, "It's in your hand; the choice is up to you."

We, each one, face decisions. Will I do this or that?
Will I take the lower road or brave the higher path?
We can't rely on others to tell us what to do.
Wisdom says, "It's in your hand; the choice is up to you."

adapted from an old story

Forgiveness Boomerangs

Forgiveness, like the blowing wind, comes again, and then again.
Forgiveness, as the warming sun, always has the vic'try won.

Even though the one forgiven may not know (the act was hidden),
Forgiveness is an act of giving that heals the one who is forgiving.

Contrasted is the act of hate that grinds the soul and has no sate:
For vengeful hearts are overcome, their joy and peace are overrun.

Like a target beyond range that wastes the shells — the mark unscathed,
The pistol's barrel glows red hot & burns the hand that missed the shot.

Seething thoughts never touch the one they're meant to scorch & crush
But sear instead the harb'ring mind & block the source of gold refined.

Forgiveness mollifies, abates, soothes the wound that irritates.
Excuses not the foisted wrong, but does defuse ignited bombs.

Forgiveness makes one stand in awe to wonder at its changeless law:
Forgiveness, as a mystic river, mostly heals the sincere giver.

The evidence of charity
Is Not
what we say we intend
But
what we actually extend.

FORGIVENESS
One Hand Clapping

Through unforgiveness, you weld to your soul
a chain that you claim is forged and held by another.
Through forgiveness, you break that chain, and discover that
it was you yourself who, adamantly, had held both ends.

Forgiveness benefits the forgiver.
Forgiveness brings release, relief, comfort and freedom.

Forgiveness or Unforgiveness
may not impact the other person one way or the other.
Chronic acid reflux in A does not produce heartburn in B —
but it may produce ulcers in A.

Why not Forgive? Let go, to receive peace with new life.
Forgiveness: It *is* one hand clapping.

BEFRIEND WEAKNESS
BE FRIENDS WITH STRENGTH

LOVE — FORGIVE

Love is the most powerful and perfect relationship that humans can express. Forgiveness is right next to it, and interconnected.

Humans are most godlike when they love and forgive. These are the two forces, the two connections, that bond and heal humans. Love and forgive! No one could express love with the fullness and selflessness as God's love. But one is able by choice and in the strength of the Holy Spirit to forgive everyone who has sinned against them — everyone. Such forgiveness is possible for a Christian.

I speak from experience. I may be, among people alive today, a most undeservedly loved and forgiven person. I have experienced, received, grace beyond measure — beyond understanding — by those closest to me, especially family and friends. I have also experienced the joy and release of forgiving others. Forgiveness is divine medicine. It is supernatural. It's enabled by the Spirit of God. It is beautiful.

As much as God enables you and me, LOVE & FORGIVE. These produce on earth the abundant life God provides within an individual, and within a relationship. The Peace of God beyond understanding.

Jesus set the example his entire life. In teaching, Jesus said: "Greater love has no one than to lay down his life for a friend." The Bible says: "God (in Jesus) demonstrated his love for us in that while we were still sinners Christ died for us." Jesus said: "God loved the world to the degree that he sent his One and only Son so that whoever believes in him should not perish but have everlasting life." Jesus said of his executioners: "Father, forgive them, they don't know what they do".

I have received the genuine forgiveness of God, spouse, family, and friends. I'll share those personal, emotional, far-reaching, reciprocal experiences at a later time. I've also personally given sincere forgiveness to others. I highly recommend that we Love and Forgive.

THE SPECTRUM of LOVE

Beauty *of Love*

Love is the beat of the heart,
the breath of the soul,
the joy of the mind.
> in Harmonic relationship

Vulnerability *of Love*

The breaking of the heart,
the vacuum in the soul,
the wounding of the mind.
> in Discordant relationship

Complexity *of Love*

Convolutes the heart
Bewilders the soul
Frustrates the mind
> in Tuning relationship

Reciprocation *of love*

Expands the heart
Overflows the soul
Enchants the mind
> in Symphonic relationship

Squandered Love

To *not* be loved is a tragedy.
To *be* loved and not recognize it is double tragedy.
To *reject* love may sometimes be a necessity.
To *abandon* true love is a multiplied catastrophe.
Love thoughtlessly squandered is a tragic waste.

LET ME KNOW YOU

Let me know what your needs are, so I like you can perceive them.
Let me know what your stresses are, so that I might help you relieve them.
Let me know your concerns, to understand why you conceive them.
Let me know what your feelings are, so I won't unknowingly grieve them.

Let me know what your goals are. As a team we can work to achieve them.
Let me know what your dreams are, that together we might believe them.
Let me know what your hopes are, so I, too, can hope you receive them.
Let me know what your pleasures are, so in unison we can perform them.

Let me know your discouragements, so jointly we can transform them.
Let me know what you're proud of, so I consciously can adorn them.
Let me know your shortcomings. Humbly, I'll with you reform them.
Let me know your hurts, so we both can help rid what has torn them.

Let me know what your dislikes are. I'll put your likes before them.
Let me know what your priorities are, so I can similarly score them.
Let me know what your favorites are, that I may arrange to encore them.
Let me know what your fears are, so that, callously, I won't ignore them.

Let me know your enjoyments, so that adversely I will not bore them.
Let me know your inferiorities, so love can assist to restore them.
Let me know your daydreams, so as children we might explore them.
Let me know what your hates are, so I, like you, can abhor them.
Let me know your loves, that together we might adore them.
Let me know your prayers, that agreed we might implore them.

Yes, trust me enough, my love – Let Me Know You.

Be Pragmatic not Dramatic
Blame is not helpful.
Hate is not healthful.
Vengeance is not beneficial.

POWER OF TWO

A smile is more worthwhile if two will wear it.
A hug can't be a hug unless two share it.
A care can lose its scare if two will bear it.
A friendship cannot mend till two repair it.
A prayer's more potent there if two will air it.
A dance — harmonic trance — when two will flair it.
A dream's a better scheme if two will snare it.
A promise is its best when two declare it.
And Love is highest love when two will dare it.

In that poem, I used the word "dare" in connection to love because not all relationships work, and because the ones who can hurt you the most are those you love. Relationships are like tennis: They must involve frequent serving and constant stroking – on both sides. *Especially* love relationships. As in tennis, if all you have is love, that's not enough. You start with love but must add quality serving and stroking by both partners. Daily serving and stroking. Practiced serving and stroking. Without these, you cannot win. Relationships are risky and worth daring.

Forgiveness occurs when guilt and grace meet.
Forgiveness occurs when confession is met with compassion.
Eternal Forgiveness occurs when a penitent accepts God's pardon.

I'M GOING HOME

The little lad had run away as small boys sometimes do.
He just had to get away from rules and chores and school.
On the trek he found a dog to share his pain and food.
But the sunset turned dark, and the dog would bark.
The boy said to the dog, "This running away isn't good."

> "You should see what I've got at home!
> More than I ever dreamed of – why would I roam?
> I'm going to the best love anyone's ever known.
> There's nothing to keep me here. Now I see it clear.
> I'm making my way straight home. I'm going home."

He wed his college sweetheart with the customary flare.
And the Tempter threw at him all the usual snares:
Sultry beauty, lovely eyes, young and comely wares.
There's excitement in lust's song, but guilt is what lasts long.
He repeated to the temptress and her fleshly dares:

> "You should see what I've got at home!
> More than I ever dreamed of – why would I roam?
> I'm going to the best love anyone's ever known.
> There's nothing to keep me here. Now I see it clear.
> I'm making my way straight home. I'm going home."

He lay upon his death bed. Machines kept him alive.
His friends and family coaxed him, "If you will only try,
You can beat this illness. Don't let go and die."
He answered from his heart through lips just barely apart,
"I'm on my way to Glory, and here's the reason why."

> "You should see what I've got at home!
> More than I ever dreamed of – why would I roam?
> I'm going to the best love anyone's ever known.
> There's nothing to keep me here. Now I see it clear.
> I'm making my way straight home. I'm going home."

REALITY

By chance, a friend sat on a tack, and, traumatized by pain,
Cried, "Tell me how to end this hurt. I'm soon to go insane."

"Sit very still," an expert said. "Don't agitate. Try humming.
If you don't irritate the point, the nerves will begin numbing."

A high-priced doctor shamelessly said, "Mask the pain with drugs.
Watch out for harmful side effects – this stuff kills beasts & bugs."

A guru said, "Just meditate, and chant this mantra oddly.
The pain will focus, crystallize, and pass out of your body."

A therapist: "This fearsome pain, beyond your comprehension,
Can be defeated only if you heed my healing session."

A hypnotist said, "Now close your eyes and do just as I say.
With mind control you'll let it go. The pain will melt away."

A preacher said, "I'll pray for you. We'll get a prayer chain going.
As this pain is teaching you: your character is growing."

A charismatic mystic said, "You really have no pain.
Whatever pain you think you have is only in your brain."

Internalize, hypothesize, spiritualize, cauterize the fact.
This answer is more down to earth: STAND UP. Get off the tack.

Choose Light

A definition of darkness is the absence of light. It's interesting that light is not defined as the absence of darkness. The fact is, darkness is nothing and light is something. There are various light waves. There are no dark waves. There are different degrees of light, therefore different degrees of darkness. But it is the light that determines the degree of darkness. Light can, and does, instantly eliminate as much darkness as desired. If you haven't got the light, you have nothing. You don't actually *have* dark, you just do not have *light*, or as much light. That's one reason you cannot project darkness into light, but you can shine light into darkness. To get darkness, you must block, reduce, reject light. It's light you must ultimately deal with, not darkness. And if the light is absolute, as is God, then whenever God chooses, **all** darkness goes.

The Bible uses light as an allegory. It says that humans reject light, turn away from the light, even try to destroy light because they choose to do dark deeds. People love darkness more than light because their deeds are evil. Today, in America and globally, many people are turning away from light, even hating light. Caution: Don't base your choices on majority rule. Don't base your choices on dark desires. Base choices on the rule of light. If people do not prefer light to darkness, do **not** emulate those people. If people prefer light, consider walking in the light with them.

Evil people call darkness light with such audacity that gullible people believe them. Sadly, there are many deceived people in the world today. Many. Their numbers and their prominence overpower otherwise reasonable thinkers. Don't be deluded or intimidated. Choose true, proven light.

EVER-NEW

Like Holland flowers in spring, or Painted Bunting on wing,
A beauty so rare cannot be compared.
Like a peacock come courting, or a Bambi cavorting,
Celtic voices in song: the thrill never gone.

The sun bursting through clouds: regal flair, bold and loud
In a glorious array, haunts my mind to this day.
Those sunbeams through clouds that raged forth so proud
And shone in our faces, etched magical traces.

Shone into the plane, while the heat of their flame
Singed the hair on my head. Thoughts of Sinai — its dread.
The shafts white and gold thrusting brilliant and bold,
Both serene and divine, overpowering yet kind.

Only seen now and then, when glimpsed yet again,
That mighty a view — each glance ever-new.
When comes such brief sight, its brutal delight
Will take breath away: ardent rush on display.

That vision when gone will yet linger on,
The image impressed and indelibly set.
Now, persistent the thought - and how could it not -
Seeks to glimpse and renew the joy of that view.
That spectacular view.

Ever-New was first written years ago after a small plane ride over the Aleutian Islands when the sun burst through clouds with unimaginable force, penetrating rays, and stunning beauty. I was not able to get a photo, but I wrote this poem to memorialize it. I always thrill to see similar, even if lesser, views of strong sunbeams piercing the clouds.
I took this photo of the sun rising over Mount Sinai: not impressive other than location.

Grief, Love, Hope

Many of us have experienced and endured the loss of a spouse, a child, a sibling, a relative, or a close friend. When a Loved One leaves this world, leaves us behind, we experience unfamiliar aspects of grief, love, and hope. Intense emotions that descend upon us as a storm cloud.

Sometimes each of these will be experienced separately: consumed by GRIEF, for example, that expels other emotions. Almost like being in the grip of a monstrous boa constrictor depriving you of oxygen. Grief that is a weight heavier than you can carry. Grief that threatens to be your constant companion from now on as the once familiar has instantly become unfamiliar and accompanied with indescribable emptiness and loss. Grief under which you cry out: "I can't do this". In one sense, grief at a time of personal loss is a cryptic expression of affection.

Grief is not bad — in truth it can be good because it enables release. A release that is necessary for one's well-being. As the release (that may be thought of as unattainable) is experienced, the grief will gradually subside. Grief, natural and reasonable grief, is not to be rejected, denied, or quenched. On the other hand, one need not exaggerate or wallow in grief. Grief probably will not totally evaporate, but will accomplish its vital purpose and retreat into the background.

Meanwhile, even in the throes of grief, sometimes you'll be flooded by LOVE: the warmth of the physical presence now absent; overwhelmed by the closeness that was known; the vivid, palpable re-living of deep affection and desire; the reality that this person cannot be replaced; the awareness that your loved one is still present in a new and mystical, incomprehensible manner. Love that defies description. Love that enables you to carry on. Love that encourages you to accept the new normal. Love that strengthens you. Love that will always remain but allows you to enjoy new relationships.

Moreover, there is HOPE. And sometimes this hope drives out all other awareness. It may be accompanied by physical sensations like a tingle in the spine, a tightening of the solar plexus, even the proverbial goose bumps. Though that will be rare, it is a beautiful sensation. This hope, in its highest and most precious assurance, is reserved for those who know the resurrected Jesus, and therefore have cause to anticipate a reunion with their loved one. A reunion that will enable a more perfect, more satisfying, and more intimate relationship with the loved one than could ever be realized on earth. (Regardless of what type that earthly relationship was.) This can bring a joy beyond comprehension or expression. Hope based in Jesus Christ is a beautiful reality.

Of course, after losing a loved one, all three of these emotions may come and go, increase or decrease, together rather than distinctly. In various combinations and intensities. The sorrow of GRIEF is bearable because of the certainty of our HOPE. And LOVE will prevail throughout eternity for those reborn into God's family.

Grief is a cry of the heart, a sigh of the soul, a despair of the mind.
Love is the beat of the heart, the breath of the soul, the joy of the mind.
Hope is the grasp of the heart, the comfort of the soul, the resilience of the mind.

I hope these thoughts bring comfort to others as they have to me.

Don't fear what lies beyond the bend.

MY FRIEND

I've heard this story told of child in war-wrecked land.
Just after terrible shelling: imagine if you can.
Defending GI's found a group of orphaned children hurt;
And one small girl was dying, lying in the dirt.

Only blood could save her, if the girl were going to live.
No GI matched her blood type – so they just couldn't give.
No GI spoke the language to convey just what they'd like,
But using signs, they tested children; and several had her type.

With awkward words and signals, they asked the orphans' help.
The GI's signed they didn't have the kind to give themselves.
To save this girl, would one of them quickly give their blood?
The children watched each other to see if someone would.

None in the room seemed willing. The girl would surely die.
But then a small boy raised his hand, apprehension in his eyes.
He got up on the table, beside the girl he'd save.
Of all the wide-eyed children, he only was this brave.

The needle went into his arm, the flow of life began.
The medic heard him grind his teeth; saw his tight-clenched hands.
He tried to ask the little boy if he were feeling pain.
The boy said "No." But something wrong was causing undue strain.

The boy then raised his free hand and covered up his eyes.
The medic thought he might have heard him utter a faint cry.
The cry was quickly stifled as the small child bit his lip.
His hand upon his face was clutched into a desperate grip.

If the medic could just talk to him, for something was not right.
The orphans' teacher, come to help, saw the young lad's fright.
She took his hand, and told the boy that it would soon be over.
Then bent her head and kissed him because of what he told her.

Continuing to comfort him, her hand upon his shoulder,
She told the lad that never in the world had anyone been bolder.
She whispered to the medics, "This one's brave all right!
He thought you needed all his blood – he'd volunteered his life."

"Now I understand his agony." The medic's eyes were blurred.

"Why would someone do that?! Why would he die for her?"
The teacher asked the little boy; and then she spoke again.
"He gave this simple answer: 'Because she is my friend'."

(adapted from a war story)

Joy Bubbling Over

I never met Miss Lydia till she had left this earth.
Instantly I saw her heart was filled with joy and mirth.
A burst of spontaneity, the real thing not an act.
As if a fragrance bloomed inside that couldn't be held back.

All she did was let it out: allow God's love to flow.
A radiance upon her face made all those present know
That she had been with Jesus, and it couldn't help but show.
There is no reason to resist when living waters flow.

Immediately, I realized Miss Lydia has not died:
Her ministry and memory are very much alive.
Her personal locality has moved to heaven above,
While friends and family, waiting here, still feel her gifts and love.

What is it births a Lydia? What builds joy unrestrained?
It's walking with the living God and mirroring his name.
It's daily faith in Jesus Christ, and yielding to his Spirit.
It's peace of God just spilling out where others see and hear it.

YOU CAN FLY
Edie the Eagle

Edie Eagle was young, and usually alone, high in her nest of twigs.
She was kept fed by her huge mom and dad, but Edie was not very big.
Her feathers were drab, her balance was bad, she was hungry all of the time.
And always obsessed that this prison nest, was keeping her closely confined.

Edie was told that eagles are bold and easily can soar through space.
But she didn't know about soaring, and so was stuck in this horrible place.
She was impressed by a worm in the nest that could leave whenever it wanted.
Could she be a worm, she'd hold the bark firm and crawl from the nest undaunted.

Though equipped for the sky and destined to fly, an eagle who thinks like a worm
Will forfeit it all, to grovel and crawl, and achieve only what she'll affirm.
Winds left her afraid, even though she was made to harness the currents for power.
For storms and hard times can focus our lives and lift us to our finest hour.

Edie stretched, and could see rabbits playing with glee way down below on the ground.
If she had her way, she'd become one today because rabbits can get around.
Edie saw rabbits run, jump and have fun – probably nothing could catch a rabbit.
Edie wished to get free from this nest in this tree, but complacency now was her habit.

Her kin had medallions for *World's Strongest Talons*, and snatched up rabbits with ease.
But she wouldn't believe that she had received the same strengths and skills as these.
She was made for the wind, to climb and ascend, but she couldn't envision that ride.
So, while others did it, Edie stifled her spirit, made excuses and swallowed her pride.

One day, without warning, it started storming. Edie's tree was twisting about.

In pitifulness, Edie clung to the nest as the wind tried to blow her out.
She lost feathers in patches, but clung to the branches until the storm was passed.
Nearly died from the fright, scared a fall from this height would certainly be her last.

Meanwhile, riding the thermals, soaring big circles, above and beyond the storm,
While Edie was whining, other eagles were flying in the splendor of sunlight, warm.
Edie had eagle wings, eagle eyes, eagle means, but she nurtured a rabbit's heart.
Instead of the thermals, she dreamed about burrows where she'd be secure in the dark.

Everyone knew that if ever she flew it would only be if she decided
She wouldn't accept a life bound to a nest, and she changed, to become eagle-minded.
And her vision conceived herself taming the breeze, just like the rest of her kind;
For the sky is the limit, & you can be in it, it's all in the set of your mind.

Edie hated the nest, but couldn't resist the comfort and safety provided.
She wanted to fly, but scared to try even though mom and dad chided.
When she'd had enough, Edie finally got tough, and threw herself out of that nest.
For fears never die, and wings never fly, until they are put to the test.

You've guessed the story: Edie flew many sorties while learning to really soar.
But once she had tried it, she said, all delighted, "I should have done this before."
Don't let comfort or fears, inexperience or jeers, persuade you not to try.
You can be regal, & soar like an eagle. Take to your wings –
YOU CAN FLY.

Lessons from Debbi

At a restaurant, we were served tasty food in large portions. I guess Debbi could tell I was full but still eating. She said: "Dad, why are you stuffing yourself?" I said: "I don't like to waste food. I don't believe it's right." She said: "Whether or not you eat it, it is going to waste directly or indirectly. Why be uncomfortable?"

I thought on that, and realized she was right. Eating everything on one's plate does not avoid waste. Food excessively eaten goes to waste, and also adds problems to the overeater. Thanks, Debbi.

At another time, we were at Debbi's home. Debbi told one of her kids to do something important. As I looked on, Debbi repeated the same instruction – the very same important thing – and then began to count rhythmically: 1 - - 2 - - - . And before she said 3, the child did the important thing.

When the child was out of earshot, I said to Debbi: "You weren't raised like that. Our kids must learn to obey at once. 'Stop! Don't chase that ball!' If they don't learn to obey immediately, they will be hit by the car that just ran over that ball. Besides, God doesn't count to three."

Debbi looked quietly at me without a verbal response.

Next day Debbi phoned. "Dad, if God didn't count to three, we'd all be dead."

I always taught my children to think for themselves and to be independent. And she was absolutely correct. I'm grateful for the patience of God! I need it more than most. Thanks, Debbi.

Daily, I am so grateful for God's forbearance. Parents need godly patience. However, for the safety and health of our offspring, for the good of society, for peace in the family, and to respect authority; children must be trained to obey commands and instructions from parents, teachers, and peace officers without hesitation. This places a huge responsibility on those in authority not to misguide children. It's the obligation of parents to be sure children have trustworthy teachers. Parents cannot be passive. This entails home school, private school, and good religious instruction as vital considerations.

Charity Beyond Reason

No Tax Deductions. No public acknowledgment. No expectation of anything in return. The joy of giving, the delight of being a blessing, the pleasure of helping a fellow person, the desire to please God: those are the only motivations for a recent charitable act I witnessed. I'd rather call it sharing a big blessing. Or living godly love in a practical, tangible way.

I witnessed tears of gratitude mixed with laughter spilling out from spontaneous, irrepressible joy and shock as the receiver grasped the reality that their life had just taken a lasting Olympian leap upward. That their life had just been improved for themselves and their family without their even asking for it. All because a generous individual whom they do not know desired out of a giving heart and a heart of godly love to share a substantial tangible blessing. Someone had related a genuine need to a genuine Christian, and the Christian acted from godly love to take care of that need and be an unexpected blessing to that family. A family that could not tangibly repay the gift – which was part of the reason for the gift.

No tax deduction. No ribbon cutting. No name on a plaque or cornerstone. No news articles. Who does that?! Who these days, just for the sake of giving, gives a large gift that will bless the lives of the receiver for the remainder of their lives? Well, it still does take place. This specific blessing was not from me, but I'm close to both the giver and receiver. Happiness was created in the giver by the happiness and relief created for the receiver. A double blessing. Plus, the collateral blessings. This kind of untainted charity is a rare beauty. Very few folks know about it here, but I think the bells of heaven joyously were ringing in celebration of a child of God who acted from selfless love beyond reason.

OVERCOMING
Going Strong

Our plane was rocked with turbulence. Potholes pocked the sky.
The cabin plunged & shuddered. Men whimpered. Babies cried.

The captain told the cabin crew. "Sit down and buckle up.
The seatbelt sign is turned on. This whole trip will be rough.
We'll try to fly above the storm or try to go around.
Be assured that turbulence won't bring this airplane down.
Now, I'll focus on the storm. I'm getting off this mic.
I promise our wings won't break: Bumps bark, but do not bite."

We bounced, we plunged, we pitched, we lurched – mice tossed by a cat.
Our heads were jerked, our seatbelts hurt. White knuckles. Palms drip-wet.
Surely there's a better way; a route around this storm.
Boom! Thunder rocked our plane. Clouds with lightning torn.

"There'll be no service on this trip. Cabin crew, stay seated.
Passengers, please be assured this plane won't be defeated.
We haven't found a better path. We're doing all we can.
This day my father drilled me for: 'Face it like a man'.
We've pledged to plow on through to reach our destination.
We feel your pain. We understand your doubts and consternation.
Give us thirty minutes, and we'll all be through this mess.
Trust us. Don't be afraid. I'm sorry for the stress."

About an hour later, we touched down – and on time.
No one hurt. Nothing lost. Everything just fine.

And so, in life we hit our storms. The path not always easy.
Sometimes there is no way around, and things get in a tizzy.
Jump ship! Uhh, into what?! A lifeboat? Parachute?
Or stay the course. Ride the bull. Overcome the brute.

Real life is tough. Real business hard, whatever you are doing.
So, buckle up. Knuckle down. Hold fast what you're pursuing.

Take a breath. Find resolve. Trust the captain and the plane.
Meet the challenge. Take a stand. You'll reach the goal. Win the
game.

My daughter, Wendi, was on this extremely rough flight, and used it as a business analogy. I took the liberty to put her thoughts in rhyme.

STAIRWAYS TO SUCCESS

A small boy with his daddy, Played baseball in the yard.
"You go catch them, daddy. I'll hit 'em to you hard."

He tossed the ball into the air, But missed it with his swing.
A second time he tossed it up; Again he missed the thing.

He threw the ball a third time, But didn't hit it with the bat.
He called out to his father: "Dad, did you see that?!"

"I tried to hit it to you, Just like I said I would.
But today I didn't hit it, 'Cause my pitching is too good'."

So we, in our adventures, can choose the view we stress.
We can curse and hide our failures, or call them Stairways
to Success.

VIP GUARANTEED

I SAW HIM near the rear door of a downtown restaurant. Just his feet were sticking out of a dumpster. I could see on the sidewalk where fluids from rotting foodstuffs were leaking from all the rubbish in that grimy container. At first, I thought he was diving for cans. A metal merchant. As I waited for the stop light to change, I saw him pop up out of that smelly dumpster with some discarded food. He sat down, leaned against the dumpster, and began eating that garbage. A man like me and you eating filthy garbage.

I know intellectually that some street people get meals from trash. I also know intellectually that 1000 free meals a day are served by Salvation Army alone, plus those served by several other charities in town. But watching a man retrieve food from waste and eat it in the flesh as it was occurring hit me like an Arctic blast. I recalled the caustic smell of a garbage truck, and wondered if that's how the pillaged stuff tasted. A reflexive shudder went through me.

Immediately I thought, I'll pray for that unfortunate man. But quickly another thought came: That man's already done the praying. I ought to be the answer to *his* prayer.

I had a sack lunch with me that day, which was not typical but perhaps providential. My car pulled over to the curb. My hand grabbed the sack lunch. My feet walked back to that hungry man. My mouth said, "Sir, I'd like for you to have this lunch. Please accept it." I could tell from his eyes that to him I was that day a VIP.

In our culture, there are many experts selling advice on how to be a very important person. Have you read books on self-esteem? Have you been to seminars on how to be the better you? Have you bought the materials? People seem to desire a professional, an eastern pundit, to instruct them. At first, students feel better just being in the class. Self-improvement gurus tell us: "Get up each morning, look in the mirror and say, 'I'm terrific. I'm wonderful. This is my world, and I'm going to win today, my way. Look out world; here comes number 1 – capable, wonderful ME!'"

Hey, if that works for you, go for it religiously, with gusto and a positive attitude. But it doesn't work for me. It seems hollow, shallow, put on. I wouldn't believe myself. I'd go away from the mirror in worse shape than before, thinking I had just watched a poor performance by a mimic who paid $200 for a seminar to become a genuine imitator. They teach, "Fake it till you make it." I'd just feel like a faker. And I don't like feeling phony.

Let me share what I've found to be an unfailing source of self-esteem. I've got the real-time fool-proof feel-good formula! Mine is an action approach. Try the other methods, then try mine. Accentuate the one that works best for you. Live the one that produces genuine satisfaction and happiness.

Here's the formula. You might write it on a card and place it on your car's dashboard. Put it in your daily reminders. Tape it on that mirror. It's not complicated, but I've discovered it is profound. I don't claim that it's original. Here it is: *HELP SOMEONE*. That's it. It's that simple; and it's that difficult. Caution: don't groan it off, don't smirk at it, don't think it's beneath you. If you are serious, if you really want to find happiness and feel good about yourself, then *HELP SOMEONE*. Help someone who cannot return the favor. Help someone today in a real-life hardship whose path has crossed yours. Do you remember the Good Samaritan? It's a winning formula.

This formula works best in person. Of course, support your religious charity. Yes, donate to your local animal shelter. Absolutely donate nice clothing to the Salvation Army or other quality group. And don't neglect to give blood. But when you get the chance, don't miss the opportunity to, in person, you yourself, hand a coat to a shivering needy person in the snow. I know they can get a free coat at several local places, but tonight they need one now. *You* can be their Good Samaritan. Do you have an extra one with you? Hand it to that man or woman or child. Go to Dollar General. I guarantee an inner rush that equals the elation of slamming shut the gate just ahead of the horns of a charging bull. You'll know you just performed the work of God on time.

I'm not suggesting that we enable someone to be lazy or dependent or take advantage. I am suggesting that we aid someone when they have an actual, immediate need and we are able to be of immediate assistance. In candid honesty, I acknowledge I have also been on the receiving end of such temporary help.

Do I practice my own message? Yes, I do in several ways. I mentioned one above, but let me relate another incident. One winter night in Tulsa as I left my office, a couple I'd guess to be in their late fifties were on the sidewalk as I stepped out to my car to go home. They looked much like any other couple that age except that they were each carrying blankets. As I was between my car and my office building, they said loudly, "Sir, can we ask you a question?" It startled me, and I automatically said, "Sure." So, they walked over to me, and told this brief story.

"Sir, we are husband and wife. We have no family in the area, and we just lost our home. We have no place to stay tonight since we choose to stay together, and if we go to a shelter, they require us to sleep in separate quarters for the men and for the women. It's cold, but we have blankets as you see, but the wind is strong. We see that there under your car port is an alcove formed by the building wall and your side-entry steps. May we bed down there tonight?"

Reality! That request jarred my mind. The step's landing was about 30" high and stood out perhaps 4' from the building. It could provide a bit of a wind break, but not much. I wanted to say to them: "Look, you seem to be such quality folks. I have a couch and a recliner in my office. You can sleep there tonight." But I've misjudged people before, and I couldn't take that chance. I did ask, "Do you need another blanket? I have one inside you could use." They said they had enough. "Do you want me to bring you a hamburger?" They said they had eaten.

I realize letting them sleep there was next to doing nothing. But it was what they asked. They were gone in the morning when I arrived at work. And they had left no trash. From time to time when I'm at that building, I think of that couple, and wonder where they are now.

Yes, I've been burned sometimes. In a Tulsa parking lot, I saw a large man in a wheelchair with one leg propped up sticking straight out. As he came closer, I noticed it was an artificial leg. He was wearing an Army Vet cap. He approached me, and asked: "Would you help a Vet with some spare change or a buck?" I said, "No. But I'll buy your lunch over at that food stand."

There was a permanent hot dog and sandwich stand at the edge of the parking lot. This Vet began wheeling that direction. I got in my car to drive there. I stopped in front of the service window, got out of my car, and walked up to the attendant. The Vet was nearby. I said to the attendant, "That guy's going to order something, and I'll pay for it." He replied, "He's already ordered. Rounded off, it's $9." I said, "That was quick." The guy said, "He's a regular customer and knows what he wants." I paid the bill, waved to the Vet, and drove off.

That evening on the 10 o'clock news (I'm not making this up!) was a story about a drug bust. There in full color on the TV was the arresting officer and this Vet in his wheelchair. The "Vet" was a drug peddler, and he used his artificial leg as a hiding place for his drug inventory. So, yes, I was duped. But God knows my heart was in the right place. We don't need to continue to enable those who are impostors or indolent takers. We should especially be careful to whom we give cash on the street. We try to help the genuinely needy as we are able.

One Christmas Season, I gathered together my kids and grandkids in the Tulsa area. We were in a couple vans with a mission in mind. We bought a few pizzas, and went to the part of Tulsa where homeless people congregate. It was easy to give away all the pizzas we brought; and the recipients were grateful. I wanted to demonstrate to my grandchildren the joy of giving, and the value of helping others, of serving the needy. To every person who that evening ate the gifted pizzas, we were significant that day in their life. A momentary VIP.

In years past, someone in our church would regularly visit a 92-year-old woman in a nursing home. This confined older lady had been a friend since her childhood. She had taught her how to knit. Then, with age, she began to gradually lose touch with reality. While she lived in the lonely, tedious circumstance of a nursing home, she valued the friendship and company of this younger visitor who tenderly expended time and effort to show love and care. This elderly friend considered her a loyal VIP.

In that same vein, when I was growing up, my grandmother took some of us grandkids with her to a nursing home to sing hymns, read the Bible, hold a lonely person's hand, and just express kindness to the confined elderly. There are routine opportunities in your regular life to help others.

Do you want to feel good? Do you want to be happy? Have lasting inner joy? Some folks may find it in front of a mirror. Everyone can find it by befriending someone who has no friend or no support. Give someone a hand up. You will experience joy. To the person you befriend, you will be a Very Important Person. Guaranteed.

I wrote a poem challenging us to help someone when we encounter the opportunity. I leave it with you hoping the rhythm and rhyme will enable you to remember the fulfilling thought: Help Someone.

Prayer Courier

When we see someone wounded, hurting and needing,
It's futile to pray if we don't stop the bleeding.
When we see someone hungry, and we are well-fed,
Our prayer will seem empty if we offer no bread.
When we see someone freezing – we with blankets to spare;
Can our prayer be sincere if we pray but don't share?

We can give our prayer wings from our excess of things!
We can give our prayer feet, give it warmth, give it meat!

When we think of the needy, we lift up a prayer.
But the needy already cried out in despair.
Let us be the answer to their desperate plea!
Usually, God uses couriers, such as you, such as me.

Help Someone. Prayer Couriers are VIPs, Guaranteed.

Commitment to My Children

To my children I will give a way to live, a love to live.
Strength of character today in the way they work and play.
Show them love from mom and dad through good and bad, joy or sad.
Build self-image so they deem their self-esteem above the mean.

It's vital that they know that God is not a fraud whom fools applaud,
But rather that he rules above in righteous love that joy's made of.
They'll learn to be a friend that's true, working through opposing views.
Forgiveness ask when in the wrong, not waiting long, 'Twill make them strong.
It's sometimes best to condescend, make amends, and keep your friend.

Love other peoples of the world when brotherhood brings out the good.
Be known for hospitality through thankfully shared bread and tea.
To recognize and value right, wrong to fight with all their might.
Guard themselves from evil fun that when it's done must make them run.
To understand the flatterer's ploys that will destroy both girls and boys.
To see behind the treacherous smiles, flashed in guile, which defile.

Appreciate the place of work, not hardness shirk nor lowness smirk.
Try to contributions make for mankind's sake to raise their stake.
Respect the right of rule by law, its honor awe in spite of flaws.
Learn the lighter side to see, laugh easily, live happily.
Not taking self too seriously, yet strive to be what they must be.
Balanced in their daily lives: don't trivialize, but seek first prize.
Yet knowing "*first*" – intrinsic worth – is well beyond this fleeting earth.
Thus, my children will be wise, in peace or strife prepared for LIFE.

My Children at 8, 6, and 4

Jenni:
The angelic, pensive kind
Who speaks more with her features and her eyes.
She's true and loyal both in heart and mind
Possessing subtle insights of the wise.

She's never quick to anger, but her sentiments run deep.
Her friendship can't be bought, but when given, is to keep.
Not a light or frivolous jester with a joke and empty smile,
Yet she reaps from life full meaning and pleasure quite worthwhile.

Wendi:
As enchanting as her name,
She bubbles like an effervescent spring.
A ready friend, a source of fun and games,
A mind that's quick, a heart that likes to sing.

A sincere gift to Wendi will purchase all her heart,
But one reproach toned harshly will pierce her like a dart.
Underneath the surface whims, her character is true
For when she hurts someone she loves, she's quick to make it new.

Debbi:
A mischievous cherub's twin.
A coy and giggling flirt, a subtle schemer.
Her eyes, kiss, similes and hugs hearts quickly win.
Her laughing charms beguile one to believe her.

When I get home, there in the hall all courage I employ,
For a running hug will catch me hard and bowl me down in joy.
When I must leave and kiss around, goodbyes are not complete
"Till Debbi *twice* has kissed my lips – cheeks, she says, are not as sweet.

Jim Foy – daddy

THE KITE

As a lad, I had a kite. Oh, I enjoyed flying my kite with its picture of a soaring, powerful eagle. How it tugged at the string while dancing on the wind, laughing as clouds tickled its balsa ribs, mocking birds with shorter tails.

I'd send secret messages up the string to my kite as it climbed, dived and shook its tail in the sky. How proud it was at the end of several balls of string, so high, so far away. I must have looked as small to it as it looked to me.

Though it was master of the sky, my kite was not content. It always struggled for more freedom. One time, with reckless abandon, it jerked so hard the string broke. My kite flew away, bursting higher, totally free for a moment, then crashing from the sky. I cried. My heart was broken over the loss.

Several days later, while riding my bike in a field not far away, I spied an object in a tree. It was my kite, with string and tail caught in the branches. Though the kite was torn, I was excited. I stuck my hand in my pocket, searching for my knife to cut loose the kite. The knife was not there. Racing home as fast as the bicycle would go, I ran to my room. It took a while to discover just where I had left my knife, but soon I had it in my pocket, riding back to that tree. Climbing the tree and cutting off tangled string and a length of frayed, twisted tail, I recovered my battered kite.

A bit of mending, a new string, and my kite and I were playing once more. It was a celebration of dancing, diving, climbing and soaring as my kite tossed its head saucily as before. With patches reminding of former escapades, my kite always tugged at the string, but never again so fiercely that it broke away.

Kites and boys don't play together forever, but I fondly remember delightful days. Periodically, I recall the lesson from my kite: Some "strings" bring most happiness; some freedoms bring disaster. With passing time, I've sometimes felt that I've been not only the carefree boy of the story, but also the kite. And, it's been the "strings" of relationships that have produced the most joy, and ties to others that enable high flight.

Good Enough

"*Good Enough*" is an attitude of simply slipping by.
The enemy of excellence. A forgery of "best".
Those satisfied with "*Good Enough*", will never know the high
Enjoyed by those still climbing in the quest.

If "*Good Enough*" is good enough to satisfy your mind,
You'll never know the thrill of breaking through to win the prize.
For the drive to be still better, giving all again, this time,
Can bring its own reward that never dies.

Some athletes wear the uniform but never play the game.
Content to ride the bench and never break a sweat.
It isn't that they never score or never achieve fame,
It's they never know the marks they might have set.

And some of us are satisfied just filling time and space.
Not knowing our potential, no inner drive to win.
Accepting ordinary effort, to never find our pace
And never do the deeds that should have been.

Be one of those who're good enough to never "just get by."
Who give to life the best they're meant to give.
Who, knocked down in the conquest, get up again to try.
Who, having done their best, can say, "I've lived.

CAN DO

Big Buzz and Jig were identical twins
    who lived in a beaver lodge.
They came by their names because of the fame
    of beavers for sawing logs.
They looked just alike on the outside all right,
    but inside had different hearts.
Buzz, a believer; Jig, self-deceiver;
    and that set them worlds apart.
To Buzz, a huge tree that would dam a wide stream,
    could be felled one chip at a time.
Jig would refuse it – knew he couldn't cut through it.
    Jig wanted the small, easy kind.
Big Buzz was a doer, but Jig a reviewer,
    who analyzed numerous trees,
Saying, "I like perfection in my selection.
    I won't accept any of these.
That tree is too tall, or won't properly fall,
    and that one's too hard to chew.
That bark's too tough and excessively rough,
    it's too fat for a beaver to hew."

Buzz and Jig were same sized, same jaws, same eyes,
    their teeth were identical length
And equally sharp to cut through the bark.
    Their muscles were the same strength.
Big Buzz found enjoyment in his employment
    and always had work to do.
But there was no pleasin' Jig any season,
    so, his paychecks were small and few.
Jig lived in a swamp, and felt like a flop.
    Few trees were suited for him.
Buzz lived in a pond, clear, deep and long,
    doing work that was turned down by Jig.
Huge trees formed his dam across a great span
    with proper packing between.
You'd never guess that one beaver built this

unless you had been on the scene.
It wasn't with ease that Buzz cut his trees,
    it was all in his frame of mind.
And no tree could last with Buzz on the task,
    for he'd fell it one bite at a time.

There is among creatures one outstanding feature
    that separates winners and losers.
Some like to blame, see the worst, and complain,
    and are expert "*success-refusers.*"
While some, no more blest than each of the rest,
    excel in all that they do.
It isn't more wit, it's they start and don't quit
    until the task is through.
They tackle today just what their plans say
    will take them one step toward the goal.
They bite off and chew only what they can do,
    not trying to bite off the whole.
They don't allow size, or remarks from wise guys,
    to keep them from nibbling on dreams.
They find reasons why to go on and try, bite by bite,
    fulfilling their schemes.
They're not scared to start, they work hard and smart,
    and stay with a task 'till it's done.
Be an entrepreneur, a step by step doer.
    Get in the race fully and run.

Dancin' in the Rain

The rain is coming down in sheets —
Caught us unexpectedly.
We could be drenched, as in complete.
We must act blithely instantly.

I've grabbed this big umbrella.
Got it for a rainy day.
Now, one gal, one fella,
Are laughing like some kids at play.

We're under that umbrella squeezed,
Rain beating out its rhythm.
We see folks curse, while we are pleased:
So close, this storm the reason.

It's not rain or that umbrella,
It's the unexpected closeness
Forced upon two timid friends
Moved from cold to breathless.

Hands join on that umbrella,
Four feet create a splash,
Delighting gal and fella
In a childish sort of dance.

It's this childish sort of dance
That lifts the hearts and spirit.
It's taking an unlikely chance
To cherish and endear it.

We did not plan a rainy day:
It forced itself upon us.
We'll take whatever comes our way
And from it make a chorus.

Why let the rain repress us?
Who cares if we get drenched.
We'll make the rain express us,

But not our spirits quench.

So, under this umbrella now
A mem'ry souvenir will last.
This one gal and fella vow
Each time surprised by rain, to dance.

Not Ashamed

My great front door neighbor says he's my friend.
But he's out there working his yard again.
Is a yard so important? Is he seeking some prize?
Is he truly naïve, and doesn't realize
It's no longer kosher making neighbors feel shamed.
But he's really so nice — he's not to be blamed.

I'll give him a book that will keep him inside.
Tell him of beautiful, long scenic rides
That he and his wife could enjoy frequently
Instead of improving his yard constantly.
Few homes, after all, will make Most Beautiful,
So why all this effort? Why so dutiful?

Here I sit, day by day, writing my poems.
Why can't he at least get his golf game goin'?
Why not get his camera: take photographs
Of birds or sunsets? Photographs last!
No. He's out there right now. But I'm not biting.
I'll move to the back porch to do my writing.

EMPATHY
Understanding

He had gotten twenty dollars among his birthday cards.
He knew just what he wanted, down the street a couple yards.
A sign said, *FOR SALE – PUPPIES*, and a puppy was his dream.
Now with twenty dollars he could fulfill his scheme.

His heart was pounding loudly as he knocked upon that door.
He'd never been the owner of a puppy dog before.
So, when a lady answered and asked him to come in,
He was the most excited in his life he'd ever been.

"I came to see the puppies. Do you, do you have a puppy left?"
"Oh yes, we have two puppies unspoken for as yet.
Just wait here, I'll get them." Now he was left alone.
He squeezed the twenty dollars. A tickle thrilled his bones.

Two cuddly, playful puppies were chewing on his shoe.
He thought: Twenty dollars – what if twenty could buy two!
Gazing on the puppies, he pet them with his hand.
"How much are the puppies?" he asked, spoken like a man.

"These are pure bred puppies from a very sturdy line.
Their brother brought two hundred, and these are just as fine."
The crush of disappointment. He'd nowhere near enough.
"I've only twenty dollars. Are there any other pups?"

"No. Well, there is a cripple. We haven't done it yet.
We're putting it to sleep; as recommended by the vet.
He said it couldn't walk right. Besides, it was the runt.
Please, honey, stop your crying. I shouldn't be so blunt?"

"Could, could I see that puppy? Could I see it please?
With only twenty dollars, I can't get one of these."
The lady brought a white fur ball and put it at his feet.
As he pet the puppy's coat, the boy began to weep.

"Could I buy this puppy? Please, could I take him home?
I'll pay all twenty dollars. Please? I love this one!"
"Son, that runt's a cripple, he never will walk good.

We'll put him out of misery. The doctor said we should."

"The doctor must not love this dog. I'd work to get more money."
The boy picked up the dog. "See, see how much he likes me?
I'd take good care of this one. I couldn't love him more.
It's okay if he can't walk". The boy sat on the floor.

The boy pulled up his blue jeans. Emaciated legs, so pale,
Were strapped in shiny braces there beside the puppy's tail.
"You see, I, too, am crippled. Without braces, I can't walk.
I know this puppy wants to live. I think I'd call him 'Chalk'."

The lady turned in tears and hurried through the door.
Never had she learned such wisdom from a boy before.
The insight of the innocent can teach old age a lesson:
Don't let a life be thrown away, judged just short of "perfection".

(adapted from a story)

Impact of Words

I can – I can't
I will – I won't
I love – I hate.
I accept – I reject.
I surrender – I'll never.
I forgive – I'll forget.
I'm sorry – I accept.
I do – I don't.
I am – I am not.
I believe – I doubt.
What we say reveals what we are
And can change what we are.

James E Foy

TRIBUTE TO THOSE WHO WEAR THE BADGE

Men and Women with the badge, stand for law across our land.
Stand for right by night and day, protecting our American Way.
Fighting crime and calming fear, making life much safer here,
With the badge they've bravely stood. Guardians of our neighborhood.

Lawlessness would take the land, if those with badges did not stand,
Keeping honest people free. Defending well our liberty.
It is called "*The Thin Blue Line*". That Blue Line both strong and kind.
It represents both hope and shield; to hate and evil does not yield.

Each cop with badge so bravely donned knows his life could soon be gone;
For as they work those thankless hours, they risk their life defending ours.
That badge they wear for justice stands. Tranquility to bring our land.
Their job is broader than it seems, as they protect the American Dream.

Many wore that badge with pride, defending others as they died.
Death too soon, so undeserved; shot down by one they swore to serve.

A widow lays her cop to rest. Pins his badge upon his chest. *
But ten, emboldened, step in line to take his place in fighting crime.
To all who wear that badge with pride, who wore it well the day they died,
We honor you & make this pledge: *We stand with you who wear the badge.*

****

* Optional: A husband lays his cop to rest. Pins her badge upon her chest.

Because of the confusion and conflict and conversations about the relationships between our police and our communities, I offer this poem to support and honor the police. I do not encourage a police state, or a military police force, but I do advocate respect for law and order, and a community that obeys the law and prosecutes those who will not. We have honorable procedures to protest bad laws and to replace bad officials.

Acknowledgment: This poem is written with the tempo of "The Green Beret" and can be sung to that tune. Let's uphold good cops.

Call of the Eagle as our Sign

Sing with me now America. Unite in freedom's song.
Our song can be the wings of an eagle.
Join with me now America, with voices clear and strong.
Our song can lift us up where we belong.

For we can soar when we're united.
We can fly when hearts combine.
We will rise with souls ignited.
With the call of the eagle as our sign.

Clap with me now America. Let's celebrate in song.
Our joy can be the wings of an eagle.
Cry with me now America: Remembrance makes us strong.
Resolve lifts patriots up where we belong.

Stand with me now America. Together we will stand.
Our strength can be the wings of an eagle.
Vow with me now America. Our promise makes us strong.
Our vow will lift above the blinded throng.

NOW we must stand for truth and right, as tyrants are within.
Vigilance has eyes of an eagle.
We do not shirk our duty now. Our loyalty will win.
Stout hearts, strong arms like eagles tame the wind.

For we can soar when we're united.
We can fly when hearts combine.
We will rise with souls ignited.
With the call of the eagle as our sign.
With the call of the eagle as our sign.

Would Anyone be Free?

What if no one stood for freedom? What if no one stood for right?
What if, in the night of terror, no torchbearer held the light?
Liberty is costly! What if no one paid the price?
Would anyone be free?

What if justice remained silent? And for honor none would fight?
What if freedom slept while terror raped and conquered in the night?
What if Liberty were helpless, and Tyrants armed with might?
Would anyone be free?

Stand and honor the Marine Corps, Army, Navy, and the Coast Guard,
Air Force, and the National Guard, who fight to keep us free.

Honor those who willingly have stopped the tyrants' might.
Honor those who selflessly have carried freedom's light.
They have given all there is to give and paid the highest price
That others might be free.

Honor those who prayed at home while loved ones fought and died.
Honor those who cheered the troops even as they cried.
Honor those who sacrificed all they had but pride
That others might be free.

THE VENERABLE VULNERABLE CAMEL

A Dromedary Allegory

A camel's a marvelous mammal
made for endurance and strength.
He's designed to tote loads over vast desert roads
no matter their heat or their length.

With extra strong back he's created to pack
the tents and food and the water.
With the humps that he's got, his hoofs and whatnot,
I'd say there's no animal odder.

He's not made to look curious, but to serve a purpose,
to get you where you are going.
He's part of your team, so never be mean
and force him to moaning and groaning.

You are right of course, he can out pack a horse
because his back is broader.
But be sure not to load more than you're told,
even of camel's fodder.

Each camel can haul only so much straw
but not any more than that,
So don't be the one who puts the straw on
that breaks the camel's back.

This truth goes for people, whether strong or feeble,
let each one bear all they will.
But don't force a bungle, creating a stumble,
of loading beyond their skill.

Now: What if it's true? What if you knew
What's worked well for others could also fit you?
You've watched some good friends live life that tends
Toward a model you'd like to pursue.

No, we don't know the future, or exactly what suits your
Dreams and desires and needs.

But you have got a back, and there's somewhere a pack
That will match your skills with your deeds.

In our life's travel – human or camel –
We impact our future and others'.
So, choose a track proven to reach where it's goin'
With convivial sisters and brothers.

Then get on that road where you each share the load,
Where you reap the rewards of your labor.
Where teamwork is real and the friendships you feel
Bring success in contentment you'll treasure.

An Axiom of Life

I've learned that once a freight train has entered the intersection, no matter what freight it carries, we must stop and wait until the very last car clears the street. We can get frustrated and angry, or we can enjoy the art (graffiti) on the cars, enjoy the train's whistle as it approaches other ever-more-distant intersections, enjoy the rhythm of the wheels on the rails, or rest our eyes (the car behind will wake us if we fall asleep). I've learned that if we start a bit ahead of schedule, then the inevitable trains will be less intrusive. I've learned that if you put the car in "park" and massage the hands of your spouse, an inconvenience will turn into a benefit — the longer the train the better. It is possible to creatively turn annoy into enjoy.

THE RITE OF LEADERSHIP

When you realize there *IS* a right and truthful pathway
contrasted to others that are false and erroneous,
you have acquired knowledge.

When you grasp *WHY* the one pathway is true and correct,
you have understanding.

When you *DECIDE* to walk the true and right pathway,
you have wisdom.

When you actually *WALK* the true and right pathway,
you demonstrate character and discipline.

When you are able to walk *AGAINST* the mob of popular error,
you display integrity & courage.

When you *REMAIN* on the true and correct pathway
in the face of ridicule and antagonism,
you prove strength.

When you do all this with *MEEKNESS*,
you are a faithful leader.

Knowledge, understanding, wisdom, character,
 discipline, integrity, strength, meekness:
these reveal an individual to follow,
to emulate, and to defend.

If godliness is that leader's foundation,
make that person your friend.

Your Life's Puzzle

What if each life were a puzzle?
A uniquely shaped piece every day?
No visible border or boundaries,
So, how wide or high? Who could say?

Yet, it's known that a typical puzzle
Will piece thirty thousand or so.
Thus, everyone working their puzzle
Can approximate days yet to go.

Some of the days make grand pieces,
Others seem trivially small:
Some days do loom monumental,
While most may not score much at all.

Of course, to think such is error,
For days that are let go to waste
Add not to eternal treasure
Nor teach those who follow our pace.

We're all looked up to by someone,
Oft' someone we don't realize,
Who'd follow us into trite trifling
Thus, getting off course for the prize.

Now, family time spent is not wasted.
And exercise time is not wrong.
Such quality times are invested
Making prominent days more strong.

It's wisdom to govern the bound'ries —
To labor how much? How much play? —
Controlling the one life we're given
As we fashion our puzzle each day!

For each puzzle piece has its value,
And each puzzle piece must be played,
And nothing of good, nothing of ill
Can make a piece placement delayed.

Now, myst'ry surrounds your puzzle —
A magical power of sorts:
You decide the weight of each piece,
Its brilliance, impact and import.

You make a piece dull or impressive.
You make this piece jagged; that smooth.
By the way you live and passion you give
You influence each day as you choose.

Thirty thousand pieces to muster
Called days in your life to be lived,
As you are constructing your puzzle
With talents and strength to you given.

Is your puzzle a map that guides others?
Will your map lead to treasure or gloom?
Is your puzzle a field or a garden?
Is it weeds or fine fertile blooms?

Each piece of your puzzle is steadfast —
Cannot be picked up and replaced.
What's done is done, time lost is gone,
No step can be ever retraced.

Yes, there is love and forgiveness
For days lived in error or waste.
But no sum of grace and mercy
Can recover lost time and lost place.

No puzzle compiled is perfection.
Some pieces get torn or bent.
So rise with the sun — get up and run.
Be loving. Have noble intent.

There's a 24-hour play clock
To shape each piece we display.
Not 23 and not 25 —
It's the wise who master each day.

Be bold at the 23rd hour.
It's easy to think it's too gone.
Make the right choice: the sound of your voice
Can change a "squandered" to "won".

For some, the puzzle is shortened:
Completion seems ended at noon.
When Providence calls be ready —
From such early call none's immune.

Your puzzle of life is your story,
Assembled each hour from your youth.
There's only one print of life's puzzle,
So, build it with wisdom and truth.

Find knowledge, then follow it wisely.
Find facts, don't believe all you've read.
Find light, don't be tripped in the darkness.
Find true life — Don't be misled.

Have fun constructing your puzzle.
Enjoy as you build your world.
Responsibly live, generously give,
As your day to day life is unfurled.

Walk with your heavenly Father.
Trust Him, be wise, unafraid.
Follow your Lord and Good Shepherd
Till your last puzzle piece is played.

Simple Joys

When fear, tragedy & plagues surround us
Amid inflated living that impounds us,
Where could one go to capture inner peace,
To lay the chaos down and stress release?

It could be found within your own back yard.
That natural, simple joy has sweet reward.
Chirping frogs join sparkling fireflies.
Crickets sing to coax the moon to rise.
The twinkling stars will join in the array,
As constellations float in vast display.

All of these provided without fee.
The kind of joy to share with company.
One never tires of such God-sent joy
Waiting just outside to be employed.

In my backyard after a good rain.

If Not For Mercy

If not for mercy and for everlasting grace,
This man could never see the Father's face.
I could not stand before his just and righteous name.
His holy light reveals my guilt and shame.

But Jesus died and paid for sin on Calvary.
He took the blame and set this sinner free.
O, praise his name, my pardoned soul shall rise above
And live with him because of everlasting love.

(can be sung to the tune of Londonderry Air aka Danny Boy)

Being a Mentor

If you say you don't make mistakes, you are kidding yourself.
If you keep making the same mistakes,
          you are called a slow learner (or worse).
If you don't learn from mistakes, you are called a fool.
If you make enough mistakes and learn from them,
          you are called an experienced professional.
If you share with others the lessons from your mistakes,
          you are called a mentor.
If you're afraid to make mistakes,
          you are called stunted by fear.

So, let's get out there and do something, learn from mistakes, and
try again in a more enlightened way; then share our progress with
others. Be a mentor.

The Rush & Blush of Life
The How & Why Our Life Goes On

In our lusty human race, it's conquest & consent.
No one knows who conquered whom, but all know the intent.
From this mystic dance of life come little girls & boys.
Thus, the population grows beyond what war destroys.
No need to curse, no need to blush — if not this interplay
You and I would not be here to even have a say.

But you are here to have your say, so look without contempt
Upon our lusty human race, its conquest & consent.
Plow your ground and plant your crop to reap a harvest full
Store, thankfully, a bit aside to always provide gruel.
Go catch a spouse, build your house — the plan is heaven-sent.
Beget your heirs within you lair, be sated and content.

For further reading: Genesis 1:27-28; 9:7; Proverbs 5:18-19
Song of Solomon; Hebrews 13:4

Note on Amorous

There's much to favor *amorous*. It's from the start decorous.
It shouldn't offend one of us. It's praised in writ and chorus,
And propagated **all** of us. (Not every parent longed for us.)
The saintliest who live with us, got here no more glamorous!
Don't be ashamed, or method cuss, God put that awesome drive in us.
He, knowing couples often fuss, made one make-up process amorous.
Do not judge it bad of us that some folks use more generous.
(My parents had eight wanted kids – the 8th one is most glad they did.
I'm sure enjoyment played a part along with tender loving hearts.
I'm told my mother's lady friends were sad the siblings found an end.
They hoped to prove it was or wasn't: Kids are cheaper by the dozen.)
Be grateful that through loving lust you got your genes to pass in trust.
Enjoy your offspring gotten thus, and thank Creator's plan as for us.
Be fruitful and be joyfulous. When proper, enjoy amorous.

POWER OF RELATIONSHIPS

Someone said, "You can pick your teeth. You can pick your friends. But you can't pick your relations." Whoever said that could have added: You **can** pick your relation**ships**. You should pick your relationships very carefully, because relationships are the power of living.

IT TAKES TWO OR MORE

A relationship requires at least two – you can't have a relationship by yourself. You need not be physically present with someone to have a relationship, although that makes it nice. One can have a relationship with God whom they have never even seen. And some wives have been sleeping with a husband for years, but have no real relationship. Relationships are more than a physical presence.

THERE IS POWER IN TWO

There is power in relationships. I call it the POWER-OF-TWO. Let me illustrate. You could walk into a police station with gasoline. You could walk in with matches. But walk in with gas and a lighted match, and you're in trouble. Now you've got a bomb. Gasoline **with** fire is too much power.

If I enter a restaurant and order everyone to give me their wallets and jewelry, I'd be subdued by the patrons and held for the police. But if some nut with a sawed-off shotgun walks in and issues the same demand, soon he has all the wallets and jewelry. Why? Because one mad man together with a loaded shotgun is too much power to argue with.

Imagine a mosquito in front of you. Reach out ONE hand and squash that critter. Get him now. Good try. With one hand, you only startled it. Try again with TWO hands. Now. How did you do? My smashed mosquito just discovered the POWER-OF-TWO in the relationship of my two hands.

That power is everywhere.

Even A smile is more worthwhile when two will wear it.

A dream's a better scheme if two will snare it.

A care could lose its scare if two would bear it.

A friendship cannot mend 'till two repair it.

A hug can't be a hug unless two share it.

And love is highest love when two will dare it.

RELATIONSHIPS ARE WORTH DARING

In that poem, I used the word "dare" because not all relationships work. Relationships are like tennis: They involve frequent serving and constant stroking – on both sides. Especially love relationships. As in tennis, if all you have is love, that's not enough. You start with love but must add quality serving and stroking by both partners. Without these, you cannot win. Relationships are risky and worth daring.

SOME ARE AFRAID OF THE PRIMARY RELATIONSHIP – WILL NOT EVEN TALK ABOUT IT

Yes, there is power when two join in a relationship. The PRIMARY RELATIONSHIP is the relationship with God. The only relationship which can guarantee eternal life is one with God. Since God IS, and since He is willing to enter a relationship with His creatures, it only makes sense to seek and to develop that creature-Creator union. We need a relationship with God. We need it here and now, and we need it in the hereafter.

Imagine the arrogance of a created being who would say "I have no interest in knowing the One who made me."

ONLY A RELATIONSHIP WITH GOD IS THE PRIMARY RELATIONSHIP AND ONLY A GOD RELATIONSHIP ENABLES ETERNAL VALUE

At a Christmas party, some folks were discussing whether or not there really was a virgin birth. Various points of view were mentioned. Oddly, the statements of Mary and Joseph were not considered. Finally, I said, "It's a simple issue with few options. Either Jesus was the Son of God **or** he was the son of some human – perhaps Joseph or a Roman soldier in Nazareth. If Jesus is the Son of God, then he *was* (had to be) virgin born, and we best listen to him. If he was the son of Joseph or some other fellow, then obviously he couldn't have been virgin born, he was at best just another great teacher, and he becomes unimportant. The world doesn't need another dead great teacher. Jesus can't be God, can't be the Savior, can't have died for the sins of the world, can't be alive from the dead, and can't have a relationship with you and I any more than can Socrates IF he is the son of any human father. If there were not a virgin birth, there is nothing to celebrate at Christmas, let's quit fooling ourselves and go home."

Truly, that is the way it is. If Jesus is not virgin born, we cannot have a relationship with him or with God the Father through him, so why play church. Let's go watch more TV. It's here that one must be a wise seeker of truth. The resurrection of Jesus proves the Christian faith is reasonable and true. Investigate it well – honestly and thoroughly.

GOD BECAME A MAN TO ENHANCE HIS RELATIONSHIP WITH US

But Jesus is the Son of God, the Savior alive from the dead, and we can have a relationship with him and with God the Father right now in time as well as forever in eternity.

It is more than a "what's-in-it-for-me" situation. If you and I establish a relationship with God, then our family and friends are more likely to do the same, and these human relationships can also last forever in heaven. You and I will only spend eternity with our loved ones if we have a union with God. Only a relationship with God can give eternal significance to human relationships.

ONLY GOD CAN HEAL SOME BROKEN HUMAN RELATIONSHIPS

God has given me the opportunity to contribute positively to many lives. I confess that in the world of my own relationships, I have also demonstrated the ability to negatively impact lives. I'm the guy in my world who pushed Humpty Dumpty off the wall. I'm sorry for that, I regret that, I wish I hadn't done that, but none of those feelings puts Humpty back together again. The story of Humpty is not just a nursery rhyme. It's a story of lives – of Relationships that get broken. Nobody can put back together some broken relationships. But God can. I believe that, since my loved ones have a relationship with God, we will all spend eternity together with God in harmony. We know little of what heaven will be like except that it will be in God's presence and complete joy. I believe that God will somehow in His mercy, grace and power, patch it all up, and "put Humpty back together again". Nobody else can. Only God gives that hope. That is why, if you have any broken, unmendable relationships, God is your only source of help.

ONLY GOD CAN MAKE SENSE OUT OF LIFE

Not only does a relationship with God prepare us and our loved ones for eternity, it is the only thing that makes sense out of this life. If this life is all there is, if there is no eternal justice, then life is grossly unjust. No objective, logical person can observe the events of this life – from the martyrs of the past, to the satanic dictators and wealthy crooks of the present, to the miscarriages of justice of all kinds through all ages – and say that evil has been overcome by good. Good will only conquer evil if there is an eternity when an almighty God sits in righteous judgment. Know this: there *is* such an eternity and such a Judge! God is in control and there is everlasting justice. If you get prepared for that judgment by the cleansing God offers, then there is a heaven awaiting you. It's called eternal life. Refuse that provision, and God has something else prepared. It's called eternal death. Eternal death wasn't intended for you, you need not experience it, but if you refuse God's means of sharing in His eternal life, then there is no other option. It's either share God's eternal life or share Satan's eternal death. Why not choose life?

THE HUMAN RELATIONSHIP THAT CONTROLS THE FUTURE

Yes, the relationship with God is the primary relationship. In inter-human relationships, to me, the most important human POWER-OF-TWO is the CHILD-PARENT RELATIONSHIP. Why most important? Because it controls the future – the future of generations, the future of nations. When two become one in a tiny baby, that new life is far-reaching power. Abraham Lincoln's stepmother had tremendous influence on Abe, and through him, participated in saving The Union. Mr. and Mrs. King had strong influence on Martin Luther King, Jr., and through him, altered the lives of everyone of us here. You and I, in varied relationships, have children and young people within our influence. How are we molding them and through them our future and our country?

MISGUIDED PARENTS DAMAGE THEIR CHILDREN

In Tulsa, three students were suspended for physically assaulting a teacher. Their parents hired a lawyer and sued the school. "You can't suspend our sons!" That kind of child-parent relationship will make those boys become honor students. "Yes, your honor. Ten years! your honor?"

WISE PARENTS EXEMPLIFY AND TEACH RESPECT

In contrast, I recall sixth grade. My history teacher misspelled the name of some exotic city. He wrote it wrong again. When he wrote it incorrectly the third time, I said, "You knucklehead." That got his attention! He sent me to the office. The principal phoned my home. That got dad's attention! Dad said, "I'll take care of it." That got my attention! Dad believed in the power of two, but he didn't need a lawyer. I don't know which of the two made the most impression on me, the belt I did receive or the meal I didn't receive that evening, but I re-learned respect.

WHAT KIND OF PARENT ARE YOU AND I

However, you judge between the handling of those two cases, I know we need youth with respect, including respect for authority. But if the parents have none, what then? America needs strong families. What kind of example are parents setting in character and discipline? What kind of training are we giving in integrity, personal responsibility, priorities, and values? We must parent and grandparent with biblical principles, with godly standards, with Christian values. In the last 50 years in America, there has been a decline, almost the elimination, of ethical and moral values. THAT is the cause of America's decline. We must get back to old-fashioned standards if we intend to save America. And reverence for God is the beginning of wisdom. We must parent responsibly, wisely; for in the parent-child relationship, there is intergenerational, enduring power.

THE HIGHEST HUMAN RELATIONSHIP

The *most important* human POWER-OF-TWO may be the child-parent relationship, but the *highest* POWER-OF-TWO is the LOVE RELATIONSHIP. No human strength surpasses the power of two in love. (I am combining two stories into one for illustration, thus some details are altered.)

Decades ago I was friends with a gymnast. You've seen gymnasts. Bobby was built like Adonis. Girls admired him, but Bobby was too busy for girls. Sports were his life. Bobby liked to skin dive. During one dive, he was hit by a boat. The prop slashed the length of one leg and ripped across his back, destroying muscle and bone. With the loss of blood and the way he was opened up, there was no chance of survival. But the boaters realized they had hit something and went back. At the hospital, no one understood why Bobby was still alive, and none expected him to live. But he did.

All doctors agreed he would never walk again without assistance. Bobby believed them. This competitive athlete gave up. His muscles shriveled, and along with them his pride and determination. Unable to even get out of bed, Bobby was defeated.

With complications and infections, Bobby was in the hospital several months. At first, scores of students visited. After several weeks, almost no one visited. Accustomed to cheers, now he had silence and the taste of his own tears, alone.

But Bobby was lucky. For it only takes one friend if it's the right friend. Jean started visiting again, and kept coming back. She had always admired him. Now she discovered she loved him. Not a previous muscular body or athletic ability. Him. Jean determined to be his encouragement. In time, Bobby fell in love with Jean.

Love changed Bobby. For Jean, he vowed he would walk again unassisted. Jean was with him in the hallway when Bobby tried to take those first weak steps without support. She watched as he stumbled. She caught him as he almost fell. She said, "You're doing great. You're going to make it!" He said, "Jean, I'm so discouraged. So afraid!"

They spent many hours together in the hallways. Sometimes crying. One time laughing because Bobby was able to keep up for a while with his 18-month old nephew. Bobby and Jean decided, it's us together against the fear, against the prognosis. There is power in two! Bobby did walk out of the hospital unassisted. Unassisted, but not alone. It was Bobby with Jean.

A RELATIONSHIP WITH GLOBAL POWER

The love relationship releases tremendous power, and the power of two-in-love is immense; yet, for growth, the most awesome POWER-OF-TWO is the doubling power – A DUPLICATION RELATIONSHIP. It's called the Timothy Principal. Paul instructed Timothy, "Find and train leaders, who will find and train others, who will do the same." (That's a very loose paraphrase.) Paul and Timothy were the first major networkers.

With that simple concept, the early church exploded. Those were hard times for church members. In those days, you'd never get church members at the head of the government. It was not politically correct to say, "I'm a believer." You could lose your head. You could be put on the program at the Coliseum. Early Christians didn't want their name on the marquee at the Coliseum. It was always the same event: Saints Vs Lions. And Lions had a perfect record. The only good thing about those events for believers was that every game was a prayer meeting and a "Homecoming". But with The Timothy Principal, Rome and lions couldn't kill Christians fast enough.

Timothy found a convert. The two each got another winner, and two plus one each equals FOUR. The four each got one, and four plus one each equals EIGHT. Eight plus one each equals 16, and so on. How potent is it? By 20 doublings, TWO grows to a MILLION. Enemies of the church saw that growth and said, "They are turning the world upside down."

How powerful can the Timothy Principle be? Its potential is total. TOTAL. Why? Because in 33 doublings, you have the entire global population. We can use this doubling power. If we EACH find one person like ourselves, work with them an entire year if necessary until we each find another person like ourselves. IF each and every one involved duplicates just once a year every year, in 33 years, we'd reach **ALL** – EVERYBODY. The last year goes from half of everyone to all of everyone. That's the potential.

We **can** make a mark on our world! We can take a stand for the Lord, for godly principles, and pass it on. It only works if we pass it on to those who will stand with us and continue to pass it on. We can do something great. This is not merely a theory! I have witnessed it, am experiencing it, in my own family in two real-life arenas – one spiritual and one mundane, though both overlap. Of course, it requires starting, and staying with it. (I've noticed that only those who begin have a chance to be an impact; and no one makes an impact who won't begin.) God gave us the tool through Paul and Timothy. We can impact family, our city, our nation, and our world.

BUILD RELATIONSHIPS

Regardless of status or relationships today, all of us face obstacles, broken dreams, challenges and opportunities. No one has a monopoly on either the good times or the bad times. Don't face life alone. Team up with someone. Whether it's with a spouse or parent, with a child or sibling, a friend or partner, with a neighbor or whomever; join the battle together – in some meaningful relationship with each other, and in co-relationship with God. When you team up with the right someone and God, when you and your friend join forces with the Creator, there is no limit in what two can do.

My Example, My Dad

I have seen faith and honesty walking the street.
I have seen self-respect and humility meet.
I've seen patience and sacrifice stretch out full length.
Compassion and love join discernment and strength.
I've seen heavy workloads for family support.
Family time and vacations given proper import.
I have seen self-control over what was deemed bad
As I watched through the years my example, My Dad.

Following Dad

I've been taught ever since I was a kid
In this life, live as Jesus lived.
But I have more – God gave another guide
Whom I can see, and touch, and walk right at his side.
I may not know what Jesus would have done;
But I've watched dad, the guide God gave this son.
I've watched dad, a wise and godly man,
And I can follow Jesus by following my dad.

Memorial to Mom and Dad

I build you this memorial, a grateful testimonial.
You are a living legacy of what good parents ought to be.
No parent needs to meet perfection,
But you earned well this dedication.

There are no words that could be penned,
No cards or flowers I could send
To thank you for the love you've shown
And all that made our family home.

But words are all the tools I have
To try to share at least by half
The grateful love within my bones
That is the message of this poem.

For praise and for encouragement
To strive to climb the steep ascent;
For strong corrections, not always heeded;
For forgiveness, too often needed;
For praying knees; for loving tears;
For patient guidance through the years;
For good examples so well set;
For humbling secrets so well kept;
For courage strong enough to wait
And let me choose the path I'd take,
Then if that path were wrong or right
To be there stalwart day and night.

Yes, there's a thought behind this poem
That's burning deep within my bones.
This is my testimonial. To you it's my memorial, for
You're a living legacy of what good parents ought to be.

Tugging on the Rainbow

One of the twins, my great grandson Smith,
Has over his head a rainbow to play with.
It's a full arch, and bowed from side to side
With colored cotton strips hanging to be eyed.

Smith was on his stomach — wanted on his back.
For a three-month preemie, still a daunting task.
He'd rolled onto his side, tottering and stuck.
His leg would not go over. But Smith has pluck.

He stretched, grabbed the rainbow. It looked promising.
Tugging on the rainbow might aid accomplishing.
Tugging on the rainbow might be the lift he needed.
And as he gripped the promise, he got the roll completed.

The rainbow is a symbol: promise straight from God.
As we grasp his promise, though our faith be flawed,
God will work his purpose to bring glory and our good.
Reach out. Tug the promise. Doubts will be subdued.

Prayer Paradox

Two college teams have met their sport to play.
One gathers, joined in heart, before the fray.
"Lord, help us one and all to do our best.
No injuries, no fouls, is our request.
We go forth in thy name as we begin,
So if it be thy will, Lord, help us to win."

The other team is anxious for the go.
All thoughts on sports, just one man whispers low:
"O, Father, though my teammates know you not,
And only victory is in their thought,
Do help us triumph, but in such a way
Each man will know You helped him, play by play."

In an election year, for office ran
A man who victory prayed would be God's plan.
"The average person does not know what's good
For his nation, state, or for his neighborhood.
Strong government must all decisions make
To keep the county fair – prevent mistakes."

His opponent held a different view.
He prayed to get the votes to see it through.
"No government should grow too strong", said he,
"The dangers have been shown through history.
Power must reside in every man,
For through the minds of all, God shows his plan."

A builder on his site observes the sky,
And prays to God in faith, "Let it stay dry.
Not for myself alone I make this plea,
But for thousands also whose work, similarly,
Depends on rain-free weeks to earn their pay.
So give us, Lord, we pray, a sunny day."

While in his field not many miles away,
A farmer on his knees has vowed to stay

'Till God in mercy sends his clouds of rain
To fill low reservoirs for waiting stock and grain.
"Not for myself alone I humbly cry,
But for a hundred farmers more whose crops may die."

Opposing nations find themselves at war.
So many die, and thousands wounded sore.
The socialist country knows it's right
That wealthy folks should fund the poor folks' plight,
By force and power to equalize the classes.
"God, win our war before the next year passes."

Free enterprise the other state espouses:
Supply, demand, hard work, reward allows us.
Who works the best and smartest gets ahead.
One should get less who stays too long in bed.
The Bible states the lazy should not eat.
God, bring that erring nation to defeat."

So, God upon his throne hears much ado
From people praying different points of view.
No matter how he answers, some will say,
"God heard me not, he is too far away.
Perhaps he's dead or doesn't really care.
I trusted him to help, but got nowhere."

The others will rejoice and offer praise
That God so quickly answers when they pray.
Does either comprehend God's master plan?
God providentially cares for every man.
Impartially gives the sun to every race;
On just and unjust sends the rain in grace.

Poor Child's Christmas Prayer

Dear God, you've promised to hear us each time we offer a prayer.
I have a request this Christmas, for this is the season to share.
Folks say we haven't got much, Lord, though daddy works lots overtime;
But I don't ask for something myself, Lord. What I do ask is easy to find.

I need a good pair of work boots, size 10. Even used is alright
As long as the soles have no holes, Lord, as long as the seams are all tight.
'Cause Daddy's have long since worn out, Lord, and can't last much past
Christmas Day.
And if some work socks could come with them. I hope that's not too
much to pray.

You know how daddy loves mamma. You've seen the tears in his eyes,
When he had to admit last Christmas, that he didn't have her a surprise.
'Cause her illness had taken the savings, and the cost of things so out of
touch.
So, help him, please Lord, find for mamma a gift that isn't too much.

Please, God, help mommy and daddy to know how much they are loved.
And help us kids to feel really, we don't need a gift more than love.
And thank you for parents who taught us, that though we've been poor
here on earth,
We've a nice place with you up in heaven, 'Cause of Christmas and our
Savior's birth.

(music for this song is in Music section.)

PRAYER COURIERS

When we see someone wounded, hurting and needing,
Our prayer will be futile if we don't stop the bleeding.
When we see someone hungry, and we are well fed;
Our prayer will seem empty if we offer no bread.
When we see someone freezing, and we've blankets to spare;
Can our prayer be sincere if we pray, but don't share?

We can give our prayer wings from our excess of things.
We can give our prayer feet, give it warmth, give it meat.

When we think of the needy, we lift up a prayer;
But the needy have already cried out – in despair!
Let us be the answer to their hopeful plea.
Usually, God uses couriers – such as you, such as me.

RIGHT OF REJECTION

It's your life. Make it pay, don't throw it away.
It's your moment. A time to fulfill, not just time to kill.
It's your talent. Feature your selections, not imperfections.
It's your occasion. To impact your world. To contribute.
It's your discernment. Judge well.
It's your commitment. To lead, to influence for good.
It's your choice. Use ambition, not your right of rejection.

75

There Are NO No-counts
Everyone can be a blessing!

It's an interesting realization to me, that at the miraculous feeling of the 5000 men plus women and children, the men were the only ones counted. Among the men counted, even among the men in Jesus' disciple group, the answer was not found to feed the hungry crowd. The answer was found with a child who had not even been counted. Sometimes the "no-counts" are the important players. In this case, it was the lunch the young boy gave to Jesus, which Jesus in turn dedicated to the Father and used to feed the entire gathering, including those who had not been counted.

The boy gave his lunch to Jesus, but didn't lack for lunch. He ate with the crowd. I have the impression that everyone had eaten their fill. While the disciples were gathering leftovers so nothing was wasted, perhaps one disciple copiously refilled the giving boy's lunch basket so that he returned home with more than he had brought originally.

Regardless of our assets and talents, or lack thereof, if we will happily dedicate to Jesus what we have, then Jesus can bless and multiply it to benefit the giver and many more people besides. If you think you are among the no-counts, please, in faith step out of the crowd, actively put into service that which you have. You will find that your ability, large or small, can be a blessing to someone in a way you may not have imagined.

ODE TO GOLDEN GATE BRIDGE

I see the Golden Span abridge the bay.
Across its stately steel crowd, day by day,
The likes of earthlings to their work or play.
An endless flow of mankind on their way.

The way they go no golden bridge could know.
Nor, if she knew, could ought do to control.
Their way of life, directed by each soul,
Prods each one surely to a timeless goal.

The fogs that swirl around this single span
In mystery enshroud full many a man,
Who, hopelessly, outside their Maker's plan,
Plunge fateful from her heights by some command.

To others, just a glimpse of Golden Gate,
Inspires their heart to sing at faster rate.
The awe that swells within none can abate:
It flows through warm embrace twixt man and mate.

Still, many a human form this arch pass by
That scarcely lift their eyes to look on high.
Perhaps their soul is dead or gone their eye
To grace this artful feat without a sigh.

And yet, this Mighty Woman, graceful path,
To friends of rank or rags, of peace or wrath,
Her faithful service yields, as in the past,
To those who cherish her or stand aghast.

Within her gaze are many sites revered:
The Cable Cars romanticists endeared,
Quaint shops, steep hills, The Wharf once wild and weird,
And Alcatraz where guest and host were feared.

O, Golden Gate, bridge over shining sea,
Your mystery and awe inspire me
To contemplate – how – when – where shall be
The bridge I'll cross from time to eternity.

Bridge to Somewhere

There is a haunting, lonely bridge.
Has allurements – bravery – this bridge.
This bridge can appear anytime, anywhere;
But the planks on that bridge lead to where?

Some are thrust upon that bridge
Through choices – forced options – not their making.
It's acceptable—their solitary right –
To punish the one who induced the taking.

That dead-end bridge is stark and cold.
Walk left, right, ahead – only silent depths.
Voices say: Make it fast, direct, resolved.
But how is this end rewarding or best?

Show strength and courage upon that bridge:
Determine to stay: boldness unswerved;
Discipline, pride, and focus of mind
Amid issues unfair, undeserved?

Could such resolve, such strength of soul,
If focused on positive thoughts of repair,
Change this sad trudge into darkest repose
Back to a happy return from despair?

True friends who see you walk those planks,
If you turn back, would celebrate with thanks.
There is this dark bridge to your somewhere:
Now is the time to choose the good *"Where"*.

BUILDING SANDCASTLES FOR KEEPS

I dreamed, and, in my dream, I was on Sandcastle Beach. A beautiful shoreline stretched for some distance between the surf and the high, steep, rugged cliffs that isolated this beach from the rest of the world. Access to Sandcastle Beach was available only by water, or by hiking a long trek along a dangerous seashore, or by conquering one of the treacherous trails that snaked sharply down the eroding cliff face. Seaweed and seashells were common on the sand, and I saw an occasional piece of driftwood as seagulls circled overhead.

On Sandcastle Beach only two kinds of people were recognized: those who were permanent residents and those who were just visiting. Permanent dwellers were called Castlers, and visitors were Ooglers.

In my dream, Castlers looked like beach bums, but yet they appeared to be an egotistical lot. It was obvious that to themselves they were elite, the royalty of the realm called Sandcastle Beach.

Living in makeshift shelters of drift wood, plastic sheeting and cardboard, the Castlers had developed a world of their own. Their huts were positioned at the base of the cliffs, as far back from the sea as possible, for on occasion the ocean had thrown a mongrel wave upon the beach which destroyed everything in its path, sucking whatever it touched out to oblivion. Even some Castlers, taken by surprise, had been caught and dragged into the eternal silence of the deep.

Beyond Sandcastle Beach, I could see in my dream that the general global population lived just as I, myself, experienced in waking hours; but Castlers never knew that world – never left Sandcastle Beach, and this beach was the totality of their experience and the entirety of their reality. To Castlers, Sandcastle Beach was the whole of life.

From time to time, a headstrong Castler would leave the beach to live in that "other world", but Castlers laughed when such deserters said they were going to experience the "real life". Any sophisticated Castler knew that such was a myth. Popular Castlers lived for today alone, concentrating on their practical beach skills, their ripped bodies with tip-to-toe tan, and making points in Castler society. The best-liked Castlers never discussed what may or may not be out there in the distant unknown beyond this familiar beach. The smartest Castlers denied the existence of anything worthwhile outside the realm of Sandcastle Beach, and by such denial removed it from their thinking.

What was the purpose of life on Sandcastle Beach? To be considered among the top Castlers, of course, by building the finest sandcastle. The only other worthy purpose was developing a killer tan to wow the members of the opposite sex. Castlers lived and died thinking only of self and sandcastles.

As I dreamed, I observed a caste system among Castlers. In the high caste were those who somehow had acquired gold-plated sand buckets and silver-plated shovels. They had genuine faux-silk flags to mount on their castle turrets, and on their fingers they wore sparkling cubic zirconias. Castlers who could erect a monstrous sand castle with plenteous sparkling gadgets were able to attract the members of the opposite sex with the prettiest tan. Some of the high caste members had gotten their wealth honestly, mostly from prize money in sandcastle-building contests. But others of the high caste had gotten their riches by deceitful means. Those who had acquired riches dishonestly were accepted in the high caste society so long as their accumulations were of sufficient substance.

Lower caste members greatly admired their successful superiors and wanted desperately to equal their status. Among the lower caste, some were filled with awe, some with envy, some with near idolatry, and some with hate, but all were filled with intense desire for the things that those above them had to enjoy and to flaunt. Some Castlers had been born with a pewter sand rake in their hand, but most only dreamed of such opulence.

I observed one well-spoken Castler lecturing to a group about *"How to Acquire Golden Buckets, Pewter Rakes and Silver Shovels"*. He spoke of making gold and silver a Castler's written goals, and of setting timetables for winning sandcastle-building trophies. Together the group chanted motivational mantras and agreed among themselves to be at the next seminar. To collect his fee for the exciting sessions, the speaker circulated plastic buckets among his disciples.

Deep in silence, I watched parent and grandparent Castlers indoctrinate their children in the importance of sandcastle building. Hours each day were spent teaching tricks of the trade and refining special skills. A child's worth was judged by how fine a castle builder that child was likely to become. Children hopelessly unskilled were allowed to concentrate on body building, tanning evenly without burning and other physical appearance enhancements, for their only hope of the good life was to capture a skilled Castler. No child was trained in skills required outside the confines of Sandcastle Beach, for none were expected to leave. And why would one prepare for a place one did not expect to inhabit – a place one denied worth even investigating? So it was passed from generation to generation that Castlers, womb to tomb, had one purpose – looking good to other Castlers, preferably by one's unique castle-building skills, but in the alternative, by one's superior tan and physique.

A Castler with no trophy or the skills to get such a trophy had nothing – unless they had the looks to entice a Castler who had trophies to take care of them. A Castler with winning castles and hoarded trophies had everything – including a gorgeous significant other.

Suddenly a kaleidoscope of colored flags and banners filled my dreams. The big event, The Sandcastle-Building Finals had begun.

Ooglers were everywhere. Some had arrived by boat, others had negotiated the cliffs. Oogler Newscasters arrived with camera crews to capture for the world Castler Sandcastles and Castler bodies. It was THE DAY. Skimpily clad Castlers were kings and queens. Today, even Ooglers would like to be Castlers – to possess their gorgeous skin and their skills, and to live in this idyllic place. It was good to be a Castler – especially a winning Castler today. Here before everybody was the supreme work of their hands, the product of their minds, the consummate purpose of their existence.

Many glittering trophies took their places on the shelves of the most astute and talented Castlers this day. How prestigious to gain the designation: "Master Builder Achiever" after one's name. MBA's, did not try to hide their pride from their peers. Major winners of the day moved up to significant others with more exotic bodies.

Sunset fell amid the joy and laughter on Sandcastle Beach casting an eerie glow on elegant sandcastles and on the trophy ribbons so proudly flaunted atop the winning castles' towers. The parties ended, and the celebrants slept proudly, contented, pleased with themselves and confident all was well with the world.

The night passed quickly, and sunrise drove the mists away over Sandcastle Beach. Daylight revealed that not one castle or trophy was anywhere to be seen. The tide in one inescapable, inexorable moment had washed away the efforts and rewards of all the Castlers. With the work and the recognition of their lives swept out to the depths of the sea, the surviving Castlers huddled in the squalid remains of a few huts beneath the heat of a glaring sun.

I awoke, and as I considered my dream, I realized that "Sandcastle Beach" has many different names in the real world; and that "Sandcastles" and "Castlers" surround each of us. Am I one? Beaches are beautiful, and days at the sea side rejuvenating, Tanned bodies can be delightful. I wondered: How many of us are dedicating our life to silly contests of our own "Sandcastle Beach", and never think of the eternal reality beyond? How many of us, seeking to impress our peers, have expended all of our efforts laboring to acquire our own brands of golden buckets, silver shovels, and ribbons? How many of us, when life is over, when too late to reconsider, will be shocked to realize we spent it all in vain building sandcastles? None of it will have value hereafter. How many, when the tide of death tests our souls and the substance of our earthly endeavors, will have anything left to take into the everlasting reality that is beyond our "Sandcastle Beach"?

Used by permission from Dan in the Sand. DanCastles.com.

ON A MISTY SUNDAY MORNING

On a Misty Sunday Morning at the lake,
A mystery-haze rises with a flair.
It veils the view yet casts a wider take
Of wonderment and fear, of hope and care.

The Lent has now begun with Ash and fasting.
God's Son, who paid the price, is resurrected.
The promise is of Life that's everlasting —
Yet many choose the dread of Christ rejected.

The TV shoves its ruse right in our room
With scandal, fraud, deceit — all called "progressing".
Their flaunted progress only leads to doom,
As faster, stronger, they laugh on, regressing.

The mirror tells the time upon my face
With bags and sags and jowls we just call aging.
As life blooms in my mind, I run this race,
But death is on its course with unquenched raging.

So, sin and death incessant surge around us;
Seem in control as Satan wages war.
Powers of evil in-fill and surround us
As they did at Calvary long before.

The murky mists today becloud our eyes.
It's not for us to know each step God takes.
But God is in control and knows the "whys",
And in his chosen time the earth he shakes.

The powers of Rome and hell did not prevail.
They took the life of Jesus on the cross,
Not knowing they accomplished each detail,
Even to the gambling lots they tossed.

Every act they made to kill God's lamb
Fulfilled the scripture as sin's price was paid.
    In hate, accomplished God's redemptive plan
    Of love, as guilt on Jesus' head was laid.

The body in a borrowed tomb was placed.
The stone was sealed. Official guards were set.
Against the sovereign God the world was braced.
The Son of God was killed, destroyed, and yet…

Death cannot defeat the Source of Life.
Lies cannot repress the Fount of Truth.
Love will overcome all Hatred's strife.
Justice conquer all of Evil's sleuths.

On A Misty Sunday Morning, Mary came
To be near Jesus at the sepulcher.
Behind her someone softly spoke her name,
And Jesus said, "I'm living; be assured."

On A Misty Sunday Morning, all was changed:
The seal, the guard, the death were all defeated.
Since that resurrection morning, God's arranged
That unexpected visits be repeated.

Doubts were dispelled. Faith was upheld.
Fear overcome. Victory won.
Christ's church was birthed. Enveloped the earth.
That message sustains. Can't be contained.

And now today we know that Jesus lives.
We know that he is sovereign, in control.
Know confidence and purpose that he gives
Both to this life and to eternal souls.

On that Misty Sunday Morning at the lake,
The sense of mystery from all around,
Recalled there to my mind a wider take
Of wonderment and hope in Jesus found.

Music of The Light

My reply to *Music of the Night*

Surely, purely, light beams pierce the darkness.
Slowly, boldly, rays of hope in darkness.
Gently wakes a new dawn; resplendent light imbues dawn,
Renewing like the beauty of a song ...

Clearer, nearer, streams the splendid light now.
Steady, heady, the sun fulfills its night vow.
Let your spirit rise as the bleakness leaves the skies,
As your sight returns once stolen by the night;
For hope pervades the music of the light.

Yes, the blaze is now breaking through the gloom of night.
All the shadowy past is put to flight.
In the glory you feel your spirit soar –
You're alive as you've never been before!

Longer, stronger, light performs its magic.
Radiance, brilliance, overwhelms the tragic
Dangers that can hide in that treacherous darker side
Where the evil lurks, where fear pursues its fright,
And steals away the Music of The Light.

Do not stay in your journey of some strange despair.
Do not stay as a slave that does not dare.
Free your mind from the image of decay.
You're reborn – love and vision – a new day.

Onward, forward, Light repels the darkness.
See it, feel it, laughing out the starkness
Of your deepest fears, of your colorless veneers,
As the power of the sun brings warm delight;
For hope pervades the Music of The Light.

There is only illusion in the tricks of night.
There is joy in the presence of the Light
Oh, be brave now and leave the past behind.

Let the Son fill that yearning of your mind.

Love and Beauty envelope and possess you.
Darker passions lose power to obsess you.
Light has set you free to the Love you're born to see,
To the Song that only leads to realms of Life.
To joy that rings in Music of the Light.
Faith, Love, Hope will make your soul take flight.
And Hope pervades the Music of the Light.

For personal enjoyment only, noncommercial, can be sung to melody of
Music of the Night by Andrew Lloyd Webber in PHANTOM OF THE OPERA

Misty Morning at the Lake

Racist Rescission

There's no Point of View that's totally new,
and most without doubt are somewhat askew.
But the concept of "Races" is fatally flawed:
just ONE human race was given by God.

The content of character, deep within,
determines one's worth, not tint of one's skin.
I'll change my "tint" by time in the sun;
but character change is much harder won.

Those screaming "racist" to stir up the pot,
are oft the most racist ones of the lot.
Those spewing "racist" for personal gain
are empty of character – mark their name.

Those who hurl "racist" as a plot to destroy
insult the image of the skin they employ.
The incessant use of the slander they sling
to the ears of the wise has a fraudulent ring.

Decreed since Adam, it's one blood, one kin –
never division because of one's skin.
Divided by language to fill the earth –
No schism based on conception or birth.

Intermarriage of skin tones – a wonderful thing,
producing the loveliest skin I have seen.
I have seen war brides from far flung nations
with children most handsome in all creation.

Away with the phony assault on mixed "races".
Welcome each other regardless of faces.
To judge one by "color" is morally wrong.
Let's be like the toddlers and all get along.

Old Friendly Barn

I remember the barn that stood on the knoll.
That's where my dog and I would go
To be all alone and sit in the hay
And wonder what makes grownups say what they say.
And think about love mom and daddy showed.
And want to be like them when I was growed.
Then I'd fall asleep lying there in the hay
And dream childish dreams. Those were the days.

We'd quarrel sometimes as kids seem to do.
I'd go to the barn, my dog would come too.
I'd watch the spiders and moths for a while,
Then pretty soon notice my face had a smile.
When I got in trouble, when the spanking was done
It was to the barn that I'd usually run.
I'd hug that old dog and cry on his coat
Till the stinging had stopped; till the lump left my throat.

We each had a horse, each horse with a stall.
A horse is a friend that is there at your call.
To jump on that friend and ride for a spell –
On the trail you forget the world mimics hell.
The smell of a horse, the touch of his hide,
The feel of his muscles, the joy of the ride.
We both loved the time away from the farm;
We both loved the thrill coming home to our barn.

Yes, I remember the barn on the hill.
In the magic of memories I go there still.
There's a hurt in my heart and a sense of alarm
That kids no longer live with an old friendly barn.

Farming My Five

Politicians say we're in a bad way, but who believes what politicians tell.
Economists shout we'd better watch out, our dollar's sick and may not get well.
When shortages come then the crowds will run to ransack the grocery stores.
But when those cities riot, I'll be where it's quiet, out on my five doing chores.

      Faming my five, there ain't no man alive enjoys life more'n I do.
      Farming my five, ain't no man alive doing more what he wants to.

Rich big city folks make a lot of mean jokes about me and my country kin.
They like driving big cars, smoking fat cigars, living near bright lights sellin' sin.
They get all impressed by how fancy they're dressed, and expensive parties that they throw.
When there's rationing and strife, they'll like our simple life, nurtured by the earth with what we grow.

      Faming my five, there ain't no man alive enjoys life more'n I do.
      Farming my five, ain't no man alive doing more what he wants to.

On my garden tractor time is not a factor. Work feels good, and man there's room to spare.
While city-dwelling cousins stand in line by the dozens paying high for what we're raising everywhere.
Got a very nice pen of good laying hens, some rabbits and a fine-looking calf.
The pastures doing swell. There's water in the well. We're grateful how God gave us what we have.

      Faming my five, there ain't no man alive enjoys life more'n I do.
      Farming my five, ain't no man alive doing more what he wants to.

Enthralled

Why so easily enthralled when before you were appalled?
Why so hard to sin resist? So doggedly allures persist.

It may not be that way for you. If so, you are among the few
Who guard successfully their mind, eye and ear gate-locks refined.

Who ardently their minds renew, focusing on what is true.
Fill their thoughts with good reports, not gossip, or malicious sorts.

Our culture is so filled with lying: love of truth is daily dying.
Anger, envy, sway of power — honesty has lost its flower.

Noxious darkness spreads each day. Exhibition on display.
Culture steeped in evildoing, Celebrating filth-consuming.

What if Christian's took a stand? Eschewed the evil through our land.
Would not pay the demon master. Would not join the dark disaster.

Why don't Christians make their own entertainments for our homes?
TV films we need not hide before our pastor comes inside.

Books and magazines to read that don't deny our Bible's creed.
Even oust the books at schools that contradict our godly rules.

Help our children know that God is not a fraud that fools applaud.
Creator God makes more sense than silly *chance-with-time* nonsense.

Never has a person witnessed "nothing" explode into fitness:
Fit exactly for our world with brain to know that concept's squirreled.

Precision drives the art of science. Doctors demand strict compliance.
No one lives his life by chance. Exacted timing just to dance.

Culture now has thrown out God. Thrown in with the godless mob.
Don't want Holy God around, So, bow to theories though unsound.

And now our country is enthralled with living we before appalled.
We love our degradating sins — and soon the consequence begins.

THE TWO COATS LIED

Two famous coats of history were both deceiving guides.
Upon those coats as evidence the players all relied.
Their evidence was simple, tangible and clear;
And, by its strength, the players were deceived for thirteen years.

The two coats lied. The evidence was planted.
The screamer lied. Her explanation slanted.
Accusers, unified, in unison all ranted.
And when the man was tried, the guilty verdict granted was a lie.

First, Jacob saw that unique coat, all torn and bloodied red.
Distinctly saw and clearly *KNEW* his favored son was dead.
The evidence, as much untrue as what the brothers said;
But yet the lie was set-in-stone within their father's head.

Next, Potiphar, in Egypt, assigned a Steward's Coat
To Joseph, and a signet ring that clearly would denote
That everything within this house was under his command,
So Potiphar could run the guard and travel in the land.

A witness heard a scream one day come shrilly from that house.
Ms. Potiphar was found inside shrieking with torn blouse.
As he ran in, he saw run out, Joseph with no coat.
And there was Mrs. Potiphar: in hand the Steward's Coat.
(Make this material note, lest there be any doubt:
The arm-sleeves of that coat were both pulled inside-out.)

The story is well known by now. Joseph had been framed.
But that coat was damning evidence: conclusive just the same.
Hard evidence was visible. Hard evidence so clear
That the guiltless went to prison, serving thirteen years.

Two Coats provided evidence upon which to rely.
That evidence as misconstrued resulted in a lie.
The evidence was easily seen, and then misunderstood.
That evidence for evil used, God turned to use for good.

James E Foy

Hidden Poison

They don't hide the poison at the end of jobs done.
It's right by your bed — you need only log on.
They don't hang the poison in the top of a tree.
It's nailed to the trunk, and entices with "FREE".
Sometimes the poison is there in your lap.
Give in to your glands. That springs the trap.

The poison is usually exciting, and fun.
It offers big wins, and quite easily done.
Usually a risk, a step out of bounds.
It's in secret, when "those eyes" are not around.

Of course, it entices with things that you like.
It's always disguised as sugar and spice.
It could be decked out as caring fruition,
Or a quick, better way to reach your ambition.

Poison is subtle. A lie that's alluring.
A bright weed that's plucked, but never enduring.
What is enduring is the consequence brought.
A result that is never the promise you sought.

A result, a cost, never earlier mentioned.
A cost far beyond your wildest intention.
 Cost that could stalk you the rest of your life
Since the poison had hidden a hook and a knife.

So, now you're dependent as long as you live.
Now you're enslaved by whatever they give.
Now you're controlled, and under their thumb.
Now you're ensnared till the day you are gone.

The poison is free and easily taken.
When you finally find out that you were mistaken
You've lost all your will to their heinous plot.
Lost independence! And that's all you've got.

92

NO GOD REQUIRED?
(written near the end of the 20ᵗʰ Century)

For years, the bicycle rode along the shore. It enjoyed the lapping of the surf on its tires. It longed to venture deeper into the waves, to explore the ocean's horizon. It became so frustrated at being unable to venture beyond the surf that changes began to overcome the bicycle. Its frame became a hull and decks. The seat became staterooms. Its tires became swimming pools. Its wheels and sprockets became shafts and propellers, while the handle bars evolved into smoke stakes. The spokes became steering wheels as the reflectors became electrical systems. The speedometer became piloting gauges and instrumentation. The chain and pedals became engines and fuel tanks. It grew in size and fashion until it became a great ocean liner. Her Majesty's Ship Queen Mary was once an English bicycle.

Don't think this a fairy tale. This is the actual process by which luxury liners came into being. Perhaps a scientific explanation of how whales developed will add credibility and help your imagination.

A scientific report condensed in *Readers' Digest* article (May '89) "Whales: Gentile Giants of the Deep" authoritatively states: "60 million years ago, ancestors of modern whales were four-legged, wolf-size animals living on the shores of estuaries and lagoons, where an abundance of fish and shrimp enticed them to try wadding ... evolution began reshaping them ... their bodies grew, forelegs shrank into flippers ... hind legs disappeared ... (they) grew tapered tails ending in ... flukes. The nose ... moved to the top on the head and ...separated from the mouth ... the insides were restructured ... as a result of these amazing transformations, they are now helpless on land." Amazing indeed! how whales evolved from something like wolves. But no more amazing than how ocean liners evolved from bicycles. By that reasoning, dolphins probably evolved from Golden Retriever-type creatures, which accounts for both species getting on so well with humans.

Picture that part wolf, part whale creature. It has become enormous – about the size of your car. Its nose has migrated to the top of the head where it is becoming merely a hole, sucking in hair and fleas, and nearly choking its mutating owner during a rain. Its forelegs have shrunk in relative size and the poor fellow doesn't know what to do with them. The rear legs are fusing with each other and with the tail in the process of

93

becoming a fluke. The thing is immobile, a beached "wuf-whale", a mutant suffering from a terrible identity crisis. It nearly became extinct for the difficulty it had foraging and mating, or even finding a partner at the same point of evolution. You MUST have a mate with at least recessive genes mutating from wolf-to-whale at the same time and in about the same step in that mutation process in order to get offspring that carries on that same odd mutation. Let your mind complete the transformation with the assurance that if you were to dig deep enough in the Arctic ice, you would find many oversized wolf-like skeletons with blow holes in the skull. Soon they will be in museums.

I was amused when in 1989 a sober debate waged over "pyramids" and a "face" on Mars. Enhancements of photos taken from space indicated these formations possessed "detail and accuracy". It divided the experts. Some were baffled; some skeptical; some were persuaded there is *intelligent life* on Mars. Though on Earth, these same experts have no difficulty crediting to *chance* such a complex object as the eye, and that eye being coordinated with and connected to the ears, nose, and throat in a harmonized operating system. But on Mars, they think a simple skull-like formation demands a designer and requires a maker. Poor Chance! It's embarrassing. On Mars, it can't get credit for an elementary pyramid – four sides with a point – while just yesterday it was credited on Earth with making all manner of things such as germs, fish, birds, trees, humans and even experts. Is ubiquitous Chance evolving backwards?

Since we've mentioned eyes and space, consider one space program in which we spent over $1.5 billion – the Hubel Space Telescope. The mirror, the telescope's eye, had the most scientifically sophisticated and technically advanced handling from design to manufacturing to installation to launching. Yet, with all that expert direction and care, it did not properly function. Many of the scientists and technicians who worked on Hubel believe that their own eyes (which work) were made by chance and focused by undirected evolution. Their own eyes (which have infinitely more complexity and overall capability than Hubel) they say, are a product of random selectivity and spontaneous generation. Is it fair to ask that, if chance is so talented, why couldn't chance, together with skills of these minds, easily make Hubel perform properly? When chance did so well solo, why did the designers do so poorly in tandem with chance? Since chance alone developed the universe, why not let chance alone develop Hubel?

Why not throw into space any mirror on any trajectory and let it send back pictures? Or was it chance that foiled Hubel? Why does chance in this modern day only seem to work in reverse? Why did chance do well when no one was there to watch, but now under observation, fails? Why, when good luck was ingenious in designing, creating and sustaining our precision universe, does only bad luck prevail in such a relatively small and simple task as Hubel?

I contend that scientists do not in truth believe in spontaneous generation and evolution by random selectivity. If they did, why engineer a Hubel? Just wait for Hubel to hatch without a designer, a cause, or maker. Imagine the stupidity of it – some highly paid technician reading and loafing all year on his government grant. When asked to account for the progress made in the program, he responds, "I expect Hubel to appear in a crude form at any time and to begin an evolutionary process to meet specifications and tolerances." Why does this statement seem too ridiculous to put in print, when it is what our textbooks teach about the origin of the universe and of life? But scientists do not genuinely believe in that kind of origination, at least not enough to bet their pay checks on it. They make Hubel themselves. They are creationists. Their career actions prove it, and belie their theoretical professions to the contrary. Only in an effort to disprove a need for God do they find the twisted kind of faith or the fantastic logic to believe that their own eyes, which mock Hubel, or their brains, which conceived Hubel, come from chance. They protest too much and they do not put their paycheck where their mouth is.

Hubel is not alone. Science built a multi-million-dollar robot, Dante, to walk into the crater of an active volcano. Dante got twenty-one feet and failed. The expertise of science could only produce 21 feet out of a planned 700-foot descent. Both Dante 1 & 2 had to be rescued by humans from their volcano treks. Luck and chance have not smiled on scientific efforts as they did on evolution.

In the April 1988 issue of *Atlantic*, Robert Wright discusses the view of prominent computer scientist, Edward Fredkin, in answer to the question, "Did the Universe Just Happen?" Fredkin contends that the universe is somebody's computer. The whole thing is too complex, too accurate, too immense to be an accident. You might do well to read the article. Fredkin asserts that "information", not matter or energy, is the fundamental, basic stuff of which all else is made; that the universe is one huge computer; and that all of reality as we know it is governed by a single programming rule. This "rule" is the "cause and prime mover of everything." The article asks, "What is the computer made of? What energizes it? Who or what runs it or set it in motion?" The article states, "This sounds like a position that Pope John II or Billy Graham would take." In other words, Fredkin's "universal rule" is God-like, and his arguments support Christian theology.

The respected computer scientist responds, "It's hard for me to believe that everything out there is just an accident ... I don't have any religious belief. I don't believe there is a God ... I'm not an atheist, I'm not an agnostic, I'm just in a simple state. I don't know what there is or might be. But what I can say is that it seems likely to me that this particular universe we have is a consequence of something I would call intelligent." That's his answer for why we have something orderly and purposeful here where there should be nothing.

Following the logic and rules he uses in his professional endeavors, this respected thinker has come close to the obvious: Something as precise, as purposeful and as controlled as our universe had to have a maker and must have a supervisor. He labels it "the programming rule" and "something ... intelligent". The Bible calls it God. Anyone can call it whatever they care to, it still *IS* God. Call the moon cheese, but it's still the moon.

Abandoning cause and effect laws which govern their work, many in the sciences have not yet progressed to Fredkin's level of understanding. I wonder if a subconscious fear of peers keeps Fredkin from confessing a belief in the true God. How could one come so close, yet miss ultimate truth? He admits in the article, "I don't know what there is or might be" out there. Yet he disavows God – the power and mind that *IS* out there. By a mix of deduction and faith, Fredkin believes in "information" as the ultimate source. It seems to me that less faith is required to accept the existence of God, which existence squares with Fredkin's view of universal reality.

Another question to Fredkin – Without a mind, how can you have information, any more than you can have uncaused sound waves? There is of necessity a repository of the information; and something already present to both understand and to react to the information. But once you allow for a mind, you've got God. Or once you assign to information a volition, an ability to act, and the ability to design and create, you've got God.

Other scientists also get close to the biblical concept of reality in their studies of DNA and related issues. They believe there is evidence which demonstrates that the entire existing human population has sprung from one woman – one mother – one originator of the race, probably in Africa. Aware of the Genesis story, they call these studies a search for "Eve", but are very careful to point out that they are not espousing or vindicating the biblical account. Whether or not the research stands up to continued scrutiny and new "knowledge" in their circles, it is interesting that when some scientists find a confirmation of the Bible, they are quick to assure themselves and their peers that they are not caving in to any religious concepts. It's almost a replay of the trite saying, "My mind is made up, don't confuse me with facts." It's like a potential juror whose mind is prejudiced before a trial, so ought to excuse himself from the case. The mind is not objective. It's as if there were some master collusion that two plus two does not equal four. All the math principles say that two plus one is three, that two plus three is five, and seem to point to two plus two being four. But the mathematicians have already agreed that two plus two can't be four. They don't know what it is, but they know what it is not. Therefore, whenever one of them sees something which indicates two plus two is four, he hastens to assure other math experts that though the evidence could be so interpreted, he is not espousing four as an answer. It is comforting to realize that though modern science may be able to prove that some "Eve" was the single womb from which originated all mankind, that will not mean we must take seriously God or the Bible. If we have enough illogical faith in fallible scientists, we need not put faith in Deity.

And they prove themselves fallible over and over again. When I was growing up, I was taught that modern humans were descendants from Stone Age creatures including the so-called Neanderthal Man. The teaching has changed. Later findings "demonstrate that modern humans and Neanderthals coexisted for several thousand years", said an authority at the Natural History Museum in London. "Even allowing for some error, Neanderthals and moderns were too close together in time to allow for one to evolve into the other," a paleontologist at the University of Chicago is quoted. "Scientists have firmly established that Neanderthals lived in Western Europe ... several thousand years after the first modern humans ... appeared there. The finding lends support to the view that modern people did not evolve from Neanderthals ... It also is consistent with the ... proposition that modern humans first appeared in one region, probably Africa, and then colonized the world," Says a NY Times article. They're full circle back to the "Eve" idea.

When one is determined to disprove the existence of God, one's reasoning can become like the logic required to prove that storks deliver babies. Columnist Joan Beck quotes Bruce Ames, professor of biochemistry and molecular biology at the University of California in an article. "Much of what we consider scientific evidence is based on links and associations – not clear-cut cause-and-effect relationships. That can lead to misconceptions and errors, as Ames has noted. 'The number of storks in Germany has been decreasing for years. At the same time, the German birth rate has been decreasing. Solid evidence that storks bring babies'."

Unlike the common perception, the world of scientific writings is a good place to find doublespeak, humor and lack of realism. Read the quote which follows. Then re-read it and transpose its logic into any other field of endeavor. It will not fit. Why should it be said to fit in the field of science? My contention is that it does not fit. It is *said* to fit because it allows its proponents to get rid of the concept of God, which concept they will not allow. As evidence that it does not fit, I offer a recognized Harvard scientific expert, the late Stephen Jay Gould as quoted by columnist George Will: "The many evolutionary factors that produced us are 'quirky, improbable, unrepeatable, and utterly unpredictable. It makes sense, and can be explained *after* the fact. But wind back life's tape to the dawn of time and let it play again – you will never get humans a second time.' So how come we humans are here? 'Because one odd group of fishes had a peculiar fin anatomy that could transform into legs for terrestrial creatures; because the Earth never froze entirely during an ice age; because a small and tenuous species (he means us), arising in Africa a quarter-of-a-million years ago, has managed, so far, to survive by hook and by Crook'." Gould is further quoted as saying we must find the meaning of life "ourselves – from our own wisdom and ethical sense."

I ask: From what would an ethic or wisdom evolve? I ask: Do you believe this man? He admits it's impossible to believe spontaneous generation and random selectivity *in advance*, but we are stuck with it *in retrospect*. It could never happen again, not even given the exact same circumstances ("wind back the tape ... you will never get humans"), and we are lucky that it happened once. To bet your eternal destiny on this reasoning takes more faith than any religion.

I belly-laughed (you might also) at a scientific article on sex: *"Is Sex Necessary?"* "Contrary to our human experience, sex is not essential to reproduction. 'Quite the opposite', explains some anthropologist. 'Sexual reproduction is insane ... like taking two parts out of older models and piecing them together to make a brand-new car.' In the time that process takes, asexual organisms can often churn out multiple generations of clones, gaining a distinct edge in the evolutionary numbers game... If (since) sex is so inefficient, why is it so widespread? Sex almost certainly originated nearly 32.5 billion years ago ... for repairing the DNA of bacteria.... Animal sex is a more recent invention. A biologist of the University of Amherst believes the evolutionary roots of egg and sperm cells can be traced back to ... organisms.... During periods of starvation, one was driven to devour another. Sometimes this cannibalistic meal was incompletely digested, and the nuclei of prey and predator fused.... The fused cells were better able to survive adversity, and because they survived, their penchant for union was passed on to their distant descendants. (You and me) Sex was maintained over evolutionary time because it somehow enhanced survival. How ever sex came about, it is clearly responsible for many of the most remarkable features of the world around us, from the curvaceousness of human females to the tails of peacocks... to enable males and females to recognize one another and connect." Read it in the January 20, 1992 TIME.

I must ask three questions: If the problem with sex is its lack of efficiency, why is our problem too many people? If asexual organisms "gain a distinct edge in the evolutionary game", why are people living longer and better lives? If this thinking is the best science can do, isn't it less ludicrous to believe that God made us the way we are as sexual creatures, rather than believe we were made sexual by some cannibalistic protozoa that only ate half its meal? To accept the nonsense put out as fact by some scientists, requires either extraordinary faith or a predetermined mind set in favor of nonsense.

Given the life span of humans, if humans reproduced like amoebas, as the TIME article author seems to prefer, the human race would have over populated the planet before the first pair had died. There would have been a starving populace devoid of the pleasure, intimacy and bonding of sex. Personally, I prefer God's plan.

Other scientific plans have gone askew. The Biosphere – a man-made environment, totally self-sufficient, ideal, sealed – had its problems. The experiment was tried twice between 1991 to 1994. After the finest engineering our best minds could produce, the place ran out of food and oxygen, and the scientists failed to figure out why. How can that be? Spontaneous Chance did a bang-up job in putting together Earth and the universe, which are self-sufficient environments that have lasted, it is claimed, billions of years. Why can't studied scientists at least equal chance? Or is this another hint that there was and is in fact a Creator more capable than the minds which put together Biosphere?

I've hiked among Giant Redwoods and Sequoias. Comprised of millions of cells, each tree is a literal growth industry. A tree continuously lifts thousands of gallons of water higher than the length of a football field straight up, without a pump, re-using water that was here before the tree was a seedling. Material that falls from the tree decomposes on the ground, forming nutrients to be absorbed by roots to feed the trees.

Chance was quite innovative on Earth. Capillarity, photosynthesis, osmosis, pollination, cell division, soil stabilization, and all kinds of marvels occur constantly, simultaneously, orderly, purposefully within and around a tree. Some naturalist will stand beside that majestic, ancient tree and explain how it all occurs by chance. As he speaks, the naturalist exhales carbon dioxide which the tree takes in while giving off oxygen for the naturalist to breathe. A lucky coincidence, this random symbiosis. Sure, just luck, but such well-packaged accidents are quite common in the real world.

In boy scouts, we'd follow trails. To mark a trail, we'd stack three rocks. To denote a turn, we'd place the third rock beside two stacked rocks. The scoutmaster said such rocks always indicate a trail, prove that someone intends to be followed, or wants to find his own way back. Three properly placed rocks prove a map, a message and a mind. Yet, hands that placed them, eyes that saw them, our brains that understood the whole scenario, our immune system that protected us from infected cuts sustained while hiking, the Redwoods we walked beneath, the diffusion of gases that enabled us to breathe oxygen from the tree rather than suffocate in our own exhaust, and the entire solar system that we slept under at night were all the result of chance. Is there inconsistency there? Three rocks are a plan – a 100-billion-cell nerve system is random selectivity.

While questioning consistency, consider the final paragraph of the first quoted article, which has the purpose of showing how whales evolved from wolf-like creatures. It says, "They (whales) are the first animals mentioned in the Bible: 'And God created great whales', one of God's noblest creatures." That is either biting sarcasm or gross nonsense. Since whales evolved from wolf-like creatures, God did not create whales. Isn't the Bible imprecise, neglecting to mention wolves eons before whales, and overlooking altogether "wufwhales". How unsophisticated for the Bible to speak of God as Creator at all. On Mars, one may need at least the equivalent of human life, or a Creator and a religion, because pyramid shapes are there. But on Earth, with one's faith illuminated by modern, unbiased science, and with our intelligence enlightened by logic that demonstrates: 1) how whales came from wolves, 2) how the universe is a computer for eternal information with no mind to originate it or frame it, or 3) how evolution occurred though it could never occur again even in the same circumstances; then is a God required?

NOTICE: Headline February 1992: "Researchers Challenge Whale Evolutionary Theory": "A genetic analysis of whales challenges an assumption about their evolution and confirms the idea that cows are more closely related to sea mammals than they (cows) are to donkeys."

It's not wolves now but cows, or something cow-like that became whales. Science changed its mind again. Can you trust it with your soul?

A Tripping Brick

His life was going fairly swell.
He kicked a brick and flatly fell.
That sudden stop his heart did quell.
Heard instantly a solemn bell
That pealed his mortal final knell.
His flight to heaven or to hell?
Among we earthlings, who can tell;
But he and Jesus know right well.

Watch out for bricks. Break from your spell.
Don't run from God. Stay off your cell.
There are two choices parallel:
Get right with God or left in hell.

Not a Chance
A choice of fools

Matters of justice have been fixed in our minds.
We're quick to opine, drawing red lines.
Yet, "matters of justice" have changed over time,
mock ancient minds, reverse the divine.

Fixed facts of nature are being called fluid:
just say you undo it, there's nothing to it.
You're breaking the law if you don't call him "girl" —
He'll steal her sports laurels. You can't overrule.

In matters of morals, good is called wrong.
Evil belongs. Just go with the throng.
In our entertainments, pure is demoted.
Desires emoted. Filth is promoted.

No one in real life can live by woke rules.
In a day, you'd be schooled that chance is cruel.
Don't stop at red lights. Why look in both ways?
Cruise blindly through. Chance guides, primers say.

Don't plan out your trip. Why mess with a map?
Chance is your escort to get where it's at.
Don't study for tests. Pick answers at random.
Let the *Chance Phantom* good answers fathom.

Engineered Genetics. Genes manipulated.
Outcomes stipulated. Results regulated.
Requires exactness! Making any revision
of a chosen design demands precision.
Make one tiny slip in the slightest detail,
Your outcome will fail. Strict observance entailed.

Yet, say all the textbooks: We got here by chance,
a quirk circumstance. No tune, yet a dance.
Nothing from nowhere, given long time,
becomes just-right design. Accidents align.

There's no logic in it. Conceptions of woke
    are serious bad jokes that deceive many folk.
It's frogs in the sauce pan: as liquid gets hotter,
    frogs stay in the water, unaware they are fodder.
Till no longer able, when the jig is up,
    to gather the gumph to escape the cup.

On Hypocrites

Yes, there are hypocrites in church. Yet, that is no reason to avoid church or to not be a Christian.

There are hypocrites in the gym. The carry membership cards but seldom work out. That is not a legitimate excuse to avoid exercise. There are hypocrites in most restaurants. They talk about eating healthy, but they don't eat according to their talk. Their pets may be on a better diet. There are hypocrites on the job and on the highways going to work.

We still go to gyms, eat at restaurants, go to our work, use the highways. Hypocrites do not prevent us from doing anything we desire to do. Laziness might. Poor choices might. Deceiving ourselves might. But we cannot blame bad behavior on hypocrites. Don't let hypocrites keep you from church. Church is the place where folks who admit their needs come to find both temporal and eternal answers. Come join us.

Christians are not perfect, but they are a work in progress, and they are forgiven. We all need improvement and all need forgiveness.

CLASS OF '59 IN 2009

Did you say 50th reunion? That's hard to believe!
That means we're getting up there. That's hard to receive!
Using meds & creams & surgeons – trying to deceive?
Will you know me, or I know you? That's hard to conceive.
Soon walkers, scooters? – All depends. Troubles to relieve,
Some pains need Oxycontin, others just Aleve.

Mostly we need friendship, as in Escondido High
Where we shared that Cougar Spirit, and love was always nigh.
So now we share our memories – a hug, a laugh, a cry.
Brag on kids and grandkids who brave things we'd not try.

Just sentimental fools making peace before they die?
No! It's love and true affection, too long hidden from our eye!
And friendship will still bind us 'til we say to earth "goodbye"
And we join that Great Reunion with our Savior in the sky.

Now we've passed 60th, and no longer counting.
So grateful for friends still with us this long.
We fondly remember those gone on before:
Still picture their faces as in The Gong.

(The Gong was our yearbook)

What's All This Clamor About Gold?

Why do people desire gold?! Gold. It's in the earth — it's found with dirt! Or found in a stream! What's the glamor of gold? Why do people desire gold, covet gold?! Answer: Because other people covet gold. That's it. The value of gold is in the fact that other people wish to have it. You have it; I think it's pretty; so, I'll give you something of actual value to take it from you. Some people will steal it from you. Some people will actually kill you to take it. Yet, it has no inherent, real value — only envy. Ubiquitous envy.

You say I'm stupid or crazy. Let's think on that. You cannot nourish yourself from gold. You cannot eat it. Gold cannot sustain you. You cannot clothe yourself with gold. You cannot wear it as a garment for warmth or comfort. You cannot house yourself with gold as in crafting a cottage. You can live in ice by making an igloo. You can live in leather by making a teepee. You can live in wood, or even straw, or dirt by digging a dugout. But you can't live in gold. Gold has no strength, and no insulating factor against heat, cold, or noise. Oddly, at bottom, the universal result of owning gold is discontent because of a drive to get more; *or*, in tragic times, frustration since your treasure is worthless. Hence, gold has no elementary, basic value when conditions are desperate. And, conditions can become desperate, have become desperate historically. Desperate is not a joke or an impossibility.

Gold is shiny. Gold doesn't tarnish. Gold is a good conductor. Gold has weight. But it has no life-sustaining value. Its value is envy. You've got it, I want it, so it has that envy value for you while it's in your possession. Until you are hungry and cold and exposed! Now you wish to trade your gold for a bird to eat, or for wood to erect shelter, or for a coat, or for tools. But those who have the bird, wood, coat, or tools do not desire your gold since it has no use for them! They and everyone else at the time desire birds, wood, coats, tools. You might trade an extra bird for a tool; or trade some lumber for a coat. Why would one trade anything for gold which in desperate times has no survival use? You can use your gold to hold down your ragged blanket so the wind doesn't blow it away. Or stack gold bars to build a protecting wall. Or pave a path to your dwelling.

Therefore, what happens when the world gets turned upside down? When truly bad times come? What will you desire then? You'll desire to build a secure shelter. You'll require food to nourish your body. You'll desire water and fire. You'll demand cotton and wool for clothing. If you own gold, you will gladly trade for a loaf of bread. With gold, you'll crave an exchange for a blanket or boards. But those with meat, lumber, clothing, or hammers have no use for gold. There's no more envy value in it. Imagine being envious of a bird, wood, coat, or tools that others have. Imagine the real value of desperately needed basic items – valuable survival necessities. Imagine the ultimate triviality of gold.

CONSIDER THE PRICE

You and I paid too much
If success cost honesty
If fame cost morality
If compromise cost character
If acceptance cost reputation
If income cost ethics
If wealth cost right
If ease cost truth
If gratification cost godliness
If thrills cost loyalty
If luxury cost family
If pleasure cost love
If life style cost life

Wendi caught the Firecracker!

Firecrackers are Hard to Eat

Of course, you never ate a firecracker. Have you tasted one? I know you've smelled their burnt, acrid aroma.

Come back with me to an old-fashioned Fourth of July celebration. In Oklahoma, it was hot and humid. Families were gathered on the school athletic field. The band informally played some rousing music. Some folks were waving small flags, and some wore flag shirts. Small kids had sparklers. Boys tossed firecrackers. There was cold watermelon and homemade ice cream. A good-natured man, wearing a veteran's ball cap, with one leg and crutches, won the 3-legged race. He didn't want the small trophy, so it went to the kids who finished next, tied together in the traditional 3-legged mode. But the main attraction was the Greased Pig Contest.

Near the cage that held the young pig, some Tom Sawyer-type boys were arguing strategy: What's the best way to hold on to a slippery pig? While the boys were boasting about how they'd win, Wendi, my 8-year-old tomboy daughter, decided that this piggy was *the cutest thing*. Well, she wanted it. And she is competitive! She'd be the only girl in the fight, but Wendi is no sissy.

She was wearing a long-sleeved blouse of cool gauzy material – brand new. Never worn before. No, it wasn't the standard pig-catching uniform. All the boys had taken off their shirts: hairless chests shining with sweat naked in the sun. In that mob, Wendi looked like a shy date at her first ever dance. The boys saw her get in place at the starting line. Oh, did they tease and laugh! Then they taunted her. But Wendi is not easily deterred.

The starting gun was – what else – a firecracker. The match was struck. The fuse was lit. BANG!! The startled pig was released. Now, I think I would have used Crisco for the lubrication; but someone had poured motor oil all over that scared pig. That little porker with adrenalin revved up and four legs cranking, was tearing though his attackers. It was obvious, no one was going to capture this piggy. Numerous boys quickly got their hands on that pig, even wrapped their arms around him, but that bacon-in-the-makin' was squealing, kicking, and twisting. Nobody could hold on to him. Falling on him worked no better, because he quickly squeezed out of the pile. He was more slippery than a politician, and totally built for escape.

Shoved around in that horde of wild boys, Wendi didn't get a chance at the pig for quite a while. But she watched it closely. When she did get next to him, she made her move, flung herself down on him, wrapped him in her arms, and held on. Yep, she held on! The material of that new blouse gave enough friction, and the pig was caught. By the girl!! Oh, how embarrassing to the tired, filthy boys with grass now stuck all over their oily skin. Wendi was now the victorious owner of a small pig, and of a greasy blouse that looked as if she and the pig had been in the same mud hole. She triumphantly put the pig in its cage; then turned, and did she ever laugh at all those embarrassed boys!! Her laugh was retaliation! (see younger version below) No one there could have guessed that two of those chagrinned guys would graduate from OU and become professional football players! Mitch and Ricky. I think another one became city mayor.

"What are you going to call it?" everyone wanted to know. Wendi popped off: "Firecracker!"

Very quickly, boys and their dads gathered around Wendi. "How much will you take for the pig?" They wanted to buy it for an FFA project. She turned down as much as $25 bucks that I know of. Could have replaced the ruined blouse. And that was just the beginning of regrets.

It's bad enough when your little girl brings home a boy, but a pig?! Or, maybe a pig is easier. It eats less, doesn't drive a car, and you need not worry when your daughter is at the barn. Well, where should we keep this pet? We put Firecracker in our chicken pen. That turned out interesting. A friend called it: "The International Ham and Egg House." But the hens quit laying. Just quit. Right then I really wanted to get rid of that rascal, but I was out voted 4-to-1. The neighbor boy was glad we no longer had extra eggs to give away. He would eat store eggs, but said: "I just don't want chicken eggs."

Of course, we reinforced the chicken pen with hog wire. The chickens had dusting holes. Firecracker rooted out all the holes. Enlarging those dusting holes was another similarity to a politician. He took something useful and expanded it to uselessness. Whenever a hen got into one of Firecracker's holes, he'd run her out.

In that pen, he consumed the most and always wanted more. He produced the most waste, made the most commotion, contributed nothing, and the only way to solve the problem was to get rid of him. But, he endeared himself on emotions, and the majority voted for the pork.

With the passing of the months, it became time for market. It was a sad day! Dad had to do what a dad has to do, with three girls and their mom crying. What's a modern man to do when four women cry? Firecracker got a reprieve. How did he use his good fortune? Like an experienced politician, he stayed at the trough.

After a few more weeks, we had no alternative. The pet was now gigantic, and he had nothing left to ruin in the hen house. It was time to send this politician to the next banquet – as ham. Wisely, this time a school day was chosen for the dastardly deed, and even the girl's mom was mentally ready to assist. I squared the horse trailer up to the gate of the pen, put up a ramp, got in the pen and invited Firecracker into the trailer. After only three or four laps around the pen, the hens squawking and feathers flying, that well-behaved pig went up the ramp. "Not such a rough job", I said to my wife as I looked at chicken droppings and the pig's political legacy on my boots. How he fit between the end of the trailer and the gate posts, I don't know! But politicians can get out of tight squeezes, and Firecracker had not gone into the trailer – he was out. Loose. Escaped. I had misread his hips.

Quickly I moved the trailer next to the barn, forming a "V" into which to drive the pig, forcing him up the ramp. What I learned was, you don't force an overgrown hog to do anything! Four hundred pounds on four legs against two hundred pounds on two legs is unfair at best. (I don't know what he weighed.) It's also ignorant – yet, I continued to try. I grabbed his ears. I grabbed them again. No use. (I did prove you can make a slip curse out of a sow's ear.) I grabbed his leg. But a pig leg is for ham, not for a handle. It's tapered the wrong way. The tighter you squeeze, the faster your hand slips off. I kept trying. I said to my wife: "I'm going to lasso him like they lasso calves at the rodeo – probably that rough rope will hold." I can't believe I thought that. I can't believe I said that. I *really* can't believe I actually tried that. There's a reason you've never seen a pig-roping contest. Look, I was fit and in good shape, but we covered all six of our acres and I don't know how many miles deciding who was boss and who was going to take what form at who's breakfast. That pig wasn't close to surrender. He had no motor oil on him today, but was tough to catch. Somehow Firecracker knew, that, for a pig, just one trip to the butcher can ruin your whole day.

I was exhausted. Perhaps delirious. I heard a voice: "When all else fails, use your head." I remembered a sedating shot a doctor had given me before a surgery. I remembered how God told Moses to use the rod in his hand. I had already retrieved a short-handled scoop to encourage this beast in the proper direction, but now, out of breath, I said to my wife: "I've had it! I'm going to knock him out. We'll winch him into the trailer." I raised the metal scoop, and BAM, whacked him as hard as I could right between the ears. The steel quivered and sang out. The handle broke off where it was welded to the scoop. The scoop itself flew through the air just missing my wife nearby. Could have killed her. I saw an instant vision of this headline: "Man uses ruse of capturing pig to murder wife." The pig let out a healthy sort of grunt-and-squeal, and took off unfazed. My jaw dropped in disbelief. Standing there with busted handle, I said to my wife: "That thing is invincible. But it IS all over! I'm going to get a shovel, and the shotgun. I'm going to shoot it and bury it wherever it is when I get back." I stormed to the house.

When I returned with shovel and gun, Firecracker was over by the trailer. My wife shrugged her shoulders. (If she had said, "I just herded him over there. Not a big deal." I don't know the damage done to my manhood.) But, she just looked blankly at me, tilted her head and shrugged her shoulders. I walked softly to the pig, tapped him on the shoulder with the gun barrel, and he walked up the ramp. "Stupid pig!" We drove in silence.

The packages from the butcher filled the freezer. One fateful evening meal, we broke out Firecracker pork chops. They looked good, sizzled good, smelled good. The women were crying good. "Eat that meat." I insisted. "Come on, eat. The pioneers would have starved if they hadn't eaten their pets." Boo hoo!! Ohoo, boo hoo. Sob, sob!! (That reaction wasn't good. The stuff I said sounded okay just before I said it. I know the clincher was true and proper because I heard it from my own father.) "Okay, girls. There are hungry children in India; now eat your Firecracker – I mean, your pork chop." More tears.

An out-of-work friend was grateful for all that meat. I'm certain it tasted great; but honestly, I, myself, can't even say how that pork chop tasted; for just like the ones on the plates of those emotional women, my beautiful pork chop was uncut. Not a bite out of it. Firecrackers ARE hard to eat!

"Long may our land be bright with freedom's holy light."

I love my Motherland every day. I love the land of our forefathers and our constitution. I love the land of my childhood. I love the land of the free and the home of the brave. "Oh, say, does that Star-Spangled Banner yet wave o'er the land of the free and the home of the brave?"

When I see a color-guard on parade with a brass band marching behind them playing the National Anthem, I get a chill up my spine, a tear in my eye, and a love in my heart that cannot be matched or contrived. I don't understand how anyone born and raised in America can see Old Glory, hear the band play our Country's Song, and not feel pride coursing through their veins, honor bristling in their muscles, and resolve stiffening their spine. How could it not stir an American to deep passion? Hearing Stars and Stripes Forever always thrills me. Singing America: "My Country tis of thee, sweet land of liberty," lifts my soul. America the Beautiful brings grateful goose bumps. I readily admit, The Battle Hymn of The Republic causes a religious, patriotic enchantment to overwhelm me.

Yet, in the years following the 70s, this special patriotism has been on the wane. I pity pallid, lukewarm, ungrateful souls. I pray that patriot pride will again grip our military, recapture our government in high places, and again be taught with genuine fervor in our schools.

If ever a nation in all history has earned the right to be called noble, generous and kind, The United States of America is that nation. This great nation is the international guardian of individual liberty and sovereign freedom. If this bastion of independence is lost, the entire world will pay dearly in governmental restrictions, control and enslavement. Mark it down.

Our fathers' God, to thee, Author of Liberty, to Thee we sing. Long may our land be bright with freedom's holy light, protect us by thy might, Great God our King." May this be our prayer, along with our pledge: "*I pledge allegiance to the Flag of the United States of America, and to the Republic for which it stands, one Nation under God, indivisible, with liberty and justice for all.*"

HAPPY NEW YEAR, AMERICA

In a way it's been a great year,
In a way a test-of-faith year.
In a way it's been "a year we will remember."
In a way it's been a down year.
A kind of smile-and-frown year.
In a way it's been the finest moments ever.

We shared the good and bad times.
We-gave-it-all-we-had times.
We kept the faith, & through the whole year shined.
Took good and stormy weather,
Joined hands and hearts together,
And through it all we saw ourselves refined.

Happy New Year, my Country!
Happy New Year, befrienders!
Happy New Year, America, brave and strong.

We remember the times we stood so proud.
Times we kneeled, like our Founders, prayed out loud.
Sang "God Bless America" with our heads bowed.
Yes, Happy New Year, Old Glory, red, white and blue.
Yes, Happy New Year, America, we celebrate you.

And now we face a new year,
A testing-of-our-strength year.
A year when we must stand strong on the line.
The best-we've-ever-been year,
When right-and-good-must-win year.
Join hands with me to make this Country shine.

Happy New Year, my Country!
Happy New Year, defenders!
Happy New Year, America, brave and strong.

(On July 4th substitute "Happy Birthday" for "New Year")

TRAVELING TIME

It's travel time: The planes and ships are calling,
From land and sea, from aisle to splendid aisle.
Now spring is here; the birds and flowers singing.
It's time to fly, yet, fate says wait a while.

But we shall soar when summer smiles have found us;
Or when the snows the trees and meadows hide.
We shall explore the grandeur that surrounds us:
Together share God's wondrous beauty side by side.

When comes the time, then better be the splendors.
Be better for the time we had to wait.
The worlds we find will flaunt delights and treasures.
We'll thrill and laugh like children through the gates.

We'll stroll the streets, canals, the parks, and cafés.
Taste bread and wine upon the grass at Rome.
We pray to God to guide our lives and pathways;
For peace and safety always on our journey home

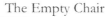

The Empty Chair

This Photo used by permission of Donna Wheat Wuerch, blogger.

The Empty Chair

Today your chair is empty where we "togethered" gently.
The "we" part, being most enjoyed, placed it where our hands could join.
The views still have their beauty, although a bit more mutely.
The places seem surreal now: your absence present somehow.

It's true that life goes on. You and I, we carry on.
Especially as a family. We planted quite a vibrant "tree".

The chair is mostly symbol; the fact more universal.
Alone yet not alone — like a favorite song well known.
The original I cannot find. The melody still haunts my mind.
Your life flows on in plenty, although your chair is empty.

Our life the way we lived it: rewarding beyond limit.
Stories stream abundantly, where now your chair sits vacantly.

Gretchen

I'll sing you a song about Gretchen.
When I met her she was just a pup,
Covered with fleas about a thousand per knee.
It's been fun watching her grow up.

I built a sturdy house just for Gretchen.
Shingled like the home of my youth.
That dog house was huge – easily lodge two –
in case some night I needed its use.

When she once fell into the swim pool,
'Twas a mid-winter night, of course,
I was so bold dashing out in the cold
dressed only in a nightshirt, or worse.

Nancy met us both in the kitchen.
Towels and 'lectric dryer in her hand.
Gretchen was so good as shivering she stood:
but then she shook, and, O my land.

When Nancy walks on our five acres,
Gretchen follows closely at her side.
To faithfully tend her companion and friend:
we're glad we don't have to keep her tied.
(Gretchen that is)

Inside lying soft on the carpet,
Gretchen's a fur pillow for the kids.
She knows she belongs as we sing favorite songs:
then all give in to heavy eyelids.

We learned the other day Gretchen's crippled.
Intense pain in both her rear legs.
Can't normally run, or jump, or quickly turn,
her condition could worsen with age.

It's hard to sing more about Gretchen –
we think of her as part of family.
When she is well, you'll be the first ones we'll tell.
Till then, thank you for your empathy.

Gretchen's House

There it survives! Weather-beaten it stands.
For it was built sturdy by caring hands.

There's moss on the shingles, holes in the roof.
Snug in that place, securely aloof,
She certainly called that house her own –
A replica of the builder's home.

That boyhood home long since torn down,
Almost like trash from a growing town.
Progress evicts what sits in its path.
Gretchen's House stands there still, and laughs.

I reached down and touched that mystic home –
Got moss on my fingers, chills in my bones.
The antique patina, the beauty of age.
No words to express it since I'm not a sage.

There it survives! Weather-beaten it stands.
For it was built sturdy by caring hands.
Memories survive like the Dead Sea Tomes
Of Gretchen's and my old childhood homes.

A QUIET PLACE

Can we find a QUIET PLACE, a respite in the endless race?
Place where more is won than lost, and stress is less a cost?
Can we find a place where we become what we could be
And let the restless, mindless crowd rush on?

Can we find a worthy plan that will help our fellowman,
Where we make our mark in life giving purpose in the strife?
Escape the thoughtless grind, create a cloud that's loving-lined
And tell the selfish, pointless path "so long"?

Can we find a peace within, beyond our culture's noise and din,
Be content in heart and mind, tangled thoughts to let unwind?
Can we satisfaction know, complete fulfillment as we go,
Assured the haunting emptiness is gone?

Can we meet the people who will be our friends forever true,
Know our faults and love us still, in our world a need to fill?
Can we help them on their way, loyal love give day by day,
As friend through need, as friend indeed, belong?

We have found there is a Friend gives a peace that does not end,
Has a satisfying plan for us and for our fellowman.
in Him the void is gone, replaced by hope, joy, love and song.
A life worthwhile, a heartfelt smile, has dawned.

I Grab His Hand

My little girl of five of six would walk beside me on the shore.
The beach, the shells, the seaweed – so much to explore.
She'd search for seashore treasures. Could never get enough.
She'd run beside her daddy in the bubbling surf.
And when the water caught her feet and knocked her in the sand
I would laugh while reaching out a strong and gentile hand.
And I always grabbed her hand. Would quickly grab her hand.
Wet and sandy in the surf, she'd grab on to my hand.

She came of age, and said, "I've got to be just who I am."
There came a love within her for sharing with a man.
There came a need to speak her mind to those who came along.
The way she found to say it best was through a poem and song.
And when she found close harmony with someone in the band
Her words fit to his melody – she took his loving hand.
She took hold of his strong hand. A new journey hand-in-hand.
Through discord and sweet harmony, she chose to grab his hand.

We all need a hand. We all want a hand.
Man or woman, young or old, it's better hand-in-hand.

When life is hard, when options few, when things get in a twist.
When things go right, just as we wish, singing songs like this.
Whether up or down, good or bad, with zesty life or bland,
We have a God who cares for us and offers us his hand.
Through Jesus Christ who came to earth another place and time
He reaches down and says to us, "I'll take your hand in mine."

And I choose to grab his hand. He holds on to my hand.
If knocked down hard or running strong, I choose to grab his hand.

TUX AND TAILS AND TRINKETS

Tux and tails and trinkets cannot enter in the Gate.
Cadillacs and Hummers will all meet the same sad fate.
You can only enter Heaven clothed in Glory of the Lamb,
Or be lost in outer darkness with the naked and the damned.

The world is called *The Jungle*, 'cause it's scary, wild and dark.
You're on the hunt, or hunted; on the run or on the stalk.
The world is called *The Rat Race*, and the rats aren't on a ride.
They're hiding for their life, or scheming for your hide.

A man will gladly sell his soul to make a pot of money,
Just to buy a bigger house and wed a younger honey.
Just to get that huge TV, a newer Jag with all its toys.
Just to satisfy his pride, and be the envy of the boys.

Yet, this life is but a vapor, a blade of grass, a mist.
So soon this life is over: you'll be gone, and seldom missed.
Your debt will be your legacy. Your plunder turn to rust.
 Your deals recalled in infamy. Your body melt to dust.

Why not lay-up treasure where no thieves can ever strike.
No rust, no dust, no pressure. Golden streets won't rut or blight.
Why not work for lasting pleasure where eternal life is won,
When the God of all the ages says: *Welcome home. Well done.*

Tux and tails and trinkets cannot enter in the Gate.
Cadillacs and Hummers will all meet the same sad fate.
You can only enter Heaven clothed in Glory of the Lamb,
Or be lost in outer darkness with the naked and the damned.

PROPER FOCUS

We who wear glasses know how vital focus is. Let's think about Proper Focus: how we see things in life, how we label events and circumstances in life. We will not talk about idealist nonsense – not talk about rose-colored glasses, but we will see that how we *perceive* incidents in our life controls how we react to our present situation and how we come out on the other side, whether it's tough times that must be overcome or good times that can be made even better. Whether the improvement is for us or for someone in our sphere of influence, we'll see how our point of view, our perception, either enables us to move upward or cancels improvement. I'll illustrate "Focus" with a story you may have heard.

A boy, playing baseball with his Dad, said, "Daddy, you take field, and I'll hit it to you." You know the story? He threw the ball straight up, swung at it as it fell, and missed. He tossed it up again, swung and missed. He tossed it up a third time, and still didn't hit it. He said to his dad, "Today, I sure am pitching good!" That's an amusing example of choosing to focus on strength! Identifying with the positive. It's our personal choice, a conscious decision, how we perceive events in life.

REAL LIFE EXAMPLES ARE PROOF THIS CONCEPT IS VALID.
I'm going to use several human-interest stories – actual, true experiences of folks much like you and me. The examples demonstrate that Proper Focus is not just a cute theory – it is a powerful tool that can help transform lives. Perhaps your life: from poor to good; from decent to excellent; from good to better; from self-satisfied to helping others. That's my purpose here.

WE CAN'T CONTROL OCCURRENCES, BUT WE CAN CONTROL RESPONSES
Things beyond our control happen in all lives. How we react to the *happenings* is within our choice. Will Rogers put it this way, "People are about as happy as they decide to be." Abraham Lincoln, at the beginning of the Civil War, when many were against him, said it like this, "I believe it is the right of everyone to be happy or miserable – and I choose happy."

WRONG RESPONSES CAN DESTROY EXISTING ACCOMPLISHMENTS
In contrast to proper focus, a wrong perspective, "improper focus," can sabotage even extraordinary success. In the 1950s, a new singing group called The Carpenters came to Disneyland in Southern California for their chance in the spotlight. That's a long time ago, but some of you may

remember the Carpenters' music: *Merry Christmas Darling; Close to You; For All We Know.* Richard and Karen Carpenter had the look and the sound that propelled them to international success. Made it big. Some of us older folks watched Karen's televised life-story. We saw an attractive, successful young woman. Karen saw herself with shame, as unattractive. Rejecting her own body, she starved herself to death. To us, she had everything (including a fine figure), but Karen focused on perceived imperfections. Her ambition lost out to Anorexia. And anorexia took her life. She lost everything because of blurred insight – improper focus.

Another example is Michael Jackson. This man had many advantages from childhood: good looks, talent to dance and sing, a charismatic personality, even married the daughter of Elvis Presley. How can you expect more than that! But he saw himself differently. It seemed that he kept changing his face, and his skin, and the style of his clothes, and his way of life. It's said he got on drugs; and drugs killed him. Somehow his extraordinary success in show business got all out of focus, and his life ended early at age 51.

WRONG FOCUS PREVENTS CORRECT UNDERSTANDING
Focus is vital. It gives misunderstanding or understanding. Over a hundred years ago, a one-room school teacher thrashed a boy soundly. The boy moaned to his dad about the beating, "That teacher is mean." His dad said, "No, he's not mean, but he does have the opinion you shouldn't talk while he's teaching." That afternoon, the teacher came to visit the boy's parents about the discipline. Before going to the front door, the teacher asked the boy, "Is that big dog vicious?" "No," said the boy. When the teacher got up on the front porch, that dog chewed his leg severely. The teacher snapped at the boy, "You said your dog isn't vicious!" "He's not," said the boy, "but he does have the opinion that a stranger shouldn't be on our front porch."

EVEN IMAGINARY FAILURE CAN SABOTAGE YOUR LIFE
How you *see* things does make a difference. How you define a circumstance, how you evaluate it, is serious. As we discussed, focusing on imperfections and difficulties, whether imagined or real, can wreck one's health, can smash a career, can ruin a life. Karen Carpenter only imagined herself overweight. Others who saw her may have been jealous of her figure. Thousands admired her; but she destroyed herself over wrong focus. Michael Jackson forfeited literally a wonderland – Neverland – due to bad

focus. In contrast, other folks, who had much less to work with, have demonstrated extraordinary positive focus, and it changed their life for the better.

EVEN ACTUAL TRAGEDY NEED NOT CONQUER US

We don't need to surrender our life or ambition to hard luck. We can suffer even enormous tragedies, and overcome – IF we hold on to a winning perspective. In 1971, a 13-year-old Texan named Jim became a human torch when a fuel can exploded in his hands. Third degree burns covered 85% of his body. He was scarred head to foot. He lost both ears – ears gone. Lost both hands. No hands! This teenager had every reason to give up and to pity himself. Who reading this would have blamed him if he had given up? Would you? But he determined to focus on his ambition to be an artist. Against all odds or expectations, he had the grit to strive for the unattainable. While still bandaged, he had a brush handle pushed into the wrappings over the stumps of his arms where his hands once were, so he could paint. Can you see it: burn-scarred arms with bulky bandages where the hands had been, and he has a nurse force an artist's paint brush in there so he can try to draw. To me, that's amazing! Eventually, two steel hooks were placed on the stubs of his arms. Fourteen years later, Jim's paintings won first place in a major art show in Dallas. When he was asked to what he credited his success, this young man said, "After I got burned, I avoided negative thinkers." If any person had legitimate reasons to be negative, this young man did! But, he kept away from people who talked negatively! Zig Ziglar calls it "stinking thinking." Jim, this incredible artist, purposefully shunned *stinking thinking,* and fixated on his noble goals. THAT'S PROPER FOCUS!

FOCUS NEARLY BEYOND BELIEF

A more recent example proves that focus and persistence can and do overcome great obstacles. Doug is a superior wildlife artist. Doug wasn't an artist until a high school wrestling accident made him a quadriplegic, paralyzed from the neck down. Doug's brother, concerned that Doug was watching too much TV, challenged him to draw with a pencil he placed in his mouth. Doug invested time and practice, and his style emerged. I'm told that to complete a drawing usually takes him 40 to 200+ hours, depending upon image size and detail. If it is a large piece, he draws half the image upside down and then flips it around because his reach is limited. Drawing is hard on his neck, and the neck wasn't built to do the amount of repetitive motions used to create these images. After many years of abusing his neck by working up to 6-8 hours at a time, he was told he had strained his neck muscles, and might have to give up drawing. He got a second opinion. He stopped drawing for several months, went through a year of therapy, then started drawing again. He began drawing 2-4 hours with a few breaks in between. Doug is the personification of Proper Focus.

We would certainly understand it if a teenager, who had lost his ears and hands, got distraught. Or if an athlete, who instantly became paralyzed, got dejected. But what use is that; what good is that? How would the depressed attitude help? Some of us, with minor problems by comparison, give up too easily. Quit too quickly. Throw in the towel almost automatically. We'll never know our potential unless we stay with it – persevere, keep on trying. Unless we stubbornly maintain proper focus, like Jim and Doug.

NOT ALL NEGATIVES ARE BAD

I want to add something about negatives. Some instructors or counselors say, "Never use negatives." That is impractical and inaccurate. We sometimes need negatives; and often negatives are the best tool to communicate the message. It is necessary, and best understood, to say to the child, "**Don't** play in the street," rather than say, "You may play only in the yard." The negative is more direct and clearer. One parent may say to a child, "Since the burner is hot, it will burn you if you touch it." Another will say, "**Don't** touch the burner." One may say, "Take only what belongs to you." Another will say, "**Don't** steal." I think the negative conveys the message better.

Out of the *Ten Commandments*, seven are negative: *No substitute for God, no using God's name in vain, no murder, no adultery, no theft, no lying, no coveting.* We break them often, which is why there is a billboard that says: "*Which part of 'Thou Shalt Not' don't you understand?*" Jesus did make two positive summary statements for the ten commands: "Love God with all your heart, soul, mind, and strength; and Love your neighbor as yourself." For sure none of us succeed in fully keeping those two positive statements.

Negatives do have their place. Don't live above and beyond your income is good negative advice. But people who are negative by nature, just generally pessimistic, depressing all the time, who look on the bad side of everything;

those folks ought to be avoided. Both negative attitudes and positive attitudes are contagious, so be wise about which you are exposed to.

ONE WISE NEGATIVE: DON'T FOCUS ON EXCESSIVE THINGS
A good sized, successful, company in the Tulsa metro area had been in business, and in the same family, for many years. When the Founder of the company died, his son became CEO. After a few years, this company filed bankruptcy. Some said that at the center of the failure was the son's poor decision-making and his extravagant lifestyle. While some company checks were bouncing, and some company credit was being denied, and company equipment was not being repaired; the son purchased a British Bentley and an Italian Maserati to drive. A Cessna airplane to fly. He bought an Italian Ducati racing motorcycle. He vacationed in Aspen and Crested Butte, Colorado; in Miami, Florida; in Costa Rica; and in the Caribbean. He lived in a $4-million house. Now the company is broke and out of business, and numerous lawsuits were filed. One alleged contributing problem: his focus on extravagant things. Caution: Don't get hooked on things. We don't need all the latest and greatest gadgets and high-tech stuff. We don't need to have more stuff than our friends. Use things as tools, not as status symbols and proof of achievement or as substitutes for self-esteem.

IT'S NOT ONLY NEGATIVE PEOPLE AND EXCESSIVE THINGS, ALSO, DON'T SURRENDER TO NEGATIVE CIRCUMSTANCES
A clergyman asked a church member, "How are you?" The member said, "Oh, I'm okay, under the circumstances." Replied the minister, "Why are you under there?" That can sound harsh, even corny, but we need not allow circumstances to defeat us. On the contrary, difficulty may bring out our best. It is said: *People can be like tea bags – you know their strength when they get in hot water.* Look! There's no shame in getting into hot water. Everyone who takes a venture, who tries anything, who seeks to improve his position in life, who stands for something, will get into hot water now and then. Just be ready. Life may be like the carpet cleaning process: It's the hot water that blasts out the dirt and grime and disgusting junk. It's the steam that cleans, and clarifies, and powers us to go higher in life. Steam is still one of the most powerful forces we know of. But, you must intelligently control it, channel it, harness it. Make it work for you. Make it move you in the right direction. We'll all get into hot water. Don't let it burn you up, or drown your enthusiasm. Let the heat motivate you, energize you. It's even okay if the hot waters, the tough times, make you mad, as long as you use the anger

for power to advance, for incentive to climb to a better place. We've got to take control, take intelligent oversight, creative power, over our circumstances. We are responsible to re-direct the "*happenings*" – to turn adversity to our advantage.

EVERYONE SHOULD STRIVE FOR ADVANCEMENT
A winning army still seeks to press on even if just to secure their position and supply lines. That's why there is the truism: *If you're not moving ahead, you're falling behind.* No one has reached such a state of perfection that he shouldn't seek for more development. Focusing on strengths and abilities does not mean you ignore the need for improvement. That would be foolish, and a detriment. Remember the boy and his dad playing baseball? The boy didn't say in defeat, "I can't hit the ball today." He did say, "I'm pitching good today." Now that's a spunky attitude; and a good coach should respond with proper insight. A dad, or coach should not say, "Kid, you're just a poor hitter." What good could that accomplish? Neither should he say, "Hey, you're hitting just fine." Why not? Because that's not true; and if the dad takes that position, the boy never will become a good hitter. A first step to improvement is admitting the need. A next step is having desire to improve. That's why a good mentor will say, "Yeah, you're pitching fine. Your hitting will be as good as your pitching when you keep your eyes on the ball better. Stare at that ball and concentrate on just meeting it with the bat. Visualize the bat connecting with the ball. Imagine yourself hitting the ball just over second base." The boy and his dad or coach will also work together on basic execution: stance, grip, swing and timing. If they are too lazy, too busy with other things, or just not serious about improvement; then that boy will never be a big hitter. But they can face reality with practical, clearly defined steps for improvement. That's how we can approach life every day: Good goals, doable advancements, proper focus, and a clear map for steps of improvement, together with confidence that we can improve. It's best to write down your goals and the orderly steps for achievement. It isn't magic, and it isn't denial of reality; but we advance and improve by taking smart, steady, progressive steps.

IN THIS PROCESS, IT'S DO OR DIE – USE OR LOSE
If that boy is to become a great hitter, two more things are still needed: Practice and Implementation. He'll need to take batting practice, using correct techniques. If you and I are to improve our position and get better,

we must act wisely on our plan of development. A practical illustration is a health club membership. I've joined a club and carried out a disciplined exercise plan that made me look good and feel better, and improve my health. I've also at another time, joined a club and carried the membership card in my wallet, but done nothing more – seldom showed up to work out. Being a card-carrying member, having a personalized workout plan, even wearing exercise gear, does nothing for the looks, the energy level or the health. Knowledge and plans and goals without implementation are valueless. It takes action. It always requires action. We must put ourselves into the plan. We must be doers, not just joiners. We must take action on our good plans, not just read formulas, or attend seminars or get enthused at motivational rallies. Excitement is good, but disciplined follow-through is also necessary. A good plan of action with persistent follow-through wins. It takes good plans with sufficient action. Proper focus together with intelligent action is the portal to the better you.

PERSONAL APPLICATION IS ABSOLUTELY NECESSARY

When I was growing up, our family lived in the country and we kept a cow for milk. And for homemade ice cream. My job was to milk the cow in the mornings, my brother milked in the evenings. To milk, we'd sit on a one-legged stool. Why did anyone invent a one-legged stool? Put it on the ground, and it falls. To make it work as a stool, somebody must sit on it. It won't stand up unless a person adds their own two legs to make a 3-legged support. I think that's a good illustration of what it takes to improve. Good *plans* by themselves, being just one leg, won't get the job done. We've got to put ourselves into the process. We must add the other two legs of *preparation* and *action*. Your best idea won't work unless you do.

AT SOME TIME, WE MUST GET MOVING

You may or may not have been a track runner, but most of us raced somebody sometime. We'd say: "Ready! Set! GO!" In life, in the race of moving along the track to a better place, too many times we never get to "GO!" We get ready – get ready – get set – re-adjust and get ready – get ready – get reset – get ready again …. But we never GO. Sometimes a desire for perfection holds us back, and we genuinely feel we are not ready. Folks, it doesn't take perfection! I've heard singers in church with better voices than many I've heard on the radio, but the better voice didn't make the big time, while the lesser voice did. Perfection is not needed, but getting moving is – getting going is required. Sometimes fear of failure holds us back. We don't want to embarrass ourselves or our family. Yet, we all know that the best baseball pros only hit around 300. That means they fail to get a hit twice as often as they do get a hit – and that's millionaire pros. Let's start swinging. We must to get going.

WE MUST BALANCE PREPARATION AND ACTION
Life requires balance. When I say don't take too much time to get ready and to get set, but rather get going; I'm not saying to disregard preparation! Getting ready is extremely important, but don't get stuck in preparation mode. There are times and places for preparation; and time for action on preparation. Employ both! If you're in 8th grade, finish high school. If you only have a high school degree, get an Associate's Degree in your off hours. Make time. If you have an Associate's Degree, get a BA. You can do it using the internet. You can go to school a couple nights a week. Find a way – Make a way! If you have a BA, then get a certification in your field. Are you an accountant? Become a CPA. Are you an engineer? Get your PE designation. Are you an apartment manager? Get licensed and earn your CPM (certified property manager). You'll feel better about yourself and you'll get paid better. You increase your value to yourself and to the workplace. Do it.

I know a fellow who finished all of his college graduation requirements, except for the last semester. He got such a good job that he left college, and began earning a very good income at work he enjoys – the work he wanted to do. But he's never gotten his Bachelor's Degree. That seems foolish when there are fine, reputable schools that will provide classes at his choice of time. They may even credit him with "life experience credits." Be a finisher. Headhunter businesses, Executive Search Firms, will tell you that if other things are about equal, the person with the college degree will get the good job. Yes, we do need to get prepared for the better place in life we envision. Prepare, but don't get mired in preparation. Let this be the starting gun right now. Get going.

DON'T JUST APPLY THIS TO THE OTHER GUY
You know what a Monday morning quarterback is. It can apply to other things beside football. It means that someone is a know-it-all – but they don't themselves DO IT. They tell others how they should have done it,

but the Monday-morning-quarterback never actually did it, and never himself does it in the heat of competition, on the field of battle. They never have their ideas tested, and they never are forced to take responsibility for their big schemes. Don't be like that! Be a player. Get in the game. Put in the personal effort. Take a chance when it matters – when it makes a difference – when it counts. Don't depend on government at any level. Take pride in your independence. Get up and get moving. Put yourself into the effort with enthusiasm and determination. It's impossible to succeed if you aren't in the running. And being a contender in the game just feels good.

I don't like gambling, but I like this illustration (you've probably heard it). A man prayed, *God, let me win the lottery.* The next week he prayed, *God, help me win the lottery.* The next week he prayed, *Please God, make me win the lottery.* God said, *Meet me halfway: Buy a ticket.* Folks, in life, we've got to do our part! Go for it in person. God isn't likely to get us a better job unless we get the ticket of more education or higher certification. God isn't likely to make our business larger unless we make more sales calls. God isn't likely to make us feel better unless we eat better and exercise. God isn't likely to give us more friends unless we are more friendly.

MAKING WORK **WORK** *FOR YOU IS HONORABLE*
Difficulties are opportunities to prove to yourself and to others that you are willing to do whatever it takes – whatever it takes while maintaining integrity – to do what others won't do to overcome or move up. Finding one's self in the middle of difficulty is not dishonorable. But complaining and blaming – that's what's dishonorable. If finances are bad, get a vacuum and dust brush, and clean your insurance agent's offices for less than the other guy will. It's not dishonorable to work. My dad and mom had eight children, so dad worked two jobs. They said all but one of us kids was planned, but they'd never tell us who was the surprise. Anyway, with ten in the family, dad had to work a bunch – work overtime. None of his work was dishonorable. His main job was driving truck. One driving job in Southern California was for a fruit company. He'd go into citrus groves and haul oranges or lemons back to the processing plant. I've been to that lemon house many times. Have you ever smelled a citrus packing plant where they clean, sort, grade and pack lemons and oranges? The aroma is

glorious. Dad would come home smelling like lemon cologne. No wonder mom hugged him at the door. But I digress.

The point I was making is this: Dad worked extra-long, hard hours at more than one job to feed and clothe us kids. Yet, he and mom found time to help others. On Saturday, they'd volunteer to drive elderly folks to the grocery store or drug store to get necessities; then they'd help them unload and put items away when they returned to their homes. Dad cooked in the kitchen at church for social events. He participated in work projects at church. As part time work, he drove the high school bus for the various athletic teams. It was a paying job, but dad made it a mission. He knew the players, and would encourage them, celebrate wins with them, hurt with them over loses or injuries. He was a friend to the kids on the bus. No matter how much he had to work to earn a living, he made time to serve others. He was a servant to many. At his funeral, over 1,600 came and many stood to honor my dad by telling ways he'd helped them. The minister had to ask folks to stop sharing. Dad was a servant who had a difficult life in many ways, yet he accomplished more for friends and neighbors than do most PhDs. When he saw hardships of others, he saw opportunities to serve. He didn't get buried in his own problems, but rather concentrated on how to help others overcome their problems. At my class reunions, I've had athletes tell me how much my dad – the team bus driver – meant to them years ago. I learned from dad that work and service to others are honorable.

SOMETIMES A CHANGE IN DIRECTION IS DEMANDED

Tulsa, Oklahoma was once the Oil Capital of the world. But times and fortunes change. During the oil bust of the eighties, one oil company in distress refused to go down without trying something different. These executives asked themselves, "What is still in demand today with potential for growth?" They examined the health and fitness market, and saw an opportunity. These executives asked, "Why not create unique exercise equipment, and capture part of this large and worthwhile market? Can't our engineers apply their skills in that booming arena?" With that plan of action, the oil company survived as *Stairmaster*, and became a major success story in the high end of the health and fitness industry. Stairmaster machines were sold everywhere; and a company was saved because those folks refused to give in. They responded to the challenge. They changed, developed new strategies, adapted to market demands. So, can we.

As Stairmaster illustrates, your focus need not be, "How can I be first at something?" There have been all kinds of exercise equipment for years. There have always been stairways to climb: stairs in homes, in office buildings, in stadiums. Michelangelo didn't invent color or paint. Handel didn't create new notes or instruments of music. Shakespeare didn't originate the idea of drama. You don't need to be the originator or even the best of anything. Ford didn't invent the car, or the internal combustion engine. He didn't have the finest product. What you must ask is: "What can I offer people in goods or service that they want, can afford, and can depend on?" Get the right answers to those questions, and problems can turn into success! Difficulties can become ladders to the best we've ever been for ourselves and others. Like Stairmaster, we can go in a different direction if need be. Like Ford, we can create a better way to use our skills and energy. We are not a statue: we can adapt; we can change.

THERE ARE UNIVERSAL QUALITIES TO BUILD INTO LIFE
Quick Trip company is headquartered in Tulsa. This convenience store chain has an excellent reputation and is known as a prime place to work and to be promoted from within. The employees make a good living – some a superior living; but there is more to the company success than well-paid employees. It seems these people enjoy making customers smile. I'm entertained as I watch them handle the line of customers, keep an eye on the pumps, count back the money, and smile at the same time. It seems they enjoy impressing customers with efficiency and accuracy while being friendly. In addition, the store is clean and the coffee fresh. It seems these people relish delivering a good image of themselves and of Quick Trip.

That's a winning formula: A strong company with employees who have a goal each day to promote friendliness, efficiency, customer appreciation, and company loyalty. Even if one doesn't work for Quick Trip, these are good qualities to emulate. A worker who brings these skills to the marketplace is a more valuable employee. Even outside the workplace, these are strong character traits: friendliness, efficiency, people appreciation, solid image and loyalty. That's a good focus.

DON'T THROW AWAY YOUR OWN LIFE, OR THE LIFE OF OTHERS

We often get our eyes off those noble goals, and instead take a poor point of view. We get overwhelmed by circumstances. Distracted by our own situation rather than thinking about helping others who are in a harder place. We sometimes not only throw away our own opportunities to serve, we also discard lives of others – label them unworthy.

How often we prejudge folks who enter our world. We jump to judgmental conclusions based on the car people drive, the clothes they wear, even if they wear the same item too frequently. We judge by the particular suburb they live in, even the kind of cell phone they use. How petty we can be. Some folks even evaluate the worth of a neighbor based on whether he does his own yard work, or hires a yard service with a horticulturist. Or if he washes his own car, or pays to have it detailed. Isn't that trite? We judge over trivia. That's wrong focus! There are people who look down on others because of the kind of work they do. It's honorable work, yet sometimes thought demeaning. That's silly. If the work is honest, it's not demeaning. Honest work is noble. Do you realize that if the president of any particular company doesn't go to work today, probably no one will notice or care that his desk is empty. But, if the receptionist doesn't get in to work, everyone will care if that desk is empty. If the janitor doesn't take out the trash or refill the towel supply, everyone will care. After a big storm that knocks down the power, the power company linemen are the most important gentlemen in the county. All work is important. Many CEOs started as a shipping clerk, and grew up in the company, and became the head honcho. Why do we judge ourselves by saying: "That kind of work is below me? I can't take that job, it insults me." Why not consider taking an interim productive job. Let's at least not judge others who do take a so-called lesser job and are productive citizens contributing to the well-being of our economy and society. The lower end job, done well, can be the entry to the higher end position.

Let's not look down on certain jobs and workers. Let's encourage instead of discourage. Let's honor productivity. Let's focus on possibilities instead of on liabilities. I conclude with an old story I put in rhyme to help us remember to see the good in ourselves and in others. It highlights the difference between seeing only what's wrong or what's weak, compared with focusing on potential and on the strengths that can be found in all of us.

The lad had gotten twenty dollars with his birthday cards.
He knew just what he wanted, down the street a couple yards.
A sign said, FOR SALE – PUPPIES, and a puppy was his dream.
Now with twenty dollars he could fulfill his scheme.

His heart was pounding loudly as he knocked upon that door.
He'd never been the owner of a puppy dog before.
So, when a lady answered and asked him to come in,
He was the most excited in his life he'd ever been.

"I came to see the puppies. Do you have a puppy left?"
"Oh yes, we have two puppies unspoken for as yet.
Just wait here, I'll get them." Now he was left alone.
He squeezed the twenty dollars. A tickle thrilled his bones.

Two cuddly, playful puppies were chewing on his shoe.
He thought, Twenty dollars – what if twenty could buy two!
Laughing at the puppies, he pet them with his hand,
"How much are the puppies?" he asked, spoken like a man.

"These are pure bred puppies from a very sturdy line.
Their brother brought two hundred, and these are just as fine."
Oh, the crush of disappointment. He had nowhere near enough.
"I've only twenty dollars. Are there any other pups?"

"No. Well, there is a cripple. We haven't done it yet.
We're putting it to sleep as recommended by the vet.
He said it couldn't walk right. Besides, it was the runt.
Please, honey, stop your crying. I shouldn't be so blunt."

"Could I see that puppy? Could I see it please?
With only twenty dollars, I can't get one of these."
The lady brought a white fur ball, and put it at his feet.
As he pet the puppy's coat, the boy began to weep.

"Could I buy this puppy? Could I take him home?
I'll pay all twenty dollars. Please? I love this one!"
"Son, that runt's a cripple, he never will walk good.
We'll put him out of misery as the doctor said we should."

"The doctor must not love this dog. I'd work to get more money."
The boy picked up the dog. "See, see how much he likes me?

I'd take good care of this pup. I couldn't love him more.
It's okay if he can't walk". The boy sat on the floor.

The boy pulled up his blue jeans. Emaciated legs, so pale,
Were strapped in shiny braces there beside the puppy's tail.
"You see, I, too, am crippled. Without braces, I can't walk.
I know this puppy wants to live. I think I'd call him 'Chalk'."

The lady turned in tears and hurried through the door.
Never had she learned such wisdom from a little boy before.
Yes, the insight of the innocent can teach old age a lesson.
For many lives are thrown away judged just short of "perfection".

We've discussed taking a positive, productive point of view for advancement. Let's get going from today forward for the benefit of ourselves and others using *Proper Focus*. Focus that isn't sabotaged by difficulties whether real or imagined; focus that seeks continued advancement even in the good times yet is not self-centered; focus that prepares and gets moving; focus that doesn't negatively prejudge ourselves or others. Proper focus in our personal lives, business lives, school lives, our friendships and contacts, and in our spiritual lives. Where is your focus?

A boy and his dog.

God Guides

Today a businessman must make a call
At an office that's two hours' drive away.
At 4 PM the set appointment falls.
He'll leave at two and drive along the bay.

A believer firm, he asks God frequently
To guide his thought and keep him in His grace.
He wants God's will to rule him constantly
As he fills his role among the human race.
"Control, oh God, my mind, my deeds, my place."

Mid-morning comes the thought, "Why not start off now,
Enjoy a slower ride and leisure lunch?"
Each time this thought recurs, he puts it down,
"I'll leave as planned though I may have to rush.
I can't spare leisure time." The thought was hushed.

And so, at two, into the road he drives.
"As in the past, Lord, haste me on my way.
Your Guardian Angel send me from the skies.
Allow not circumstances to delay.
To be late would cause losses and dismay."

So hastily he joins the traffic flow
Along the freeway leading to the town
Where waits a vital meeting which will show
If his career is heading up or down.
If he were late, he would appear a clown.

The cars were moving speedily along
When suddenly a traffic jam appeared.
Then, stop and go – just creep – what's wrong?
Ten minutes lost before the jam was cleared.
He must recoup that time, or else, he feared.

He urged his car along at faster speed
Above, by far, the limit of the state.

The only reason he allowed this deed
Was to keep his word and not be late.
"God, I can't afford to make those people wait."

As if God didn't care about his plea,
Behind him flashed a red official light.
A competent policeman ends his spree.
The law has moved his error to requite.
"God, couldn't you have spared me from this plight?"

Again, upon his way, he looks to find,
Between the time made up and lost to law,
He totals sixteen minutes still behind.
Nervously he grinds his teeth and jaw,
"Lord, why have you allowed my plan to flaw?"

And then the unbelievable occurred.
God must not care at all about this child.
The tire that's flat he aired, with vision blurred
By tears that flowed, by thoughts gone wild,
"What have I done, Father, to be reviled?"

With *Fix-a-Flat*, again he sped away
Six minutes more – in total twenty-two.
He pondered in his mind just what to say
His lateness to excuse. What should he do?
"God, don't you care enough to see me through?"

And now he sees ahead the blue, blue bay.
As soon as it is crossed he's nearly there.
But, at the bridge approach, again his way
Is blocked by cars whose drivers stand and stare.
"How can it be that God heard not my prayer?"

Discouraged, hurt, he jumps out of his car
And rushes up to see why is this pause,
Why traffic stopped. He sees ahead not far
A policeman who will know the cause.
"How could one day contain so many flaws?"

"Officer, what's making this delay?

Why are these folks not moving on ahead?"
"The bridge is out. It's fallen clean away.
Some freak of nature; folks involved are dead.
Was just twenty-three minutes ago," he said.

With sudden shock this statement pierced his brain.
Twenty-three minutes – the time that he has lost.
Humbly, hushed, he turned to God in shame.
"Had you given me my wish it would have cost
My life upon that bridge as I had crossed."

God saved his life by well-placed obstacles,
Yet to the meeting wanted him on time.
So thoughts put in his head, he now recalls,
To leave quite early – no traffic jams, no fine.
As he had asked, God led him through his mind.

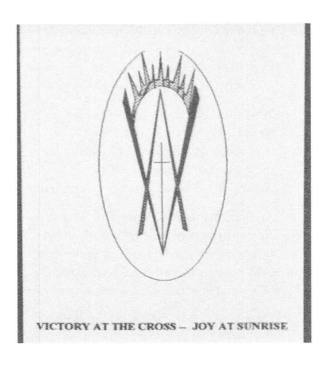

VICTORY AT THE CROSS – JOY AT SUNRISE

THANKSGIVING

We thankfully gather the family together
So grateful for love that binds us forever.
And grateful that all in the bunch are quite normal –
Well, there is that one who seems so hormonal.

Any group expects that, so we are quite lucky,
Though you-know-who always seems to feel yucky.
Yes, we're normal and lucky and generally great –
It's just that one in-law's habit I hate.

Sure, overlook it, just let it slide by,
But this time nobody brought pumpkin pie.
Really! What is Thanksgiving without favorite foods?
The tasty traditions of holiday moods?

Okay, folks, forgive me. I see what I've done.
I've stopped being thankful, though that's why we've come.
So many reasons sincere in my heart,
Yet, petty distractions – thus, here's a new start:

God our Father, I'm thankful for all of your blessings.
The big ones and small ones. And, yes, I'm confessing
I just don't express as much I ought
My thanks for the fabulous family I've got.
And so many friends who add to my life
The joy, the interest, intrigue, and spice.
And thanks for the ways you show your love,
And the home our family has waiting above.
Thanks for the time to hug 'em and kiss 'em,
And to tell the ones absent how much we miss 'em.

NIGHT AFTER CHRISTMAS

'Twas the night after Christmas, and all through the house
Not a Creature was happy, not even the mouse.
The stockings were flung in the trash without care --
With no hope to find a small gift tossed in there.
The children were fighting for toys on their beds
Though none matched the visions they'd had in their heads.
Mamma had a headache; and we had a flap
About my watching football while taking a nap.
I thought of work done by that Jolly Old Elf,
But the stuff that got done I got stuck with myself.
I thought of how everyone put up the tree
While fighting and fussing about how it should be;
But no one will help to take the thing down
Several days after the needles turn crispy brown.
I thought how this season sure brings out the gimmies
For all kinds of stuff that won't go down the chimneys.
Of the hours and cost to get the gifts wrapped,
But torn off with greed in twelve seconds flat.
When out on the curb there arose such a clatter
As overworked trash men collected waste matter.
Away to the window I flew like a flash,
Tripped on my coin purse and fell on my cash.
Outside, in the light of the moon's crystal glow,
All over the lawn and starting to blow,
My wandering eyes saw spilt trash everywhere.
I started to holler, but, then, didn't dare
'Cause the back of that mobilized crushing machine
Was less than a foot from my sleek limousine.
And the short, balding driver, so easily, so quick,
Could put in my paint job, any moment, a nick.
The driver had helpers all scurrying the same;
And he whistled and shouted and called them by name;
"Hey Flash! Knucklehead! You guys know what I'm fixin'
To give you, if you don't watch where you're pitchin'?
Ya got the trash scattered from the porch to the wall.
Now go pick it up. Dash away. Go get it all."

A Strange Bouquet

Unexpected Gift for no Particular Reason.

Pretty leaves, flowered weeds, berries, thistles.
A strange bouquet you've never seen before.
I give them to you now for your window, and
To bring my outside heart inside your door.

*This was written when we moved to an Oklahoma
rural area in the Coweta school district. I was doing a
bunch of work outside on our small acreage, such as
fencing, contouring of the land, working with a contractor
to put in a double tornado shelter, then using the dirt
to build a decorative outcropping of rock, with a fire pit
to roast hot dogs and sing under the stars. So, I was
outside much of the time. I gathered an outdoorsy "bouquet",
put it in a vase, wrote the above poem on a piece of paper,
and gave it to Nancy. Thoughtful gifts for "no reason at all
except I was thinking of you" may be the finest gifts of all.*

A WISE LIFE-OBSERVATION

"He is no fool who
gives up that which he cannot keep
to gain that which he cannot lose."
Jim Elliot, missionary.

Jenni, my oldest daughter, and her husband
were missionaries for sixteen years.
They own our original Oklahoma home
and the Old Friendly Barn.

ESTEEM MACHINE

Jerry was a young giraffe who found his long neck awkward.
His neck was so unusual, it made him shy and backward.
He banged his head on tree limbs. He had to duck through doors.
And long-necked fashions weren't in stock, not even at Zoo stores.
Sore throats were huge, drawn out affairs. If he'd stick out his neck
To try to get ahead in life, he'd cause a traffic wreck.

The Zoo put on a seminar called "Looking On The Bright Side".
Jerry didn't want to go, but where could giraffes hide?
Jerry didn't try to, but he had a lot of fun,
And found a whole new attitude before the class was done.
When the sessions ended, and evaluations read,
The Zoo staff opened Jerry's, and this is what it said:

> *"Because I have a long neck, I am closer to the stars.*
> *I can see above the obstacles, even over Zoo bars.*
> *I can see beyond the crowds, and be a guide to those around me.*
> *I realize friends and family, and those whose love surrounds me,*
> *Think my neck is handsome, and one of my best features,*
> *And in this world of specialists, I am a special creature."*

Now, if you're feeling ugly or handicapped or odd,
Or if you know of someone who doesn't like their bod,
Try thinking about Jerry, and go to any length
To see that "perceived weakness" might instead be "strength".
Share words of true encouragement with genuine respect.
Find the good that makes you "*you*", as Jerry did his neck.

Doug Octopus: The Hugging

In the zoo lives Doug the octopus, who felt sorry for himself,
Since, having only head and arms, he looks like no one else.
The giraffe, he thought, is stately — so slender, sleek, and tall.
But Doug: "I'm short and ugly — no neck or legs at all."

The birds can sing such pretty songs, and soar on open wings.
The elephants have handy trunks that do all sorts of things.
The lion has a curly mane. Doug Octopus, "I'm bald.
My reflection in the water always leaves me so appalled."

One day another octopus came put an arm around him.
It felt so good, Doug got a thrill and found out he could grin.
It felt so good, he hugged her back, and she hugged him again.
With 16 arms, four hugs at once, it hugged some pride in him.

Today, Doug Octopus is happy and thankful for his luck
That he has arms, not wings or legs or mane or neck or trunk.
Now, if you know somebody feeling low, as once did Doug,
Go get your arms around them, and teach them how to hug!

Doug learned important lessons with his extra arms that day.
He realized every one of us are special our own way.
We each must use the talents given purposely to us;
Stop with the complaining; put an end to all the fuss.

What we've seen as hardships that have us set adrift
Can focus our abilities and prove to be a gift.
We'll find we have advantages as we have seen in others;
Advantages new thinking and new efforts will uncover.

Doug craved to be like others — then he could do big things.
First needed the advantages of legs, neck, mane, and wings.
If people's thoughts and actions were identically the same,
Then life turns dull and boring, as if all shared just one name?

If all of us were so alike, then why would I be needed?
But each one fills a certain role to make our world completed.

141

Yes, each of us is differently equipped in our own way,
And each of us, with what we have, is valuable today.

So, anyone discouraged or who's envious, like Doug,
Remember how his life was changed the day he learned to hug.

Baby's Lullaby

Baby of mine, you've had a day:
Growing, watching, stretching, play.
Now comes the night on silent wings,
Go to sleep and find sweet dreams.

Baby of mine, tomorrows come.
I pray to God, "Protect our home."
I sing and watch your heavy eyes.
Wake up strong with happy skies.

Baby of mine, don't be afraid.
Angels guard where you are laid.
Mommy and Daddy by your bed.
Snuggle close, you sleepy head.

Baby of mine, there's no one knows
The wonders that your future holds.
I pray you find a faithful love.
And bask in blessings from above.

(music in Music Section)

The Healing Hug

There's a hug that just goes limp, loses energy, yet hangs on. That needs to empty gusts of emotion and despair into the person clung to. A drowning person's grasp on the life preserver. But it's more. It's a hug of exchange: "Please absorb my weakness and lend your strength. I need your support". The accompanying tears seem to release desperation through the eyes.

Have you received this hug and held on to let it become a healing hug? Hold that hug longer, until you sense a spiritual relief. Don't be embarrassed or cautious and let go too soon. Wait for a sign of release from the loved one.

The best healing hug is a hug from a mother or dad, from a husband or wife, from a daughter or son. It cannot be duplicated or substituted: no stand-in fully satisfies. A close friend or minister tries and is very helpful, even indispensable, but comes just short of equivalent fulfillment. Yes, be a hugging minister or friend sincerely, faithfully. Don't be timid. Be that friend indeed. But if you are the parent, spouse, or child, now is the time, the defining moment, to BE that unique role. YOU are needed — and wanted. Don't miss or neglect the silent plea of your loved one for your embrace. This hug benefits both ways. It's a hug of undisguised honesty and trust with a tinge of hope. It cannot be feigned. It must not be denied.

This clinging hug may be from someone in your life who is tired, "going on empty". Someone exhausted, depleted, at wit's end — but empty cannot be the end. So, they slog on. Beyond empty hide deeper forces often called abiding love, compelling duty, tenacious loyalty, brute stamina, irresistible commitment, genuine love. Yes, it all comes back to agape love. Love that stays the course because it will not tolerate anything else. Love that serves, gives, responds, or is just being there, being present to smile, touch, hold a glass of water, or just quietly wait. This loved one can't run, can't quit, can't let go, so continues — somehow. And they crave a life-giving hug.

The Last Fare

It would be my last fare of a long day.
With nighttime shadows making their play,
I thought I'd let the next guy take this ride.
My back was sore. Home calling me aside.

I don't know why I mapped the address
And headed out. Just old habit I guess.
A body sometimes reacts on its own.
Without a thought, I glanced at my phone.

A short and uneventful trip I hoped.
Preferably not a talkative bloke.
Why do they need to tell their problems?
As if a cab driver really could solve 'em.

That's the house number on that rustic old place.
A little paint would easily years erase.
I honked and waited. Then honked again.
"I don't need this fare." But honked again.

I didn't drive off. I went to the door.
That started a ride like never before.
When I knocked on the door, I heard this voice.
"Just a minute". By now I had no choice.

The voice sounded weak, maybe old and frail.
And a dragging sound, like a gouging nail.
Now in suspense, I waited still longer,
My heart speeding up a bit, in wonder.

"Definitely not the ride I was hoping"!
Now, with a creak, the door was opening.
There before me, somewhat bent, almost sacred,
Stood a lady with class, nearing a hundred.

A pillbox hat softly sat on her head.
"Dressed for a reason", her appearance said.
My quick furtive glance: Stuff a bit dusty.
My sensitive sniff: Nothing too musty.

That faded hat had a veil fastened to it,
Like a character actress in an old classic.
She's in a print dress. I'm no longer wary.
I thought of Clara, Bee's friend in Mayberry.

There by her side, a small dated suitcase.
It looked as if no one lived in this place.
No decorations or pictures on walls.
A box held photos and very small doll.

Everything valuable arranged in that box.
As she glanced its way, I could read her thoughts.
All the furniture covered white with sheets.
Only the box had stuff she would keep.

"Would you help carry my bag to the car?
Don't think I could manage although it's not far."
"Of course I will, ma'am. I'll come back for the box.
I'll come walk with you so we don't slip on rocks."

She carefully laid her hand on my arm.
Something about her spoke class and charm.
We carefully, steadily walked to the cab.
Looking back, one of the best walks I've ever had.

She repeated her thanks on the way to the curb:
"Some other driver might by now be perturbed."
"I just want to treat you the way your son would.
Why all can't be helpful I've not understood."

"You're a fine young man", she sweetly allowed.
I'd be proud of you if you were my child".
She leaned on my arm, sliding into her place,
She couldn't weigh more than a prayer filled with grace.

I got in my seat. She gave the address.
"Could you drive through downtown for this old guest?
"That's the long way around," I replied, being kind.
"Well, I'm going to hospice, so I really don't mind."

I glanced at her face, and her eyes showed tears.
I'll always remember those eyes through the years.
"I've no family left, no one to care for.
Can't remember names of friends that I pray for".

I noticed her eyes looked far in the distance,
As catching a vision that very instant.
"My doctor says I've not long to be here."
I reached up: stealthily turned off the meter.

"What route would you like us to drive?" I wondered.
For hours we drove by sites that she pondered.
We passed a place where she ran elevators.
Said "Made many friends who walked in those doors."

Said "Most of them now have gone on before.
You learn about people in that kind of chore."
We passed a place where she'd danced on a date.
A worn-out old warehouse where they'd roller skate.

Another old building: once furniture store
Where they got good items after the war.
In one neighborhood they'd lived much of their life:
The first house they bought as husband and wife.

In two places she had me slow and stop.
She sat there in silence, alone with her thoughts.
She reviewed her life's story, gains and losses.
Her loves, her family, her joys and crosses.

The sun began hinting arrival of day.
She said, "Better take me to where I'll stay.
I'm a bit tired, no doubt you are too.
So much to think on, and days so few."

We silently drove to a place with no glory
Where alone with mem'ries she'd finish her story.
Drove to the entry where a wheelchair stood.
Took her hand, and without being rude,

Placed a kiss on her forehead and one on her hand.

Told her "There's much that I don't understand,
But I'm certain our meeting was part of God's plan,
And she'd made a difference in the life of this man."

She wanted to pay me for bringing her there,
But I said for her ride we charged no fare.
She said I gave her several hours of joy,
And wished I had been one of her boys.

I told her I'd thank her for years to come,
And be grateful she chose me to bring her home.

(put in rhyme from a story I'd heard a few times)

Unexpected Call

Did not expect the call so soon
when Heavenly Father bid me come.
But in my heart the fear is gone
replaced by joy I'll soon be home.

This life on earth is almost done,
the crown of life will soon be donned.
Eternal life with Christ, the Son,
since Jesus has the victory won.

Salvation won on Cal'vry's cross
where Jesus paid the total cost.
My Savior took my sin and loss:
and there my pardon did emboss.

I'll look for you near heaven's gate,
to joyfully rejoin my mate.
Together praise the Lord above
Who saved us by redeeming love.

AT LA JOLLA

On the beaches of La Jolla, the gulls and guards enjoy the
Way you sun, cavort, and laugh as in a dream.
Nature teaches at La Jolla, no stresses need destroy ya:
Spirits rise as froth blown wild off waves that gleam.
Fond mem'ries of La Jolla, persist, and still enjoin ya
As their magic plays an oft repeated theme.

Fleshly pillars ply La Jolla — they walk the sands to toy ya,
And stretch from earth toward heaven quite serene.
Silent speech there at La Jolla, taunting talk that can annoy ya,
Lauding beauty that surpasses Neptune's Queen.
On the beaches of La Jolla, the rhythmic swells can buoy ya
To most any mystic place you dare to scheme.

"Since I was born and raised in So California
about 30 miles north of San Diego and 30 miles
east of Oceanside, our family often went to the beach.
Usually we took the back road through Rancho Santa Fe,
and came out at Del Mar. I love the beach and the surf.
La Jolla (pronounce La Hoy-yah) is a beautiful beach with
caves, seals, cliffs, tall pine trees that stand near the beach, etc..
There is a hand-gliding port atop the cliffs.
I like to play with words, so tried to write a poem using La Jolla.

LEGEND OF THE CENTURY BIRD

Never is there more than one pair of Century Birds alive within one century. Two of these mythical birds are hatched every 99 years. Both male and female mature rapidly, providing a dazzling beauty and delightful song for one year. Then, nature compels the couple to enact two missions.

Their first birthday, Century Birds mate and deposit two eggs in the sand. Their first mission is fulfilled. It is decreed that in precisely 99 years, one egg hatches a male, the other a female. Providence protects the progeny of the Century Birds.

Leaving their eggs to the care of destiny, Century Birds are driven to perform an inexplicable feat – a final mission. The two birds each scoop sand into its beak, and begin one instinctive journey. They are enabled to fly continuously many days to an immense canyon into which they drop their granules of sand. Exhausted, they are lifted by thermals to the canyon's rim where side by side they die.

Time passes without the song or beauty of the Century Bird. But at the turn of the Century, two hatchlings break from leathery shells. They delight in the sun and rain, in the wind and sky for one year. At the appointed time, driven by fate, they mate, bury two eggs in the sand, scoop some of that sand in their tiny bills, and follow intuitively the unknowable path of their parents to that same yawning chasm. Just as their kind has done each century for eons past, once above that vast gorge, they drop their paltry burden of sand. Then, spent from their irrational journey, together they die. Again, the world will have no Century Birds for 99 years.

When every last grain of all the sands of all the lakes, rivers, and oceans in all the world shall have been deposited by the Century Birds into that one great, boundless abyss, so that it has been built up into a mountain higher than any other on earth, the shadow of which shall cover a continent, then not yet will one-tenth-of-a-second have begun in eternity.

Home This Day – Tom's Theme

This day, I'll meet my Savior inside the white pearl gate.
This day, I'll see his glory, brighter than the sun.
This day, I'll greet my family on a golden street call Straight,
And find unfathomed joy that's just begun.

We will visit saints of hist'ry. And on new arrivals wait
Whose service on the earth is not yet done.
The very life of Jesus will our own lives animate   •
Because our full redemption he has won.

"Awaiting new arrivals" is not to say we're idle.
We're each assigned responsible endeavors.
Endeavors you don't recognize, with unfamiliar titles.
Assignments here are satisfying treasures.

I've found the ultimate reality of our faith and truth.
I'm in the greatest story ever told.
I'm living the reality. If anyone needs proof,
I'm living where the rubber meets the gold.

There is no fear, no envy, no selfishness, no hate.
No illness. No kindness left undone.
The morning stars sing songs their winds and light create
With tones on earth unknown, unheard, unsung.

I will join the happy choir with the saints of ages past.
The harmony of voices pure and true.
Songs since Eden to the Heavenly Feast ringing from a ransomed cast,
Echoing though the eons ever new.

Earthly exclamations stutter, for there are no words that utter
The glory and the wonders of God's throne.
In the presence of our Savior, be assured, it is far better
Than any dream the world has ever known.

I'll be waiting here up yonder with an invite all must ponder.
Jesus said: "Whoever will may come."
He died and rose to buy our pardon. He calls from heaven's garden:
"Choose life. My hand will lead you surely home."

So long, Tom. Till I see you again.
Love you so very much. Your Brother, Jim.

A Planted Seed

Today, I leave you in such a different home.
Seems dark, seems still, alone, and all unknown.
So cold. How can I turn and walk away?
But I must go. I must. And you must stay.

Could I just see you, hold you one more time.
Together do the ordinary things – the daily grind.
But how, when the spirit leaves the flesh behind,
And you're no longer here – not here to find?

So fast we race through checkpoints of our lives.
So soon we reach the passage points in life.
So blithely test the breaking points and stays.
So brightly smile and laugh along life's ways.
Till comes today. All our lives compressed into this day!
Our love and dreams, our fruit – all join today.
Everything we lived for in this moment focused.
Everything we'd die for at this moment taunts us.

Confirm my hope! Blessed hope I hold on to!
Is there some symbol here? Some solid clue?
And then I glimpse a flower, bright, windblown.
That flower, once a seed and planted all alone,
Is now a living voice, a message strong
 That's singing in the breeze a happy song:
"Death is not the end; it's planting of a seed
So beauty can burst forth." You took the lead.

No tiny home, no dark, no cold, no loneliness!
Eternal life, in glory of his holy bliss!
I know you are not gone, but waiting just next door.
We'll bloom & grow together in God's presence evermore.

Togetherness Never So Sweet

When the angel called death
Came to take me from you,
Then I rose to the land of the living.
Now your days will bring change
And the usual seem strange
As you travel alone with the grieving.

You will still sense my touch,
Hear my voice, as so much
Of our time was together.
Let the promise we share
Ease the weight of despair
Till we join in the realm of forever.

In our bright home above
In the warmth of pure love
In the home Jesus built, we will meet.
Where our lives we are told
Will never grow old,
And togetherness never so sweet.

It's not long till when
I will hold you again.
Then, togetherness never so sweet.

The Waves of Galilee

It's wild! A stormy season on the Sea of Galilee.
It's loud! The thunder roaring intends to cower me.
It's dark! The clouds are angry. They hide the raging waves.
It's cold! The wind is threatening to take us to our graves.

Not long ago 'twas peaceful. We were unconcerned, content.
But now our pleas are fervent. Of small faith we repent.
Not long ago our prayers contained no urgency or passion.
We cry out to you, Father, now in bold yet humble fashion.

My boots are filled with water as the waves wash in the boat.
How much more can we withstand and keep our lives afloat?
How much more can we take on and keep from going down?
God, we need an answer soon, or surely we will drown!

The only light we're seeing here could strike and take our life.
The progress we are seeing: rising water, added strife.
We want to trust your power, your wise and loving care,
But all we see around us taunts and temps us to despair.

"MY SON IS WITH YOU *in that storm.* Struggle will not last too long.
I will give you grace and strength, and reasons why to carry on.
In all this there's a purpose, a joy you do not see.
Your legacy is not beneath the waves of Galilee."

Few walk on the water with Jesus.
As did Peter when Jesus said, "Come".
Most wait in the boat soaked and chilled.
As did Matthew, James, Thomas, and John.
All in the care of the Father, covered by his perfect will.
Each reach the shore safely on schedule
When to them Christ says, "Peace be still".

"MY SON IS WITH YOU *in that storm.* Sorrows will not last too long.
I will give you faith and hope, and reasons why to carry on.
In all this there's a purpose, a joy you do not see.
Your legacy is not beneath the waves of Galilee."

FIRST CHRISTMAS CANDLE

Think of the tallest candle you've ever seen. Make it taller, more elegant and expensive. Imagine it as white as an Angel's robe. Now, throw it in the ashes of a hot fire.

It wouldn't mean a thing to you. You wouldn't care because a candle is nothing to you. But what if something very special to you had been destroyed?!

My father owns and operates Michael's Candles, Cards and Candy Store. Our specialty is unusual candles. I love the fragrance and elegance of our candles. So do our customers.

One day during Christmas season, I dropped an especially exquisite candle that I was taking to place at the top of a small manger scene in our store window. This candle was intended to cast a star-like light over Baby Jesus, Joseph and Mary, the shepherds, and the wise men on camels. (We all know the wisemen actually came later to see Jesus, but our manger scene included them at the first Christmas). As the candle hit the floor, my foot came down on it, breaking it in several pieces. I suppose it's because of that incident with this manger scene that I had an unusual dream about a candle when Jesus was born. In my dream, I was the son of a Candlemaker in ancient Palestine...

Two thousand years ago, candles were always born twins. Tapered wax icicles hanging on opposite ends of a wick string, heads to the center.

In his shop, a master candlemaker worked before his pot of molten wax. He selected the longest wick string and began dipping. When the dipping and drying process was finished, there were candles such as he had not seen before. Pearly and unblemished, like the white of a baby's eyes. Though they were the tallest candles he had ever made, they were perfectly straight and smooth.

"Beautiful!" he said aloud. "Exquisitely formed. These must be used in service to God! These will stand gracefully in the center of the holy candlesticks, inspiring worship as their flames leap upward."

Surprised at catching himself talking out loud to no one, the candlemaker carefully picked up the majestic candles and hung them in a place by themselves.

A few days later, the candlemaker selected several of his best candles for the temple. He chose only the finest for this holy work, and the finest of all were the tall, straight, glistening twins. He cut the wick strings to separate the candles, giving each its own individual identity for the first time. Carefully he laid them on the table to be prepared for delivery. He then went to attend to duties in another part of the shop.

As the chandler's son was bundling candles, the owner of an Inn from a nearby town came into the shop. As usual, he selected candles of various sizes and colors, each suited to the job it was to perform. As he looked over the candles for sale, his eyes fell on the exceptional twins.   He was captivated at once.

"I'd like to purchase these two delightful candles to use at my table when I have special guests. I have never seen such lovely ones," he said.

"Yes", replied the son. "They are elegant – my father's finest. He has dedicated them to the temple. They are not for sale."

"Listen," said the inn keeper. "I will pay double the usual price. Surely your father would rather have the extra profit, and donate less valuable ones."

"I'd like to sell them to you, but these are definitely not available. Father wants to give the best to God."

"I have the answer, then," said the inn owner. "You send one of these perfect candles to the house of worship. For the other, I will pay three times the normal figure. Your father could donate a third of the price to the temple, and still keep twice what such a candle usually brings. What could be better? You are in business to make a profit, and surely the religious leaders would rather have a cash donation than a pretty candle."

"Yes, indeed, they probably would," admitted the son. Shaking his head, he sold one of the irreplaceable candles.

At closing time, as the son and his father reviewed receipts of the day, the lad boasted how he had gotten such a high price for one of the perfect twins.

The master candlemaker was visible displeased.   "Son, some strange instinct tells me that those candles were destined in a special way to honor God. I would not have sold them at any price. Such stateliness and grace. They were like ivory, and instilled a sense of awe as they pointed to the heavens. There were to serve God. But now, one is gone. It is gone! Why was I not more careful?"

Not long afterward, finding himself on business in the nearby town, the candlemaker decided to pay a visit to the innkeeper who had purchased the special candle.

After a brief chat, the candlemaker inquired, "You will recall that unique candle which you acquired from my son on your last trip to my shop?"

"Oh, yes!" replied the owner of the inn. I will never forget it. I was captured by its radiance -- and I paid dearly for it."

"Never have my hands produced such excellence," stated the chandler. "I believe God helped me prepare that candle and its twin for divine service. I must have it back for its dedicated purpose."

"So, you think that candle was destined for godly greatness?!" Was the innkeeper taunting? "Well, I think your insight is correct," agreed the innkeeper. "Let me tell you what happened to that candle. A memorable story indeed!"

Both men quietly walked outside and sat in the shade of a big tree.

"One evening not many days after I had purchased the candle from your son, just as it grew dark, a young couple came here seeking lodging. Due to Rome's tax edict, my inn had been full for several hours, and I had already turned away other travelers. Yet, something tugged at me. I knew there would be no vacant rooms in the entire town, so I offered this couple shelter in my shed adjoining the stable. Having been already refused at other lodging places, they gratefully accepted.

"Since it was getting darker, I said, 'Wait! I'll get you a candle.'

"Now, Chandler, I would not have parted with your luxurious candle for anything. I was saving it for some celebration, or to honor someone - - perhaps dinner with the city elders. Yet, an irresistible force compelled me to take THAT candle. I lit it from the one burning at my door, then handed it to the couple to light the path and to illuminate the shed. As the man passed the candle to the woman sitting on a donkey, I noticed that she was going to have a baby, and quite soon if the silhouette of her clothing was an accurate indication.

"Why I gave them my prize candle I can't explain. But then, it was a night of inexplicable activities.

"Shortly after they had left my doorway, I decided to be sure the couple had fresh water and bedding. Taking a jug and two blankets, I walked to the enclosure. After knocking, I opened the door. The man had gathered some kindling and was lighting a warming fire in a kiln once used by a potter. The exquisite candle, laid on its side, was catching the kindling on fire.

"I gasped, hardly restraining myself from rescuing the candle, for it was becoming dirty and bent. I saw its grandeur evaporating with the smoke that curled out of the loft window. I handed them the blankets and water. The lady certainly looked as if the baby could be born any time. Having done all I could to be hospitable, I excused myself and went to bed.

"About midnight, I was awakened by barking dogs. I looked out. There in the moonlight were shepherds making their way to my stable. I quickly dressed, but by the time I got outside, the shepherds were in the shed near an old, small manger. They were surrounding the couple, and, yes! the young woman had a new baby in her arms. It must have been born shortly after I had left the couple.

"I wanted to see if there was anything I could do, but the shepherds stayed and stayed. Since all seemed well, I went back to bed, planning to find out in the morning why these visitors had come, and what needs the couple might have.

"I had hardly gotten back to sleep, when barking awakened me as before. Some sort of small caravan was in the street! Hastily dressing, I hurried to determine what all this meant. Before I could get to them, the leaders of the caravan had joined the others in the large shed. They were now next to the couple, with the shepherds quietly in the background. The bent candle was illuminating the baby's face as they gazed upon him. The mother looked tired, but peaceful and happy. The father appeared watchful, proud and amazed.

"The caravan leaders had the air of royalty, and were giving presents to the baby. Expensive gifts! The flame of the candle glistened brilliantly on gold. A pleasant aroma of incense and myrrh permeated the musty shed. What was happening, I wondered?! This was obviously a poor couple. I hadn't even charged them to use my shed. But these lavish gifts, if sold, would make them quite comfortable for life.

"Now, nothing could tear me away until I found the meaning of all this. With determination, I approached the man in charge of the waiting caravan. 'Who are you, and what are you doing here? I own this place and must know.'

"His reply stunned me. 'Our leaders, rulers from the East, are here, directed by a constellation of stars. Look if you will.'

"He pointed out a truly amazing position of the stars that I had never before seen. He said his leaders were 'kings' who were learned in astronomy and prophecy. He said their studies and these stars told them that here, today, in this place, was born a new King who would be King over kings! He said that they had traveled here to honor and to worship Him, and to celebrate his birth.

"I was unable to speak. In amazement I quietly left him, making my way around the shed to the stable. There I came upon one of the shepherds. Regaining my voice, I asked him why they had come here. His reply was equally astonishing. Said he, 'The other shepherds and I were on the hills just out of town when the sky lit up with strange lights, and the quiet was broken by frightening sounds. Quite honestly, we were terrified. A voice said, "Don't be afraid." It was angels talking and singing. Since we all heard and saw, we knew it was real. An angel instructed us to come here, giving directions. He said a baby had just been born Who is the Savior of all mankind – the Prince of peace – the Son of God. We came and found just what the angel had said. It's a miracle!'

"My mind was reeling, thoughts racing, searching! I remembered the power that seemed to force me to give the wonderful candle to this special couple. I remembered holy writings, prophecies of an unusual birth. I shrank down against the fence post to regain my senses. My eyes closed.

"Shortly, I put a hand on the rail, struggled to my feet and made my way to a shed window. Streaks of gray dawn were beginning to christen the Eastern sky. I looked through the window. The man and woman were asleep. The baby, wrapped in swaddling cloth, was asleep on hay in the manger. The precious candle was flickering its last light. Then it was out.

All that was left was a small puddle of grayish wax speckled with dirt and straw.

"I don't know, Candlemaker, what fate made your twin candles so luxurious, or why one of them came to be here in a small inn at Bethlehem, or what convinced you that they had a divine destiny. But I know that those candles have touched me. And one of those candles stands centermost in the Temple candelabra while the other humbly burned itself out here. First it lighted the way for the couple. Then it fired the kindling to keep them warm. Then it illuminated the face of the baby so that he could be adored by the shepherds, by the royal visitors, and by me. I believe that this candle, in this lowly place, was expended in worship to the King over kings, the Savior. Perhaps God arranged – even used us and your son to make sure – that this perfect candle would be here to serve His Son, and that this unknown candle was the most blessed and honored of all!

The photo of a Shepherd's Cave near Bethlehem may be like the place Jesus was born.

First Christmas Candle
REPRISE

In a Bethlehem stall, a candle stood,
That was used to light a fire of wood.
That flamed to warm a baby, said
To be a King in a manger bed.

In a cattle shed that candle burned
At the place to which the shepherds turned
From tending sheep on the hills that night
When angels caused them such a fright.

When a thousand angels sang on wing
That He was born, the promised King,
To bring goodwill and peace to all,
That He humble lay in a borrowed stall.

In that rustic room, the candle shone
Upon his face in His "manger-throne",
That those who came to this hallowed place
Could honor Him – God's gift of grace.

As the candle gave its blessed light,
The shepherds praised this glorious sight,
And wise men brought Him gifts to say,
"We worship You this holy day."

In a lowly place, that candle died
Where Mary slept at Joseph's side,
Content that she could be a part
Of bringing hope to human hearts.

Just so, some serve with wide acclaim,
As public lights for Jesus' name.
While others serve, not known at all,
Like this candle in that stall.

The Lord rewards all who obey
Regardless of their place or fame,
But specially honors those whose labors
Are quiet and faithful in lowly stables.

MOSES, THE GAMBLER

MOSES HAD IT ALL

Moses was the biggest gambler of all time. Here is a son of slaves, who through providence found himself the adopted son of the Pharaoh of Egypt when the Pharaoh was the most powerful ruler in the world. Everything a man could want came with that position. Wealth, fame, power, women, leisure, and any pleasure known on earth. Moses had everything the mind could imagine.

HE WALKED AWAY FROM EVERYTHING THIS LIFE OFFERS

He bet it all on one wager when he chose to forfeit that position to rejoin his slave kinfolk. He chose to suffer with the people of God, over luxuriating in the pleasures of sin for a lifetime. He valued the stigma of being in God's family more than the status of being in Pharaoh's family. Why?! Because he believed the end result of his choice would be better. He gambled that the palace of God is better than the palace of Pharaoh. He bet his life that the eternal life God offers is more sure than the royal dynastic life Pharaoh's daughter offered.

Jim Elliot, a missionary who gave his life spreading the gospel, said, "He is no fool who gives up that which he cannot keep, to gain that which he cannot lose." Elliot and Moses thought alike. You and I – how do we think? What is our price? On what value are we betting our eternal life?

WHAT IF MOSES HAD STAYED AT THE PALACE OF PHARAOH

Shelly, in his classic poem, had a Pharaoh say: "My name is OZZIMANDIAS, king of kings, look on my works ye mighty and despair." All around, lay only rubble of the kingdom and of the statue of the boastful Pharaoh. Had he stayed with the dynasty, Moses could have been that Pharaoh – a memory, a mummy and crumbled mortar. I've seen in Egypt such monolithic, crumbled statues. And I've seen the Holy Land built by the descendants of Moses. I've seen the tombs of Pharaohs, and I've seen the empty tomb of Jesus. There is a vast difference.

HE WOULD HAVE MISSED SOMETHING BETTER

But Moses chose God. And God has something far better for Moses – a kingdom which cannot be shaken or destroyed. Moses met God on Mt. Sinai, and visited with Jesus on the mountain when Jesus was glorified before selected disciples. Moses will inherit the New Jerusalem eternally where he will, as an adopted son of God, participate in governing. Remember how Jesus said that there will be believers to whom Jesus will say: Be ruler over five cities? Or: Be ruler over ten cities? Pharaoh won't be there, and eternity is a long time. Moses had his priorities straight, his values right, his choices correct. He wasn't stupid, and it wasn't that he didn't want to be the son of royalty. He just knew who IS King of kings.

ARE WE AS WISE AS MOSES

Today, we see people sell themselves for a few thousand dollars, for a bit of fame, or for a taste of power. Would anyone today give up a kingdom for a godly mission? Is there a Moses among us? Probably. But each of us must determine, am I a Moses?! Again, remember that Jesus said: What is a man advantaged if he could gain the entire world, with all its wealth, fame, power and pleasure, but lose his own soul? What can a man trade to recover his soul from eternal destruction? The entire universe has not enough wealth to buy a single hour of enjoyment in the presence of Almighty God. The entire world has not enough pleasures, though experienced a lifetime, to trade for an eternity without God. Are you gambling with God? Better ask Moses if that's wise; he knows the odds. He knows the payout.

An un-staged, live photo taken in Egypt not far from Pyramids.

IT'S ALL BY FAITH

FAITH IS THE FOUNDATION OF ALL RELATIONSHIPS

Why should it seem unusual for one's relationship with God to be based on faith? All relationships are based on faith. From the trivial to the mundane to the profound, faith is the basis of bonding.

Pets have a faith relationship with their masters. In exchange for the pet's protecting us and loving us, they completely trust their owners to feed and care for them. Farm animals trust the farmer to nurture, protect and provide for them. That may seem petty, but it illustrates how common is a faith relationship.

LIFE ITSELF IS FAITH IN PROCESS

In everyday living, we operate by faith. We believe the other drivers on the street are safe and sane. We trust the car we drive, and also trust vehicles others drive. Sometimes that faith proves ill founded, and we pay the price. We trust our children to a bus driver, to a teacher, to a day care center. Children trust adults for all of life. In the first few years, that faith is unquestioning, hence the idiom, "childlike faith". A child trusts mom and dad for proper food, clothing, shelter, health care, education, guidance, culture, values, discipline and training – everything. That's one reason child abuse is so heinous. When one takes advantage of the complete trust of an innocent child, that one is justifiably worthy of horsewhipping first and prison next.

Life itself is lived in trust. We breathe believing the air is good. We eat accepting food as healthy. We sleep believing the premises safe and companions trustworthy. Life is a pageant of faith. One reason crime is so terrible is because one person wrongfully takes advantage of another person's fundamental faith. Society cannot allow the destruction of trust, and must protect the ability of mankind to function in rational faith. The incorrigible criminal must be removed, for he violates the faith of everyone.

BUSINESS AND THE PROFESSIONS FUNCTION ON FAITH

Employers and employees must be able to function on mutual faith. An employer must be able to trust employees to do a good job and to protect industrial secrets. The employees have the right to trust the employer for fair wages, job security and a safe workplace. Similarly, business trusts customers to pay with good checks, and customers expect business to supply quality products at fair prices. Both believe the other will fulfill their respective expressed and implied promises.

Faith is the basis of a physician-patient, of a financial advisor-client, of a counselor-client, of a real estate broker-client relationship, and of an attorney-client relationship, and others.

FAITH IS REQUIRED IN A LOVE RELATIONSHIP

Faith is fundamental in good marriage relationships. If it is not based on mutual faith, a marriage does not have much, no matter what else it may have. Rich, beautiful, talented, famous, powerful, friendly, loving, likable people with pleasing personalities get divorced every day. Those desirable factors do not make a stable marriage. Faith in practice does. Both spouses must be able to trust the other not only with fidelity, but also with such things as self-image, personal idiosyncrasies, personal insights, confessions of one's deepest thoughts, commitments and expressions that open one up to hurt from the other, and the things that go on when one is totally relaxed behind closed doors. If a spouse will not or cannot trust the marriage partner, their union is certainly wounded. Love and faith in each other will be evidenced by fidelity and genuine caring. Joint trust must be present, and deserved, for a marriage to be happy, fulfilling and successful.

ATHEISTS ARE ATHEISTS BY FAITH

To claim there is no God requires great faith. No one can know there is no God, and there is more evidence and logic in favor of a Creator than against one. There's a book titled: I Don't Have Enough Faith to Be an Atheist. To know there is no God, one would need total, universal knowledge – which no one has – and one would have had to examine all parts of things infinite – which no one can do. Therefore, to believe no God exists, requires immense faith. To live and die as if no God exists requires more blind faith than intelligent faith.

THAT GOD REQUIRES FAITH IS CONSISTENT WITH ALL REALITY

God has set it up so that humans have the ability to relate to him in faith. He has set it up so that we are accustomed to faith relationships. Faith is a gift from God. "Trust me. Believe me," says God. "Rely on me alone, and I will give you eternal life. An abundant and satisfying eternal life." The hymn "Trust and Obey" is a powerful formula for life.

FAITH IN GOD ALONE

It's an insult to Deity for a created being to reply, "Yes, I will rely on you, supplemented by my own abilities and resources where yours are insufficient." That kind of faith is not faith. Faith that is not total is to the same extent unbelief. Faith that is not 100% is the inverse percentage doubt. Faith and doubt are antagonistic. Faith is vital. Just trust God. That is the requirement. Rely on him only. Believe. The Bible puts it this way: "As many as receive him (Jesus), to them he gives the power to be children of God; yes, to those who believe in his name." And: "You are saved by grace through faith. A faith that is not of yourself but is a gift of God; not by human activity that deserves being saved." (Ephesians 2:8-9 paraphrased)

left James E Foy

James E Foy

OUR LIVES SHOWCASE OUR FAITH

Real faith in God will evidence itself by a life that looks like a life God would produce. In contrast, a life that looks like a life which sin, self and Satan would produce, is not a life from godly faith. Your actual faith and your actions are consistent – they are twins. Conduct is a mirror of conviction. Your actions that are seen describe your faith that is unseen. Outward actions declare actual inward belief. Really! If you definitely do not believe your car breaks are going to stop your car when you press the brake pedal, then you will not drive that car! If you do get into the car of your own volition and drive onto the highway, that is proof that you truly believe the brakes will perform adequately. Similarly, if you and I do genuinely believe that God is our Creator and Savior, then our life choices will demonstrate that sincere, actual belief. If, however, we consciously and volitionally live like a demon, then we are not a child of God.

WHERE HAVE YOU PLACED YOUR FAITH

Of course, salvation is by faith. Of course, relationship to God is by faith. All of nature and relationships therein are of faith. And God is the Creator of nature. Faith relationships in nature are teachers to bring us to God. God functions in the realm of faith. You know God by faith. Intelligent faith, not blind faith. The Bible says: "Come, let us reason together". Biblical, saving faith is reasonable belief, rational trust. That is normal. In our world, it's ALL by faith. The big question in life is: Have you chosen by deliberate act of your will to put faith in God? We must not deceive ourselves. Our daily life is the proof of personal truth.

On the Sea of Galilee with approaching storm.

Loving Eyes

The girl was blind – and hated herself.
Her sightless eyes had poisoned her mind.
But not just herself – she hated the world,
Save one special friend who was loving & kind.

This man was a pillar, and his words of support
Included, "I love you. Will you be my wife?"
She said that she would if she only could see.
"I can't burden you for the rest of your life."

This girl was so blessed, for one day in spring,
Someone donated eyes – she'll be able to see.
When the surgery was done, a complete success,
She could view the world, and her husband to be.

While in loving embrace, he smiled in her face,
"Now marry me, Love, you have your best wish."
She gazed at her man. He had hollow, blind eyes.
Stunned by his visage, and shocked by his kiss,

She thought of awaking each day to this sight –
A man misshapen, dependent and blind.
"I can't marry you. Not who I now see.
If insisting I do, you couldn't be kind."

In tears the man left – left the one that he loved.
Then sent her this letter: "I know you'll see fine.
You truly are loved. Enjoy your new sight.
Take care of those eyes: Before yours, they were mine."

(Adapted from a story heard)

Paradoxes of life:

Pleasure is entertaining while teaching little.
Difficulty is staggering while teaching much.
Suffering is bewildering while drawing one to God.
Healing is joyful while yielding gratitude otherwise
unknown.
Separation is lonely while heightening comfort of friends.
Reunion is delightful – magnified in heaven without end.

The Manual on Life
The 10 Commandments

You shall have no other Gods before me.
"Before Me" has two concepts:
Not prioritized ahead of Creator God.
Not before God as not before the court:
therefore, not honored as another God
You shall not have any idols.
You shall not take God's name in vain.
Remember the Sabbath Day to keep it Holy.
Honor your father and mother.
You shall not murder.
You shall not commit adultery.
You shalt not steal.
You shall not bear false witness.
You shall not covet.

SECTION THREE

3 RRR ON ROMANCE

THESE HANDS

These hands try to say that I love you.
To imprint the feeling that I care.
These hands try to reach to your spirit
As I'm tracing the softness of your hair.

These hands want to learn all about you,
The little things that pleasure you so.
These hands want to lift you uniquely.
These hands want to give you that glow.

These hands want to do good things for you,
Protect you from any kind of harm,
Provide all the things you have need of,
Make a house of wood into our home.

Please listen to the love in my fingers,
For spoken words are limited so much.
These hands will convey, as they linger,
Through the unspoken language of touch.

If my words are losing their foliage,
There's a way to renew the youthful blush.
These hands will deliver the message
That my voice finds is just too much.

May Her Day be Beautiful

When I wake up in the morning, and see her lying there
Her eyes still closed against the light of dawn.
Although I wouldn't wake her, I lightly touch her hair,
And watch the rise and fall of lace that she has on.

God, keep her sweet breath coming, her pure heart beating strong.
Protect her from all evil, and from every kind of harm.
And may her day be beautiful, as mine will be for me
Because I held close her this morning in my arms.

When she walks each day beside me, I'm happy I'm not free.
She glows a radiant beauty in the sun.
I've seen the secret splendor, and know the ecstasy.
The web we wove and held together glistens on.

God, keep her sweet breath coming, her pure heart beating strong.
Protect her from all evil, and from every kind of harm.
And may her way be beautiful, as mine will be for me
Because she walks, today, beside me arm in arm.

When I lay down in the evening, I know things are alright
Because we'll be together through the night.
When moonbeams through the window cast halos 'round her face,
I know God loaned to me an angel in this place.

God, keep her sweet breath coming, her pure heart beating strong.
Protect her from all evil, and from every kind of harm.
And may her rest be beautiful, as mine will be for me
Because I held her sleeping safely in my arms.

(music for this song is in Music section)

BEAUTIFUL ANGEL
Two Dreams Together

(male solo)
He said, "I'm no angel; I'm only a man.
I only can give you the best that I am.
I could never be perfect, but would always be true,
And always be grateful for an angel like you."

(female solo)
"I've been called an angel by others", she said.
"But I hope that the saying hasn't gone to my head.
If I could be an angel, if good dreams come true,
I'd give all my love to a man such as you."

(duet)
Than this beautiful angel and this heaven-blest man;
Both regular people – just a woman – just a man;
Tied two dreams together with help from above.
A new kind of happy, in the old kind of love.

(male solo)
He said, "It's a pleasure just seeing you smile.
But there's no way to measure what I find all the while
That I'm trying to please you – to give you first place –
The fabulous treasure that I see in your face."

(female solo)
"You do bring me pleasure, and happiness, too.
But my real, lasting treasure, is just being with you.
You say I'm an angel – in the life we'll explore,
What you'll get from this angel is forevermore."

(male solo)

He said, "We both know there is no endless bliss.

There's no perfect dream – life as one endless kiss.

But in life as it takes us – when we're up – when we're down,

I will try to be worthy of the angel I've found."

(female solo)

"I'm not thinking of 'worthy'. I'm thinking of gifts.

As we both keep on giving hearts just like this.

I give all I am, and you give all to me.

As we live for each other, the dream comes to be.

(duet)

Than this beautiful angel and this heaven-blest man;

Both regular people – just a woman – just a man;

Tied two lives together with grace from above.

A new way of living, as two become one.

Yes, this beautiful angel and this heaven-blest man;

Both regular people – just a woman – just a man;

Pledged total commitment that fully intends

To go right on giving love without end.

(music of this song is in Music section)

Autumn Leaves

While traveling in the spring time of our lives,
No thought of changing seasons in our heads,
Every urge and instinct set in over drive,
Impelled us to cavort on leafy beds:

We played awhile today on Autumn Mountains.
What sweet delight to taste the Fall with you.
Bare feet on leafy carpet climbed the ridges
To feel the ecstasy and see the view.
We chased the floating leaves as you were laughing.
I flicked a leaf that settled on your hair.
Then, like the glist'ning dew, I saw a tear drop
because of such delights we captured there.
Then, like a falling leaf, a tear of joy dropped
Because of mystic beauty that we shared.

*This fun chasing falling leaves occurred in Gatlinburg TN
where we stayed in a motel along a beautiful creek in the
Smokey mountains. Below shows the romantic place.*

I Haven't the Words

I confess precious darling you capture my thoughts
Too many lingering hours.
You dance in my daydreams — a frolic untaught.
You burst into flames as the flowers.

I feel your fond touch in the brush of the air.
Your whisper I hear in an echo somewhere.
I sense our love song in the call of the birds.
I so want to tell you but haven't the words.

The ducks on the pond are coupled,
The card'nals are paired all day.
The Eagles are nesting together.
The sunbeams to you point the way.

The ducks on the water are gliding along
In synchronized waltz with their mate.
The song birds in chorus are paired as they sing
With luster that does not abate.

Of you I'm reminded as the world turns:
I so want to tell you but haven't the words.

Autumn Reverie

Autumn colors everywhere, autumn briskness in the air.
Reds and oranges, browns and golds, yellow flame amid the cold.
She goes walking by my side. She's my pride, autumn eyed.
Watch the wind blow her hair, she's so fair few compare.
Soon the world will all be white, and we'll be by the fire light,
Dreaming of the coming spring when the world and love is green.

*The best things in life
are not things.*

172

Our Journey Round the Sun

In our journey 'round the sun
I have the feeling that I've won.
I've won first prize – like gold refined
Because you are my Valentine.

My Valentine, you fill my head
As you dazzle, all in red.
All in red to celebrate
A love that time does not abate.

Does not abate: 'tis no surprise
What with your image in my eyes.
In my eyes the vision told
Cannot portray the depth of soul.

Depth of soul that melds with mine
And dances as my Valentine.
My Valentine, you're my delight;
I choose you still each day and night.

Day and night, I pray not done
In our journey 'round the sun.

Moments with You

Life is an hour in time and space in which to live.
Moments to laugh, to love, to work, to get, to give.
Moments of fortune and fun, of failure and fears,
Moments to share with one you love in joy or tears.

In my brief hour, moments I've held above the rest,
Were moments with you, moments of climbing to the crest.
Moments of oceans and lakes; running in the sand;
Planting a tree; carving our names; just holding your hand.

Moments with you, dreams realized.
Fleeting and few, so highly prized.
In my brief hour, most precious it's true are moments with you.

Then with the kids there came a different love demand
Sharing with them the lessons of life the way God planned.
Sometimes we laughed, sometimes we cried,
sometimes we swelled up with pride.
Moments too short, the years too fast, but memories abide.

Moments with you, as in a song,
The melody sweet though some notes played wrong.
This is our hour, this is our song: Moments with You.

And now today have you and I this moment of time.
Though it's so brief it will endure within our mind.
Let it be joy, let it be good, let it be graced from above.
Let it be hope, let it be happy, let it be love.

Addendum -
Now you are gone, gone from my arms but not from my heart.
There by your stone, here on my wall, our memories impart
Nearly a touch, nearly a hug, nearly a palpable kiss.
Memories fond for the life we found in moments like this.

Marriage Love

It's beautiful, wholesome, this thing we have: *Love*.
A beautiful gift from our Maker above.
Who designed you for me; designed me for you;
And designed that true love makes one out of two.

Now, it's no easy task, making one out of two.
It requires the right formulation and glue.
The glue is commitment: "'til death do us part",
As each of us promise: "I give you my heart".

The formula's strange: "As we each love our self".
A love that is steadfast in sickness and health.
Through richer or poorer. On good days and bad.
Through thrills or depression. Through happy and sad.

Through typical times — and that can be roughest:
Monotonous schedules are usually the toughest.
The everyday work day, being home every night,
Can dull our love's glow if we don't get it right.

As we work out our Love Plan — each day a new start —
It's wise to include both laughter and art.
Some un-special days, surprise something special.
"No reason" gifts are uniquely essential.

We'll look past the problems. Help each other look good
In spite of the failures — the way a self would.
We'll show special care, to assume what is best,
Acknowledging no one can pass every test.

To defend and protect as I do my own self.
To let this love show — not be hid on a shelf.
It's lifting each up when one's fallen down.
It's to aid and encourage whatever comes 'round.

It's a gift that's enduring. Stamped in our heart.
We each give this love "'til death do us part".
Yes, we'll too often fail, and not always show it,
So, pledge to forgive each time that we blow it.

I do love you, darling. You are my life.
I'm so very grateful we're husband and wife.
May God help us live in actual time,
The genuine love portrayed in this rhyme.

I Think of You
To my Wife

If I don't know what to do, I call on you.
When I've got the doggone flu, I turn to you.
If I'm in the doldrums where it isn't any fun,
I know just what to do: I come to you.

To think of all the best, I think of you.
Whether serious or in jest, I think of you.
No thought fills me so, and I'm certain that you know:
If I've got a thought at all, it includes you.

Love is an essential dimension.

The pond I see from my home office window.

Cozy by the Fireplace

We're not spring chickens, we're not summer hawks.
We're not much like sheep that run in their flocks.
More like the swans or cooing doves in pairs.
Preferring quiet hours huddled in our lair.

Cozy by the fireplace, cuddled with my mate.
Just a bit of dancing as the hour gets late.
Need no other pleasure to set our hearts aglow.
Just time and song and fireplace with one I know.

I see the flame's reflection glistening in your eyes.
Loving contemplations. This is paradise.

Cozy by the fireplace, being with my mate.
Moments more enchanting as the hour gets late.
Need no other pleasure for our love to grow:
Just time and song and fire place with one I know.

The flame's warm radiation: some embers do not die.
Love's anticipation. This is paradise.
Need no other pleasure, for I love you so:
Just time and song and fire place with one I know

Love loves without requiring a reason.
Love is strongest when most selfless.
Love is vulnerable without regret.

When With You

When you fix your eyes on mine, nothing matters but your love.
When your touch responds to mine, we connect to heaven above.
When your lips perform their charm as your kisses say you care,
When your unobstructed beauty in its furtive splendor there…

When you say, "I love you dearly. Darling, you're the only one.
You're the one I want to be with every day till life is done."
When you say, "Now, life's fullness – now we write the book of us.
Ours the present, ours the memory, passion, family, dreams & trust."

Oh, just realizing you're mine. Just to know you're wholly mine.
Just assured that you see "*us*" now, and to the end of time…
And just to be with you. Just to see your smile.
Just to hold your hand and heart as we traverse this little while…

The yesterdays are precious: In them we're sealed together.
Tomorrows – grand anticipations: You and me forever.

Without You

A day at the beach is just another sunset
    without you there.
A museum, zoo, or park, just another spree met
    without you there.
A mountain creek or ghost town, wasted gambit
    unless with you.
Camp sites or travel times are lonely vignettes
    without you.
You are the substance and the spirit.
    In my balloon, you are the air.
When I'm most content and happy
    It's because you're with me there.

Happy Anniversary

Another year! It's as a sigh:
Another blinking of an eye.
Another mist chased by the sun.
Another book of Said and Done.

The struggles & cuddles etched in our hearts.
Not fleeting bubbles, but life's puzzle parts.
In so many ways we two are now one.
The true math of love: $1 + 1 = 1$.

What is time that quickly passes?
Like fine wine low in our glasses?
Another laugh, another tear?
Our puzzle pressed into a year?
Whatever happens, this is clear:
It is our love that makes it dear.
This, too, is clear year by year,
Your love & God's love cast out fear.

At times we took it on the chin.
At times I said: You're right again.
The moments of forgiving mean
Love is real – real people living.
Hours of selfless giving, prove
Love is deep in joy and grieving.
Sure, we seek the fun and thrills,
But are drawn close by hills and spills.

If granted choice, this I'd pursue:
I'd walk remaining years with you.
Not said as well as some could do,
But still, I'm glad you know it's true.

Another year! Another sigh.
Another blinking of an eye.
Then, when next year is said and done,
Let's make it best – with more to come.

YOU ARE

You are the first startling drop of rain.
You are the first stream of light each day with its promise & joy.
You are the first flower of spring bringing beauty and fragrance.
You are the blast of an airhorn jolting me to sharpened senses.
You are the song of a melodious bird.
You are the purr of a contented cat.
You are the uncontrolled wag of a dog's tail.
You are the kaleidoscope of a thousand gem stones.
You are a painting that cannot be fathomed or duplicated.
You are the shade of a tree in the heat of summer.
You are a cool drink of sparkling water.
You are the surprising strength of a gossamer web.
You are the pillow for my head.
You are serenity in the cacophony of life.
You are the voice of contentment and confidence.
You are my partner who is irreplaceable.

Love loves even when loving seems foolish.
Love is not necessarily logical.
Love doesn't demand a fair exchange – this for that.
Yet, for the good of the loved one,
*   love makes high demands.*
Love and gullibility are not synonymous.

The 12th Ringing of the Gong

In the LA County Ballroom, we joined the celebration.
The dress you wore — a yellow song — soft-flowing intonation.
In romantic sculptured gardens, we lingered just past midnight.
Why time being squandered? The question would be asked that night.

That very hour I asked my question: "Will you marry me, my love?"
Slipped a ring upon your finger — fit you perfect as a glove.
Then, you asked of me your question: "Why did you wait so long?"
"It became my mother's birthday the 12th ringing of the gong."
"It was on my mother's birthday, dear, you promised me we'd wed.
This day is ever-hallowed by the promise you then said.
You pledged that day your solemn vow: To me you would belong.
It became our sacred day at the 12th ringing of the gong."

This life is but a journey — it's the shortest leg, in fact.
We took our trip together, though at times I left the map.
You took an early exit, dear. There's no one wanted that.
You found eternal glory first. Nothing fills the gap.
No one knows how long they'll linger, nor the last verse of their song.
'll hold you soon in heaven The 12th Ringing of the Gong.
Since to the Heavenly Father each of us belongs,
We'll join hands there together The 12th Ringing of the Gong.

True Love is concealed in the heart and mind
but is truly revealed in daily actions and reactions
to the one loved.

Love is not by sin repealed
when repentance has been sealed,
and by forgiveness love is healed.

My Love is Yours

When it comes – and it must come –
Then I must leave this place.
Sad, the fact I won't return,
And how I'll miss your face.

When it comes – and it must come –
That I go on alone.
Then, until you come to me,
I'll miss you and our home.

Oh, what joy to gaze again
Into you loving eyes.
To hold again, embrace you close,
To see your smile: First Prize.

I never did deserve you.
Could a pauper claim a queen?
What could I do to earn you?
Yet, our love is ever green.

When standing on the ocean sand,
One foot already in the surf,
We'll both find solace holding hands,
Because our peace surpasses earth
And reaches to our heavenly berth.

When it comes – and it must come –
That I have left your side.
The only cause will be that came
The revocation of life's tide.

We Have Love

When the sun is shining bright and everything's alright,
we have love.
When the sun is sinking low and we can't see how to go,
we have love.

When our bank account is full and our fortunes like a bull,
we have love.
When our bank account is slim and our future looking dim,
we have love.

When our friends are all around and popularity abounds,
we have love.
When our friends are just a few, if it's only me and you,
we have love.

When we have the strength of youth, when the good news is the truth,
we have love.
When our strength and vigor fail, and the news a frightful tale,
we have love.

When your face is bright and fair, when it's easy showing care,
we have love.
When the sparkle starts to dim, when we're not so fit and trim,
we have love.

Ah, when our vows are young, and easy on our tongue,
we have love.
Then, when we're growing old, and our story has been told,
we have love.

With our ideal wedding dreams, and with our hopeful schemes,
we have love.
When our dreams and schemes are spent, we'll cherish how they went,
And still have love. Yes, WE HAVE LOVE.

Dessert's Dessert

I like chicken fried steak and potatoes, biscuits and gravy and greens,
Butter and bread and tomatoes. And then I loosen my jeans.
'Cause, I like dessert after dinner.
A little sweetness each day doesn't hurt.
Then, as an encore, there in the door, is standing Dessert's Dessert.

> She's the apple of my eye, she's my lemon meringue pie,
> She's frosting on my lip, she's chocolate chip.
> She's a big banana split. I'm gonna have a fit.
> A little sweetness never hurt, she's Dessert's Dessert.

It seems that my hunger starts building each day on my way home from work.
I think of the meal that she's fixing. Try to guess what we'll have for dessert.
Hey, I'll like whatever she's cooking. And with the chef I will flirt.
'Cause, When the meal's done, it's sweetness & fun. It's time for Dessert's Dessert.

> She's the apple of my eye, she's my lemon meringue pie,
> She's frosting on my lip, she's chocolate chip.
> She's a big banana split. Now, I think I'd better quit.
> A little sweetness never hurt, she's Dessert's Dessert.

There's Nothing Like Waltzing With You

When a waltz stars to play,
Then my feet want to stay
Caught up dancing away the night with you.

When the song's one, two, three,
And you're flowing with me
Then my spirit soars free, waltzing with you.

As the music takes flight
And our hearts become light
Held by smitten delight: so in love with you.

Now I'm lost in your arms,
In your beauty and charms
As your dress takes your form, I'm taken by you.

Yes, I always love you,
To be held next to you,
And while dancing the waltz, I melt into you.

My heart melts into you,
Whirls and twirls right with you,
There's just nothing like waltzing with you.
There's just nothing like waltzing with you.

NEAR PARTING?

You are in my dying heart
And in my falling tears.
You have been my love, my art,
Desire through the years.

Now the pulse may soon depart.
My bier is nearing view.
But without doubt no Cupid's dart,
Has ever flown more true.

Do not our memories abort,
But hold them warm and near.
They'll take a hue of richer sort
As time makes each more dear.

We are composed of all things past:
Our love reposed in memory's scenes.
This truth I know: our love surpassed
The fires others merely dreamed.

Never better than us paired,
In real life or in storied rhyme.
Let's celebrate the love we shared
Until that last hill we have climbed.

When, then, our last hill has been topped
Our love will climb to find new life.
The ocean surge cannot be stopped,
Nor our refrain: husband and wife.

Love Garden

My heart's an idyllic garden, for in it I shelter one rose.
Oh, what a fragrance surrounds it – the prettiest flower that grows.

I've noticed other men's gardens are dulled here & there by green weeds
Sown by a hypocrite lover; or lust or distrust spread bad seeds.

Inside the wall of some gardens, men cultivate more than one bloom.
Both have less fragrance, less splendor. Probably destined for doom.

Inside a few garden fences are rogues who just want to play.
Thoughtlessness damages blossoms as a thief who would steal it away.

I see in many a garden, hurting petals, bruised and torn,
Injured in unwelcome fondling. The gardener now sits and mourns.

There are some exquisite blossoms adorned by colors quite gay.
But the soul and heart of the flower, unnourished, has withered away.

Having seen numerous flowers, yet, sparkling with heaven's dew,
I think my rose the loveliest bloom that a love garden ever grew.

In the seed plot of my garden, my heart of arable sod,
I'll nourish this splendid flower given for my caring from God.

I'll work to keep safe my garden, keep love content, without doubt,
So, my flower of love will keep blooming 'til life itself flickers out.

So quickly we pass the tunnel of time.

THE DUET OF LIFE

There's a lot can be said for a one-man band
      and a guy crooning songs in solo.
It can make one's hair curl when a beautiful girl
      with a haunting voice makes it a duo.

They each please one's ears, even bring one to tears,
      and the melody thrills the senses.
But it transports the soul and makes the heart whole,
      when both voices join in consensus,
Beyond mortal strife to the spirit of life,
      to the source of all melody,
Where no one alone can attain the full tone
      that is reached in sweet harmony.

On this wedding day bright, as your lives now unite
      to more fully express your life's score,
May your home find God's best as you follow your
      quest, making music forevermore.

*(this poem is based upon a grandson's life; and
dedicated to him & his bride at their marriage)*

The Ultimate Gifts

I give to you the ultimate gifts, the best gifts one can give.
The gifts, bereft of which one dies, yet giving of them, lives.

The gift of VOWS I give you first, by pledging you my heart.
The promise that no force but death will ever see us part.

Then, LOVE I give of every kind, of body, heart and soul.
Affection, care and passion blend, and halves become a whole.

A LIFE I give to you, through love – a miracle of two.
A child because I gave you me, because you gave me you.

Then, HONOR next I choose to give, for you I will protect.
If called upon to spend my life, I would without regret.

The gift of TIME I give to you as lover and best friend.
As hours and days turn into years, my life with you I'll spend.

Good HEALTH I give by taking you for jogs along the sand,
Or riding bikes to take a swim, or walking hand in hand.

Then, finally, I give you FAITH. Assurance is a must.
As confident and satisfied we share a mutual trust.

These gifts I give – the Ultimate Gifts – to you alone, my love.
The blessings that create on Earth the bliss of Heaven above.

AWESTRUCK
Reminiscing

You flashed in my sight so young.
As lightning in a dark storm.
Dazzling, brilliant, contrasting,
Complex, alluring, untamed.

One could gaze, but not comprehend.
Enjoy, but not conquer.
I felt the current in the air and
Sensed the heat in the elements.
Flames of desire unquenched, controlled.
Frustration, impatience, fidelity.

Our eyes and smiles met – lingered.
Our words and thoughts engaged – linked.
Our lives complimented – connected.
Through many years – love gifted.

I've known the joy of being with an angel;
The satisfaction of bringing you satisfaction;
The fulfillment of fulfilling your heart;
Days and nights contented and savoring love;
The enjoyment of the light of your smile – and of you.

Some observed and wondered at the joy.
Some looked in silence. Some commented.
When the snare and fall were seen,
Some laughed, and some wept.
You endured as confidant and friend.
You kept unfading beauty,
A serene comradery and forgiving strength.
A personification of love – unconquered love.

In Beautiful Light

She wears her beauty subtly;
She shuns a glaring show.
She struts not proudly on parade,
Yet still her beauty glows.

Her mystery she does not flaunt.
Her glamour is restrained.
And yet allure is unconfined;
Her charm a bright refrain.

The beauty is real and flows from within.
Each time I'm near her I'm smitten again.

Her Maker chose to form her well;
Her face with light imbued.
The awesome song her presence sings
Gives honor where it's due.

Her countenance is prism-like
That gathers light received,
And casts a rainbow, obviously
By Deity conceived.

It's The Thought

Someone thought of you today.
It was a lovely thought.
If doubting implies otherwise,
Don't give that doubt a thought.

Someone prayed for you today
In heartfelt words of care.
Should someone come to mind today,
Lift that soul in prayer.

Someone was your friend today
Expressed in words and deeds.
Blessed joy: a thoughtful friend
Who for you intercedes.

Someone reached for you today
With caring, loving touch.
You thought you sensed a hand today?
It may have been this touch.

You inspired one today.
You could be unaware.
You're a joy in someone's life
In thoughts that someone shares.

If the content of this page makes you uncomfortable, then skip it. However, this practice can be extraordinarily satisfying and effective in establishing and reinforcing a loving connection. Plus, it is health-giving. So perhaps return to this concept later.

Regain the Passion

Advisement: this is not a very good poem,
but is about a very effective practice.

Has warm romance slipped down a notch or three?
Is long embrace not what it used to be?
Is fun flirtation absent for too long?
Perhaps kisses routine, or not as strong?

Then take this book together on the couch.
Turn it to romantic poems. Don't doubt!
She reads some poems aloud. You gently rub her neck.
(Along with the next move, you steal a little peck.)

This move entails an extra special feat:
You shift enough to take hold of her feet.
(It's best if you had told her this before.
There is no sexy way to do this chore.)

Reach gently for her feet, as said above.
Place them in your lap — an act of love.
If you have planned ahead with towel made warm,
Wrap her feet awhile for special charm.

In your hands now put some slippery lotion,
Then rub your hands together in fast motion.
(Baby oil might be better used.
I tried to rhyme the words, and got confused.)

Massage her feet conveying love through touch.
The tops, the sides, the soles, the toes — a bunch.
There is no need to have an on-site lesson,
Just make your thumbs be clear — a firm expression.

A well-rubbed foot conveys your deeper feelings.
Work slow and firm. Sore spots special kneading.

Ask frequently what's feeling best to her.
Massaging well will bring all sorts of cures.

Complete one foot, then move on to the other.
You should by now the chemistry discover.
Hear romantic sighs your touch elicits?
If not, repeat tomorrow till you get it.

Note: If your spouse doesn't feel comfortable having her feet massaged, then give a similar manipulation to the hands. If foot calluses make her self-conscious, make them smooth with a coarse file made for this purpose. On the hands, the fleshy web muscle between the thumb and pointer finger may be especially sensitive, so observe reactions to your touch and to pressure points. Rub the entire hand, tugging lingeringly on each finger as you did each toe. The hand and fingers have many nerve endings, and can yield serene pleasure from attentive massage.

Caution: A close college friend of ours was once traveling through our town, and spent a night with us on his journey. We couples had double dated in younger days, and he and I were connected to the same business. As we visited that evening, from habit, I put my wife's feet on my lap and begin massaging them without giving it any further consideration. No lotion or towel, just casually, naturally, routinely, rubbing her feet.

After breakfast the next morning, going on his way, he said to me: "Jim, it can be very frustrating to a guy sitting in a room without his wife to watch you massaging your wife's feet." So, I learned to be considerate, more cautious, with this pleasurable task.

Love That Does Not Die

As the near-stranger left her bedroom he said, "See you next time, Gomer." Both of them knew, if they would have allowed the moral thought to occur, that there shouldn't be a next time. There shouldn't have been this time, or a first time, or any time. But there was – and there'd be other times, unless one of them ran across someone else who enticed them more. Their relationship was wrong, immoral, selfish, but it temporarily quieted their lusts. Both knew there'd be other men, because nothing excited Gomer like the thrill of a new man in her bed. It wasn't the free meal, or a few day's trip, or even the gifts. She had entertained many men, because giving herself to a stranger pleased her as nothing else. Yes, it pleased her, but only for the moment; it didn't satisfy; didn't bring contentment. Her appetite always drove her to others. And still others.

Gomer was a very attractive young lady with a pleasing personality, fun to meet, easy to get along with, and alluring in the extreme. Her eyes, her figure, her smile – all so lusty, so powerful, so magnetic. She could have anyone she wanted. Gossip about Gomer and her bed was neither kind nor scarce. "If you want a quick tryst, see Gomer." Numerous men who heard the rumor experienced the reality. Gomer didn't shun many.

Of course, Gomer's "lovers" were not the moral stalwarts of society. All were loose-living creatures willing to take advantage of a beautiful woman, in order to enjoy illicit thrills. They were braggarts who boasted of their sexual exploits to other men. And that boasting resulted in yet more men seeking Gomer's favors. Some were one-nighters, some weekend affairs, some longer relationships.

In stark contrast, Hosea was a prophet. He was reasonably handsome, successful in business, and desirous of a wife. He was kind, a man with a natural way with people as well as with God. He was upright yet humble; both liked and respected in the community. He was not thought of as rich, but was well off through work and prudence.

Not only was Hosea quite comfortable financially, he was also a very eligible bachelor never before married. Every matchmaker in the region had tried to pair a young woman with Hosea. It was well known that parents of marriageable young virgins hoped it would be their daughter who was fortunate enough to wed Hosea.

Hosea was in love with Gomer. His attraction was physically easy to understand, for her alluring beauty was nearly irresistible. But spiritually, his adoration of this loose woman raised questions. Hosea, who had reserved his physical passion to be gifted to only one woman – his future wife – loved this woman though he detested her lifestyle. Is love blind? Can love conquer all? Should he wed Gomer? What would people think? What would God think? Hosea wasn't sure what to think, but he knew he loved Gomer, and loved her enough to make her his wife. A more unlikely pair couldn't be imagined.

God didn't leave His opinion a mystery. God got directly involved and instructed Hosea to proceed with his desire. God said, "Hosea, take Gomer to be your wife."

God's message to Hosea, however, didn't stop there. God went on to say. "Yes, take Gomer to be your wife as you desire. But know this, the children of your marriage will not be your own. Though you are faithful, attentive, and giving to Gomer, your children will each be fathered by other men in adulteress affairs. The wife whom you love will not be faithful to you." God knew Hosea would be good to Gomer, and good for her, but He knew Gomer would be unfaithful to Hosea.

Hoping that real love and the marriage vows would change Gomer, even though God had warned in advance that she would continue her salacious ways, Hosea married Gomer.

Hosea, the prophet, and Gomer, the girl with a reputation, had a delightful wedding. Hosea was excited to have as the recipient of his affection and generous gifts this beautiful girl who was so easy to live with, so easy to love. He forgave her wayward ways, and he anticipated years of mutual fulfillment and contentment. He was naïve.

Their life together began in wedded bliss. They experienced a bit of heaven on earth secure in love, committed in love, sheltered by love. Wanted, needed, enjoyed by each other exclusively, this couple experienced love's magic. For a short time. Though Hosea's love had provided everything she wanted and needed, including the satisfaction of her physical yearnings, Gomer's passions began again to desire other men. Gomer wanted to really live, to be really free, to have it all. Gomer returned to the degrading habits of her previous immoral ways.

Forsaking the genuine, faithful love of Hosea, Gomer repeatedly gave herself to the lusts of other men. She was merely a pleasure tool, but her strong desire combined with some kind of emptiness drove her to the arms of despicable men who were always willing to play with stolen goods. And then she found herself pregnant.

Turning back to Hosea, the expectant Gomer was welcomed home and cared for by this forgiving man. Hosea was chagrined. Yes, he knew of the talk around town. Yes, he knew Gomer was probably just using him as a meal ticket until this inconvenient child was weaned. But undying love compelled Hosea to be caring, tender, loving.

Three times Gomer left Hosea. Three times she got pregnant by another man. Three times she returned to Hosea for help. Three times he took her back. Three times she bore a child — two boys and a girl. Three times she left again after the child was weaned.

During these years, Hosea longed to hear Gomer say, "Hosea, I truly do love you. Love you as I've loved no other man. Love and respect you, and honor you for who you are, for what you believe, for how you live, for your kindness, and for loving me so deeply. For your sake, for the sake of our mutual love, I wish I had lived differently. If I had my life to live again, I would live differently, saving myself for you alone. I would gladly and willingly give myself to you as a pure and chaste virgin, if I could rewrite my script. I can't undo what's already happened. I can't change what's been done. But I love you exclusively, totally. You are my one and only. I am, and will be, completely yours."

Such words were never spoken. After weaning the third child, Gomer left again and began to live with a no-good scoundrel. Why she would trade all Hosea offered her for the pit into which she cast herself, no one could ever understand.

In time, hardships hit Gomer and her current man. They were short of money, wore tattered clothes, lived in squalor. And through it all, from a distance, Hosea kept himself aware of Gomer's plight. His love for her continued even through public humiliation and hurts. Seeing her poverty, Hosea arranged to meet with her "lover". Hosea gave this poor-excuse-for-a-man a substantial sum of money for food, clothing and basic necessities. He assured the man that if he misused the money, it would be the last. But if Hosea saw that Gomer was eating well, dressing well, and being properly cared for, then Hosea would provide funds each month for their living.

Gomer's "lover" took the money. Back with Gomer, he told her that his fortune had changed, that luck had smiled upon him, and that they could again enjoy the good times. Not letting her know the true source of the money, and letting her think it was money he had earned, this pitiful, wretched man, took Gomer to buy fine food, good clothes, and a flagon of well-aged wine. Month after month the money was given. Gomer was grateful for the apparent success of her partner. She never knew it was Hosea who was unselfishly, graciously providing for her needs.

Greed is cancerous, persistent, and ugly. Gomer's hideous man wanted more money. A lump sum of money. Who could comprehend why he took the course of action he did? But this cowardly creature determined to sell Gomer as a slave in order to raise a goodly sum of cash. Gomer was no more to him than a possession, an object to use or to discard, or even to sell. He took her to the slave auction to hawk on the open market.

Someone alerted Hosea that Gomer was to be sold as a slave. Perhaps people thought Hosea would want to gloat over the pitiful condition and misfortune of his unfaithful wife. Perhaps he'd want to spit on her as she was led away, a collar around her neck.

At the slave auction, Hosea stood at the back of the crowd until he saw Gomer was next to be auctioned. He elbowed his way through the crowd as workers stripped Gomer of all her clothing. A buyer had the right to see merchandise in full view. Any deformities or broken bones. Any apparent weakness. Any tell-tale scars from frequent beatings that would indicate an incorrigible slave.

Gomer now stood stark naked upon the block in view of the curious, the mockers, a few joking previous lovers, and the prospective buyers, one of whom would soon own her, and have absolute control of her life, her conditions, her actions, and even, should they so choose, her death. Seeing Hosea nearing the front of the crowd, bystanders may have thought he was there in the spirit of revenge. He had cause. The bidding began.

The final bid seemed to be fifteen pieces of silver. The auction was about to be stopped and the sale done, when Hosea raised the bid to 15 pieces of silver and enough barley to double the price. No other buyer was willing to pay so much. Hosea had purchased Gomer as his slave for the equivalent of 30 pieces of silver.

He put no slave collar around her neck. He curtained her with his cloak as she put on her clothes. He had brought her clothes because he knew that whatever the price, he would pay all it took to redeem his wife. Now, Hosea put his arm around Gomer, and led her threw the crowd away from the staring eyes, back home.

Who can know the amazement, questions, and fears in Gomer's mind as Hosea purchased her, dressed her, protected her from rude, hostile people, and took her home. What did she expect? She deserved nothing good. She deserved whatever punishment her owner decided upon. She knew she didn't want whatever it was she deserved.

At home, Hosea provided Gomer a bath and nourishment. As they ate together, Hosea said, "Gomer, I have loved you all these years. I have never stopped loving you. All I ever wanted in return was your exclusive love. Just all your love. Though you have told me you loved me, you were unable to give me your total love. You were unable to forsake the false thrill of fornicators and their gifts. While you were free to come and go and do as you wish, you were unable to be my faithful wife. Now, Gomer, you are no longer free to come and go and do as you wish. I have purchased you. You are my slave. Yet, it is I who am your servant, for I love you deeply. I love you still. I want you still. And what I want now is what I have always wanted – your exclusive love. All your love. As my slave, I give you total freedom in my house. As the one I love, I will one day give you everything I have. All I require is your faithful love. You will find in me that Love itself is your master; and genuine love, when submitted to, is what you are really seeking; and this undying love will bring you contentment and will set you free."

Comment:
The Hebrew word Hosea means "salvation" or "the Lord saves" and is similar to the names Joshua and Jesus.

The love Hosea showed Gomer pictures God's love for his people. Gomer's unfaithfulness pictures the waywardness of many of God's people in straying from his love and care. This straying is usually expressed in three ways: a lower concept of God than his holiness and power demand; mixing false religion with the True; and willful disobedience in either thought or action. Sin is never as good as it seems it will be while it entices us, and its fleeting thrill comes with a price. Sin pays off in death. Death in one or more of the following: death of purity, death of freedom, death of innocence, death of love, death of hope, death of trust, death of one's soul forever. Only God can resolve the sin issue. And He has. He has paid the price of sin, and welcomes us back to Him. Do you, do I, lovingly repent of sin, and accept and receive his salvation? Jesus has paid our sin penalty, our price. It is finished. Jesus said: "One who comes to me, I will not reject."

SECTION FOUR

4 RRR ON RELIGION

A PARDON MUST BE RECEIVED

In 1830, George Wilson was condemned to death for a capital crime. He was pardoned by President Andrew Jackson as follows:

"I, Andrew Jackson, President of the United States of America… have pardoned, and do hereby pardon the said George Wilson the crime for which he has been sentenced to death… In testimony where of I have hereunto set my hand and caused the seal of the United States to be affixed to these presents. Given at the city of Washington this 14th day of June, A.D. 1830…"

However, Wilson, of record as follows, declined to accept the pardon, "… This 21st day of October, 1830, the defendant, George Wilson, being in person before the court, was asked by the court… whether he wished in any manner to avail himself of the pardon referred to: and the said defendant answered in person, that he had nothing to say, and that he did not wish in any manner to avail himself… of the pardon."

To determine whether Wilson should be set free or executed, his case was heard by the highest court in the land. In the case The United States v. George Wilson, the US Supreme Court ruled, "that a pardon is a deed, to the validity of which delivery is essential; and delivery not complete without acceptance. It may then be rejected by the person to whom it is tendered; and if it be rejected, we have discovered no power in a court to force it on him… It may be supposed that no being condemned to death would reject a pardon, but the rule must be the same…"

Wilson was executed. The sentence of death was carried out even though the defendant had been pardoned and freedom made available.

****

Jesus has paid for our crimes, and provided each of us a pardon for our sins. He offers the pardon to us. In order for that pardon to be valid and effective for each of us individually, we must personally accept it. If we do not accept it, our individual penalty will be carried out just as if the price had not already been paid by Another, and just as if the pardon had never been offered. Jesus says: "I am the way, the truth, and the life. I am standing at the door knocking." Let each one of us respond affirmatively to receive his offer of pardon.

Jesus said: God the Father sent his Son into the world in order that those who believe in him would be saved to everlasting life. Jesus did not come into the world to condemn the world, but to save us. One who rejects Jesus is already condemned, but Jesus came to rescue and to pardon those who believe him and receive him as their Savior and their Lord. Forgiveness of sins and the gift of eternal life await those who will confess their sins and come to Jesus to receive his gift of life everlasting.

OUT OF DEFEAT

Let Him take your disappointments, and turn them into faith.
Let Him take your biggest nightmare, and all the fear erase.
Let Him take defeat and failures, and cover them with grace.
Stop staring at the problems – look up into God's face.

I Saw Jesus

I see Him in the Bible. I see Jesus, God the Son.
As a Baby in a manger when the angel songs were sung.
As the Teacher of the ages who taught the seeking throngs.
As the Healer of the hurting who filled hopeless hearts with songs.
As the crucified Redeemer when he hung there for our sin.
As the dead and buried Jesus when it seemed that death would win.

I see the resurrected Jesus — the eternal God the Son.
As the glorified Redeemer who had the victory won.
As the infinite Creator, the Beginning and the End.
As the Judge of all the ages before whom none unbowed can stand.

Just the terror of His Being caused all hearts and breath to stop.
Just the brilliance of his visage caused every knee to drop.
His piercing eyes, beyond description, brought other eyes to tears.
The power of his presence wrought gripping, crippling fear.
His voice, above the oceans. His face as many suns.
His essence fills the cosmos. His power — inexplicable by tongues.

His sheep were on his right hand, the goats were at his left.
Eternal life, eternal death: His children blessed, the lost bereft.
All fell as dead before him. Silent worship filled the place.
Every heart was praying "mercy". The only hope was grace.
To his own, the Judge is Savior – the One who gave his life
To buy his children's pardon – paid their eternal price.

His nail-scarred hand he lifted. His once-pierced heart he bared.
He said: "Arise, my children. All I have I'll share.
My glory is your glory. Look at each other now!
My power is your power. You're my brothers and sisters now.
My life is now your life. My wisdom is your own.
My family is your family. I love you. Welcome home."

I saw Jesus, and I worshipped. Saw the One on earth reviled.
Saw his majesty and power, and thank God I'm his child.

OVERWHELMED WITH GRATITUDE

I'll be overwhelmed with gratitude to wake up in that place.
Overwhelmed with gratitude just to see His face.
It will demonstrate His mercy, forgiveness, love and grace.
And I'll be overwhelmed with gratitude to wake up in that place.

When I contemplate the magnitude of God's redeeming grace,
It brings a humble attitude, that I was given space.
There is no worthy platitude, but I will sing His praise,
And I'll be overwhelmed with gratitude just to reach that place.

Since salvation's power was able in my case
To make me fit for Heaven and all my sins erase,
God will redeem, save, anyone in the human race:
We'll be overwhelmed with gratitude when we reach that place.

DANCING IN HEAVEN

On the streets of gold forever
    I will dance in joyful song.
As King David danced triumphant
    singing out the victor's Psalm.
Dance to His glory; dance to His honor;
    Worshipping Father, Spirit, Son.
Dance to mercy, love and power that
    brought this pardoned sinner home.

(Can be sung to the tune Ode To Joy)

COMMITTED

Have you ever wondered how best to serve the Lord?
How best to live the Christian life, a doer of the word?
How best to share with others your substance and your faith?
How best to do God's business, until you see his face?

He said, "Just be committed. That's all I require today.
Ready to follow the Word, to witness and pray.
Just be committed. Willing to trust and obey.
Just be committed each step, each decision, each day."

You want to share God's message, but neither sing or preach?
To make a mark on others' lives, but neither write nor teach?
Do you want to make a difference, but haven't much to give?
Do you want to be a blessing, to please God as you live?

He said, "Just be committed. That's all I require today.
Ready to follow the Word, to witness and pray.
Just be committed. Willing to trust and obey.
Just be committed each step, each decision, each day."

Now, I'm not saying it's easy, I'm saying it's right -- worthwhile.
By faith it will be easier during the second mile, so smile....

Each of us can put our own life story in this verse.
Some have been a little better – some a little worse.
When we come to God with questions, no matter why we came,
Specifics will be different; the basic answer is the same.

He'll say, "Just be committed. That's all I require today.
Ready to follow the Word, to witness, to pray.
Just be committed. Willing to trust and obey.
Just be committed each step, each decision, each day."

THANK YOU, JESUS

Five thousand men were hungry, their wives and children, too.
Jesus looked at Andrew, and asked him what he'd do.
He said, "A little boy is with us, who has a lunch he'll share,
But what is that among so many hungry list'ners here?"

The boy gave all to Jesus – gave the lunch made just for him.
He watched as Jesus blessed it – saw a miracle begin.
That lunch soon fed the thousands, with basketsful to spare.
From the children, moms and daddies, happy cheering filled the air.

"Praise to Jesus! Thank You, Jesus! You satisfied our need.
Praise to Jesus! Thank You, Jesus! You are a friend indeed."

A hundred eyes were staring up at Jesus on the cross.
Those who hoped He was KING JESUS, felt a cold and bitter loss.
A hard Centurion had commanded, "Now drive the nails in place."
His soldiers cursed, had raised the cross, and spit in Jesus' face.

The crucified Creator paid for sin mid taunts and jeers.
But earthquakes, storms and darkness turned the mocking into fears.
That tough Centurion watched in awe this Man whom he had flogged,
And said, "In truth, I crucified the sovereign Son of God." *

"Praise to Jesus! Thank You, Jesus, for saying You forgive.
Praise to Jesus! Thank You, Jesus! You died so I may live."

It is now the judgment morning at the final Great White Throne.
Jesus' majesty and power pierce each creature to the bone.
They recognize *Creator*, and their hearts are turned to stone.
All fall in fear before Him, and confess him Lord, alone.

Elsewhere, the saved, in wonder, raise a grateful whispered prayer.
For Jesus took their judgment, and a home for them prepared.
That courtroom is now emptied. Savior, Judge, smiles to the wise.
Then His children join in chorus – a mighty anthem fills the skies.

"Praise to Jesus! Thank You, Jesus! Praise the Savior, God the Son!
Praise You, Jesus! Thank You, Jesus! By Your cross we've overcome.
Praise to Jesus! Thank You, Jesus! Worship Father, Spirit, Son.

Praise You, Jesus! Thank You, Jesus! By your grace the victory's won.
Thank You, Jesus! Merciful Savior. Thank You, Jesus!"

*

Note: In the middle of this above poem, I portray as converted the Centurion in charge of the crucifixions. Some people claim the centurion only said: "This was a son of the gods." However, Jesus was a prisoner in the care and custody of this officer of Rome. He was with Jesus that entire day. My portrayal of him takes into account all he saw and heard. The alternative portrayal disregards the events of the day and what was said by Pilate to Jesus ("are you a king"?) and Jesus' reply ("My kingdom is not of this world"). There was no discussion of, or allusion to, Greek or Roman gods. The Roman soldiers while mocking Jesus did not mock him as a mythical deity in the pantheon of gods; they were mocking Jesus as King of the Jews, knowing the Jew's God was the Creator. On the scene of the crucifixion, the soldiers, for hours, heard the Rulers of the Jews taunt Jesus: "If you are the Son of God" – that is, of the God of the Jews. "If you are the Savior". Even one of the crucified criminals, who heard the same words that the centurion heard, turned to Jesus in faith, believing he was in fact the King of the Jews, the Son of God, and the Savior. The centurion heard Jesus say to the dying, penitent man: "Today, you will be in Paradise with me". No one thought Jesus, or the criminal, was referring to some mythical crossing of the river Styx on the way to Elysium. The centurion heard Jesus authoritatively announce from the cross: "It is finished." Then Jesus went on to intentionally, purposefully dismiss his own life: "Father, into your hands I commit my spirit" and simultaneous give up his life. Witnessing all this, the centurion believed in Jesus, the Savior, the Son of God, who controlled life and death. It could be, we don't know, that one of the centurions mentioned in the Book of Acts either was this centurion, or was an acquaintance of this centurion who crucified Jesus. In any case, the centurion on Mt Calvary would not have believed Jesus was in the family of Roman mythological gods.

Another Look at the Via Delarosa

It's Good Friday. The day of crucifixion. Have you ever considered at length what may have taken place between Pilate's courthouse steps and the arrival at the place of the skull? At the place of Jesus' crucifixion?

We know that at Pilate's Pavement the crowd was agitated, irritated, and loud. They occasionally screamed: "Crucify him! Crucify him. Release Barabbas — crucify Jesus." Hate was literally in the air in the form of these shouted sound waves.

At Mount Calvary we know that the taunting, mocking, reviling continued. Do you think it was quiet along Via Dolorosa? Not a chance! We know Jesus had been publicly scourged so severely, that, with the loss of blood, he was so weakened that he fell under the cross along the way. We know that some women cried out in pity for Jesus. We know soldiers forced someone else, Simon of Cyrene, to carry his cross. I think that the horrific trudge, intended by Rome to create shame, may have been something like the below in the mind of the one condemned criminal who would be crucified with Jesus, who would mock Jesus, and then change his mind and be born again on that cross.

If the below narrative would bother you or offends you, please don't read it. I believe it is put softer than it probably actually went down.

Slogging, even stumbling, trying to hold on to a brave front, this condemned rebel's hateful thoughts were raging as Roman soldiers humiliated him on the road to Golgotha: "This bloodied, stinking cross is the heaviest thing I've ever carried. I wonder who else has died on it. So much rotten blood soaked in these beams. Why, in the name of Caesar, do they have to put a chain around my ankles? With soldiers everywhere, I could run away? Ohhh! Ohhh! And why do they have to slash me like that? I'm keeping up with the others. These stinking soldiers. That stinking Roman laughing at me: If I got him in the dark, just him and me, I'd break his neck in two seconds. But I'm forced to listen to his laugh. This stinking cross is already killing me!

"Barabbas was our fearless leader, but how he got off free — it's crazy stupid. He's our great leader, he goes free, and I'm gonna hang on this stinking, cursed cross for how many days? And this Jesus. Even Pilot said he was innocent. He lets Barabbas go and crucifies Jesus anyway. Stinking Roman authorities! I'm being treated worse because of the hate for Jesus. I've never seen anybody whipped that bad before being crucified. I hate Rome! Curse them all.

"Listen to these religious leaders walking along side, saying,

'Blasphemer, Blasphemer'. Saying: 'So you are the son of God?!' And that centurion said, laughing: 'He's the king over you Jews!'

"Ohhh. Why did he slash me again? Curse him. He can't hear my thoughts. I despise them. When these stinking soldiers drive spikes through my hands and feet, I am not gonna scream! I'm not gonna give them that satisfaction. I will not yell out!

"Why are they treating Jesus worse than us? I guess what they would have done to Barabbas in revenge they're taking out on Jesus. Oh, no! He fell down. Quit slashing him — ohh, quit slashing me, you stinking Romans! They're making that big Ethiopian take his cross. A lot of women crying.

"That Sanhedrin Guy just yelled: 'If God is your father, why doesn't he save you?' That priest roared 'He saved others but can't save himself'. I won't scream out when they nail me. I won't give thug soldiers that pleasure.

"If Jesus is the savior, why doesn't he save himself and us?! If he's the miracle-working Son of God, why doesn't he rescue us now? If he is King David's son, where is his army? Why doesn't he show Rome now, if he is the king? Why!"

And slowly they trudged to the place of execution, the place of the skull, Mount Calvary. There, the derision continued. There, this criminal believed that the words being said in mockery were in fact true. He believed in the innocence of Jesus, and that he was going to be king in an eternal kingdom. The criminal said to Jesus: "Remember me in your kingdom". In reply, Jesus said: "Today you'll be with me in paradise."

Note: I've been to the place of the skull. A clear skull impression is still in the stone cliff very near the garden tomb. This very old photo is displayed there. Mt. Calvary is from Latin for cranium.

Today You'll be in Paradise

A MOCKING REBEL on a cross to Jesus turned that day.
He turned, and said, "I'm guilty. I deserve this debt to pay.
I'm crucified upon this cross for all the crimes I've done.
But you are fully innocent. I know you are God's Son.

Would you remember me, in your kingdom, on your throne?
Would you remember me, when you come into your own?
Remember me…. Remember me."

And Jesus said:
"Today, you'll be in paradise. In my kingdom, at my throne.
Today, while soldiers played with dice, a lost son has come home.
Your crimes are all forgiven. And your pardon has been read.
So, you'll be with me in heaven, no matter what the mockers said.

"You can't be held by Roman spikes. No more fears, and no more dread.
For you'll be with me in paradise before the guards confirm you're dead."

AND NOW THIS SINNER in this place to Jesus turns today.
Turns and says, "I'm guilty, with a debt I cannot pay.
I am trusting only in the Savior's love for me
And that he paid the total price there on Calvary.

He will remember me, in his kingdom, on his throne.
He will remember me, and prepare for me a home.
Remember me…. Remember me."

And Jesus said:
By faith you'll be in Paradise, in my Kingdom, at my throne.
Because I paid the total price: my child you have a home.
Your sins are all forgiven. And your pardon has been read.
So, you'll be with me in heaven, no matter what the doubters said.

You can't be held by cancelled vice. No more fears, and no more dread.
One day you'll be with me in paradise: keep trusting what my promise said.

Bodily exercise profits a little: but
godliness is profitable unto all things,
having promise of the life that now is,
and of life which is to come.
1 Timothy 4:8

TROUBLE WITH TRUTH?

*IF TRUTH GETS IN YOUR WAY,
YOU'RE GOING THE WRONG DIRECTION.*

*IF TRUTH CAUSES YOU TO STUMBLE,
YOU'RE IN THE DARK.*

*IF TRUTH EMBARRASSES YOU,
YOU'RE CAUGHT NAKED.*

*IF TRUTH BURIES YOU,
YOU'RE DEAD WRONG.*

A PRIVILEGED PLACE

Was he in a privileged place? How could the criminal, on a cross beside Jesus, exercise saving faith and believe?

Let's consider one of the miracles that took place on Good Friday. And indeed, it was a good day for a criminal crucified on one of those three crosses on Mount Calvary – the place of the skull. (The word Calvary is from Latin, meaning cranium.)

There is no mention in the Bible that the two criminals crucified with Jesus had previously seen or heard Jesus during his three-year ministry. They were likely members of the rebel gang led by Barabbas. Because of the huge crowds that followed Jesus to participate in his miracles, the Roman Crowd Control Detail may also have often been in attendance. Rebels against Rome would not wish to be observed by them. Zealous rebels would stay out of sight. Therefore, the implication is that this was the first time those criminals personally encountered Jesus. With that in mind, how could one of the men executed with Jesus be so quickly, dramatically and publicly changed, come to saving faith, and express his belief in Jesus as King and Living Savior?

It is my thinking that, as he hung on a cross next to Jesus, this converted criminal heard in that place all that was necessary for him to make an informed decision about who this Jesus truly was. Though this admitted criminal at first mocked and jeered at Jesus – "Save yourself, and us" – he became convinced that Jesus was in truth the Messiah.

What enabled this dying criminal to repent and confess and convert on the cross? Consider what this distressed man heard for hours that intense day. He could read the sign on Jesus' cross: "This is Jesus of Nazareth, King of the Jews." He listened to "King" jeers screamed at Jesus.

This man was right there, and heard Jesus say of his executioners: "Father, forgive them; they don't know what they do." (Luke 23:34) He heard Jewish rulers scoffing: "He saved others; let him save himself if he is the Christ (Messiah; anointed one) of God, his Chosen One." (23:35) He heard soldiers mock Jesus and laugh: "YOU! King of the Jews! Save yourself!" (23:37) He heard the mob and passers-by deride Jesus: "Look! You said you would destroy the temple and rebuild it in three days. Save yourself. Come down from the cross."

He heard Chief Priests and Scribes mock Jesus: "He saved others; but can't save himself. Let the Christ, Israel's King, free himself now from the cross. When we see, we'll believe." (Mark 15:32) At this point, he and the other criminal both joined in to revile Jesus: "Save yourself and us!" Inadvertently, in ridicule, they reiterated that Jesus was the Savior.

He heard the Chief Priests and Elders say: "He trusts in God; let God rescue him now, if God wants him. He said: 'I am the Son of God'." (Mathew 27:42-43) This derision and repulsive mocking continued at least three hours, repeated over and over. "You said you are the Christ. You said you are the Son of God. You claim to be the King of Israel. You trusted God and called God your Father. You saved others: save yourself." Repetitively, loudly! Then, the other crucified criminal again, through a parched throat, spat a challenge at Jesus: "Are you the Christ?! Save yourself, and save us!! Now! Now!" (Luke 23:39)

By then, the repentant criminal had heard enough, and realized that all this spewed derision and hate about who Jesus was, and what Jesus had said, was in fact the message which Jesus had preached as the Christ. The truth Jesus had taught in love was being hurled back at him in mockery and hatred, but the message itself was true. And that truth penetrated this criminal.

With conviction, this repentant criminal rebuked the still-taunting criminal, saying to him: "Do you not fear God at all, seeing that you are being executed in the same manner?! We are receiving justice for our crimes; but this man, Jesus, has done no wrong!" Then, the repentant criminal looked to Jesus and said: "Jesus, remember me when you enter your Kingdom." (40-42)

Clearly, the repentant criminal confessed himself a sinner, recognized Jesus as King and Savior, and realized Jesus would live again to remember him and rescue him from death. As he called out above the raucous noise, this guilty, naked, dying rebel expressed saving faith in Jesus Christ the Savior. He believed Jesus and trusted Jesus. He put faith, the only thing he had, in Jesus. And he was immediately reborn into the family of King Jesus. Jesus replied to him: "I tell you, this very day you will be with me in Paradise!"

This specific criminal asked Jesus to save him, not from death on the cross, but from eternal death in the realm of the damned. Jesus told this man that his request would be granted. That promise brought peace to this man dying in pain and humiliation. As hideous and tragic as was the life and death of this criminal, yet, at this crucifixion scene, he was in a most advantageous place to hear and understand the gospel of Jesus Christ expressed by envious, hateful, foolish people who rejected Jesus. As he is in Glory now, this guilty but pardoned criminal is exceedingly glad that he met Jesus that day, and trusted Jesus as Son of God and Savior who paid the penalty for his sins.

The Centurion who was in charge of the execution, was probably also converted. Having seen and heard the events of the day, he believed when he observed Jesus dismiss his earthly life by saying: "Father, into your hands I entrust my spirit." This soldier had watched many men die. None like Jesus. The centurion said: "This was a righteous man; surely he was the Son of God." (See also previous note following "Thank You, Jesus".)

Much later, when people satirically imitated Paul's preaching, the Apostle Paul, who was another converted enemy of Jesus, explained it this way: "What is going on here? In various ways, whether in satire or sincerity, Jesus Christ is being revealed. I rejoice in it." (Philippians 1:15-19 my paraphrase.) Paul was pleased the gospel message was being told even in mockery. That occurred at the cross: the message Jesus preached was retold in ridicule. In addition to the criminal who was executed and the centurion in charge, surely others who observed Jesus on the cross and heard the mocking, also believed that day. It was a Good Friday.

Never has another man lived as Jesus lived; or died as Jesus died as a substitutionary sacrifice for others; or literally rose to life from the tomb never to die again; or ascended back into heaven as did Jesus. Let us follow the example of the repentant criminal, and confess our sins, believe and receive Jesus as our own personal Savior and Lord, and trust Jesus for everlasting life. Jesus, I believe.

The Vast View

Sitting by the ocean gazing out across the sea
It's a quiet, poignant moment that scares and comforts me
Out beyond horizons, a distance deemed so vast.
Am I contemplating future, or studying the past?

I said the view is vast, yet, it truly is so small!
So tiny is the view that it's almost none at all.
Compared to the Pacific, the distance that I see:
A paltry speck of ocean! How that humbles me!

One of seven billion people on this planet we call Earth.
My foot: a nanoscopic dot of the global total girth.
The "greatest" ones among us based on assets or invention:
So minuscule a factor they're barely worth a mention.

When I speak of "mention," a custom validates my thought.
There are signs on roads and bridges naming folks who nobly wrought
Major deeds among us: brave, heroic, selfless acts.
Statesman. Writers. Industry. Philosophers and quacks.
Folks pay a thousand dollars to have a name etched on a brick
So that, by chance, it might be seen as someone steps on it.
Maybe pay ten thousand to inscribe a plaque at church.
(It's counter to religion but that incentive seems to work.)
You get into big money for names on Alma Maters.
Pay a hundred million naming walls for sons or daughters.

We read a dedication sign: "Lincoln," "Captain Smith".
In truth, it's just grouped letters, a sound, conceptual mist.
Yes, we know that sound, those letters – part of history,
Yet, we do not KNOW that person – they're still a mystery.
We hold some fading honor, some concept of respect;
But, if not friend or family, sans recognized content.

How soon a drop of water is absorbed into the sea.
How soon the generations are a blurry memory.
Family photos kept within their special, musty book
Are unfamiliar faces — if not labeled, are mistook.

So, in this voyage of life, we chase the final port
Wishing to contribute some good value of import.
We'd best consult our Maker about what truly lasts,
So our "drop" will not just dissipate within the oceans vast.

Daily Celebrate His Resurrection

Every Easter we celebrate his Resurrection:
Christ arose to life from out of death.
The death of Jesus Christ paid for our redemption.
Resurrection proves eternal life and breath.

Every Sunday we celebrate his Resurrection:
He arose the First Day of the week.
We celebrate new life and his Ascension,
Rejoicing in his strength, for we are weak.

Every morning we celebrate his Resurrection:
We rise from slumber back to conscious life.
Every beating heart is attestation
Of God's grace to us each day in peace or strife.

Every death we celebrate his Resurrection:
Believers pass from death into Christ's Home.
This everlasting joy and consolation
Is from the resurrected Christ alone!

Prayer in Stillness
Psalm 46:10

Prayer is not always in words.
Sometimes it's a silence of awe and wonder and awareness in the presence of God. Being overcome with humility and gratitude.
Sometimes it's being quiet, contemplating God's universal greatness, absolute holiness, total omniscience, realizing one does not know what to prayer or how to pray, therefore is quiet, intentionally relying upon the un-duplicable prayer of the Spirit of God.

SAY IT — PRAY IT — LIVE IT

How can I indicate **trust**? How can I emulate **love**?
How exemplify **grace** and **mercy** God grants from above?

TRUST
Say it! In words that are clear: "Jesus, I fully trust you."
Pray it. As the Lord's prayer: "Thy will be done" through & through.
Live it by casting your cares on God: don't retrieve or renew.

LOVE
Say it! Again and again, expressing the beat of your heart.
Pray it aloud together. More fervently yet when apart.
Live it by deeds small and clever: Love is commitment and art!

GRACE
Say it! With meaning that's strong: "I forgive you". Yes, for that!
Pray it: "Forgive me my sin as I forgiveness grant".
Live it: Forgive oft again, never to take it back.

LIVE IT
Words can be cheap, or prayers weak. A life manifests the real.
Some tricky tongues deceive, and true motivations conceal.
Say it — Pray it — Live it. The **doing** the truth reveals.

We all need to trust more fully. More truly express God-like love.
Forgive as we've been forgiven in words and deeds hand-in-glove.

Overlooking Sea of Galilee

217

HEAVEN'S ABOVE

There's a heaven ahead where God it is said
Provides joy beyond earthly fulfilling.
There we'll join the blest throng
      where the theme of our song
Describes glory and love and forgiving.

God himself paid the cost to ransom the lost
And redeem us from sin's terrible wages.
He himself took our strife to give us his life
For he means us to shine through the ages.

Is it hard to believe? Or hard just to leave
Earthly thrills, though their pleasures deceive you?
Only God is the way beyond death and decay!
Trust Jesus to save and receive you.

Yes, trust God the Son, the one who has come
To seek and to save the receivers.
Respond to his love. He'll forgive from above.
Hear, now, as he calls the believers.

A receiver has heard, and takes God at his word,
Accepting the pardon he proffers.
Now, as child of the King, there's a reason to sing,
For heaven's the home that he offers.

There's a heaven ahead where God it is said
Provides joy beyond earthly fulfilling.
There we'll join the blest throng
      where the praise of our song
Describes grace and love and forgiving.

Changed to God's Life

We must be changed so we can live before Him.
Must be reborn – His glory somehow share.
Those who are His, who dwell with Him forever,
Will all be changed. His image we will bear.

God is Light – light far beyond our glory.
Ten million stars would bow their flames in shame.
For God is light – The Absolutely Holy.
No lumen less could stand before His Name.

God is Fire – an all-consuming fury.
Ten million suns would bow their flames in shame.
For God is Fire – The Absolutely Holy.
No lesser glow could stand before His Name.

God is Truth – all knowledge from Him solely.
All other minds will bow their heads in shame.
For God is Truth – The Absolutely Holy.
No rebel thought can stand before His Name.

God is life – all life flows from Him only.
There is no life outside his sovereign reign.
For God IS life – the Absolutely Holy.
The power of death can't stand before his name.

We must be changed so we can live before Him.
Must be changed – His glory somehow share.
Those who are His, who dwell with Him forever,
Will all be changed. His image we will bear.

Through Jesus Christ, eternal life is offered.
Through Jesus Christ, peace with God is gained.
Through trusting Him, there is His pardon proffered.
He died and rose that we might His name claim.

Now, day-to-day, He dwells within his children.
We can't know how His Spirit lives within.
We humbly bow, surrender to his leading.
And daily choose to follow after him.

This Side of the Bridge

On this side of the bridge there is a sunset. Every day we know the sun will go down and have the expectation, although it is not an assurance, that we will see the sunrise in the morning. Sunset, sunrise: the cycle of life this side of the bridge.

Soon, we will reach the other side of the bridge. On that other side, there is no sunset — perhaps there is no sun to set. We are told there's no need of the sun, SUN, because God the Son, SON, will BE the light on the other side of the bridge. When God makes all things new, it's an eternal day — no night there. No day-night cycles. No getting tired, no need to rest. I can't imagine how that functions, but that's exactly what we are told: no one can imagine, or even comprehend, what's on the other side of the bridge.

When Paul the apostle was given a preview of heaven, he said there are no words which could describe it, and that it is "unlawful" to try to describe it. Perhaps, by the term unlawful, he meant that if one did try to describe it, they couldn't help but be misrepresenting the facts, ie: lying, which is against God's law.

In any case, God allowed Satan to foist upon Paul some kind of humiliating affliction. God's purpose was to prevent Paul from being proud. What Satan's purpose was, we can speculate, was to cause Paul to lose his faith. Satan did not succeed. God gave Paul grace to sustain him in the affliction. Paul never did try to elucidate his heavenly vision of the other side of the bridge.

At the end of life,
success is measured more by the level of one's contentment
than by the luxury of one's corporeal containment.

Come see a Cross

Come see a cross upon a hill.
See Roman soldiers casting lots.
See the garments that they got.
Now, look more closely, if you will.

Hanging on the center Cross,
Where that sign says The Jew's King,
Feel the hatred menacing.
Why the laughter? Why the scoffs?!

Do you see those women there?
Gasping sobs, so ripped apart
As if a sword had pierced their hearts.
Gripped by love and by despair.

What's this I see occurring here?
There's something hanging in the air!
It's something evil. Something grand!
Is this some orchestrated plan?

Could callous evil work for good?
Could heinous death be somehow life?
Much as the bread sliced by a knife
Provides our needed daily food?

As the juice stomped from the grapes.
As water from the beaten rock.
Could this be the son of God
Dying for we sinners' sakes?

Yes! Here God worked amazing grace.
Here mercy, love and justice met.
Eternal life was here foreset.
The way was made to see God's face.

Now, look inside that empty tomb.
The very place his body laid.
The empty grave clothes still in place.
Now, we sing a different tune.

Jesus rose just as he said.
The tomb became a kind of womb.
Death no longer need be doom.
By faith, there's hope and life ahead.
We trust, and follow where he led.

THERE IS ONE GOD

There is one God, and he is righteous.
There is one God, and he is justice.
We praise your name that you have paid our ransom.
Oh, just and pardoning God, we come to you as children.

There is one God, and he is holy.
There is one God, and he is mercy.
We praise your name that we have been forgiven.
Oh, holy, mighty God, we come to you as children.

There is one God, he is all-knowing.
There is one God, and he is with us.
We praise your name, your power, and your wisdom.
Oh, wise and present God, we come to you as children.

There is one God, and he is loving.
There is one God, and we believe him.
We praise your name, we have a home in heaven.
Oh, loving, Father God, we come to you as children.

(music for this song is in Music section)

COME HOME

Find a church identity
In a close community
Assembled by Divinity,
Possessed of strong affinity
For following God's Word.

An atmosphere that glows serene
In reverent awe of Christ, the King.
Where hymns impel the saints to sing.
From sincere hearts their praises bring
In worship deeply stirred.

Where, preached with passioned clarity,
With faithful regularity,
With love and reasoned gravity,
The Bible holds priority
To each one's conduct gird.

No fear to teach what Jesus taught,
The preacher, clearly, as he ought,
The free salvation Jesus bought
Proclaims, to those The Shepherd sought.
Not parroting the world.

With just the right temerity,
Compassion and severity,
Frankness and humility,
The Pastor labors fervently
To ever please the Lord.

The message of the Bible still
Is held aloft for all who will
See God's light and love revealed,
Receive by faith the truth instilled:
Eternal Life secured.

Where people gather genteelly
To worship unabashedly.
Their friendships show sincerity,

No matter their diversity:
The love of God conferred.

The welcome mat is not concealed.
The fellowship indeed is real.
Forgiveness is a warm appeal.
The family seeks to bear God's seal
To a fallen world.

Yes, find a church identity
In a close community
With welcome universally
In down-home cordiality;
And with them seek the Lord.

Note: When I lived at Grand Lake for a couple years, this poem was originally written to highlight and recommend the people and ministry of Trinity Baptist Church in Grove Oklahoma. I continue to love and appreciate that Pastor and those people. For this book, I altered slightly the original poem in order to describe the kind of church I would recommend to believers.

When I was a visitor to Trinity, I went to the Sunday School teaching session under the practical, applied teaching of Bob Plunk; then to Sunday Church Services both morning and evening, and to Wednesday evening service all under Pastor Robert Carter. When you hear his life story, there is no doubt of his genuine dedication. I was serious about finding a quality church.

The third time I attended Trinity, a man named Charles (who now walks the streets of heaven) stopped me as I was departing the morning service. We exchanged names, and Charles said: "Jim, a few of us regularly go to lunch together after church. I'm inviting you to join us today." I replied: "Thank you. That's really kind of you. But I'm a bit shy and somewhat of a loner. I probably will take a pass." Charles said: "You'll fit right in, and I'm going to get your meal. So, come on." I again replied: "Wow. That's so nice, but I don't know." He said firmly: "Jim, it's called *fellowship!*" I was impressed, actually surprised, with his polite yet almost gruff insistence, and said: "OK. I'll follow you to the restaurant." He said: "Today, it's the one right across the street, so we're walking. Just follow me." I'm so glad I did.

That assertive, authoritative invitation changed my life at Grand Lake for the couple years I lived in that area. To this day, I attend services there from time to time, still have dear friends there, and eagerly recommend this church to anyone in that vicinity. "It's fellowship." And, it's clear preaching, teaching, from the Bible. They still sing many of the gospel hymns. If I'm there when you visit, come introduce yourself. I look like the guy pictured on the back of this book. I'll get your lunch.

TO FIND HAPPINESS

Happiness may be counterintuitive.
It is seldom secured by seeking it.

To be happy, make someone else happy.
Personal happiness occurs on the pathway of
contributing to the happiness of others.
If one tries to make themselves happy,
it will prove to be elusive and fleeting.
When one adds to the happiness of someone else,
happiness subtly takes root within, and
blossoms inside and outside as a natural byproduct.
You catch joy you sought for the wellbeing of others.

WHY?!

It's the question of the ages
Asked by poets and by sages
Of a story so outrageous:
TELL ME WHY?

Why would one who had no need,
No thought of gain, no hint of greed,
Leave his throne for Adam's seed?
TELL ME WHY?

Why God the Son should leave his throne?
Would he forsake his heavenly home?
Why would God take flesh and bone?
BECOME A MAN?

Why would God descend to earth,
And then submit to humble birth?
Bear execution, scorn and mirth
AS A MAN?

Then comes the answer loud and clear,
He brought hope and conquered fear.
To be our Light shined from above.
To be our Savior sent by love.
To be the Way we can be sure of.
THIS IS WHY!

To be the Father we can see.
To be the Truth that we believe.
To be the Life that we receive.
THIS IS WHY.

Redeemer paid the full decree.
The Savior came to pardon we.
The Judge himself has set us free.
THIS IS WHY.

He is the answer through the ages.
He is the riposte to sages.
It's written on the Holy Pages.
THERE IS A WHY.

Two Fishes — Five Loaves — or Ten

Of course, you can't feed the five-thousand,
plus women and children, too!
The masses create a need so great —
and assets impossibly few.

Of course, you can't help all the hurting —
can't reach the scope of their need.
The world's so wide; time's not on your side.
Starvation grows faster than seed.

Of course, you can't reach all who're hungry
starving for God's gospel truth.
But God's on his throne. You don't act alone.
God's plan may prove much more profuse.

God gifted his children with talents:
some two, some five, even ten.
Invested they grow in abundance God shows.
The harvest's entrusted to him.

When children of God join together
seeding the hearts God prepares,
The yield multiplies in souls justified
Through talents invested with prayers.

Don't wilt at the size of the problem.
Don't say: "I would if I could".
The need, so large, is not *all* in your charge.
Just joyfully do what you should.

Of course, you can't feed the five-thousand.
And yet, consider again
the talents you have, and what if you gave
Two Fishes — Five Loaves — or Ten.

CIRSQUATRI" ™

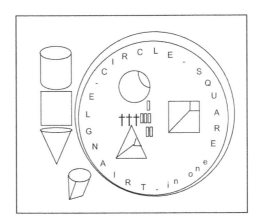

Imagine one solid object which is at the same time a circle, square & triangle. You can create it.

Obtain a one-inch dowel. Its end is a one-inch circle. Clamp the dowel securely. Mark a point exactly one inch from the end of the dowel precisely in the center looking straight down at it. Cut from the outside edge of circle on the far end, to the middle of the center mark you made on top of the dowel. Do the same to the other side. You see a 1" triangle. As you make the triangle cut, the piece falls from the dowel. The ends of the cut piece, together with the sides from the top of the triangle, form a 1" square.

Stand the piece on its circle. Position it as a **triangle**, turn the piece one-quarter turn. You see the **square**. (the extreme outside border only) Of course, the round end is a **circle**. I call it "Cirsquatri". Three-in-one is possible. For God to be a **three-in-one entity** is no problem.

Say the word "three". That word exists as a sound wave in the air that hits your inner ear, or no one would hear you say "three". The thought of "three" exists in your mind giving you the concept of three. Write on paper the word "three". "Three" is then a physical entity visible to your eye. As you write and speak it concurrently, "*Three*" is soundwave in air, concept in the brain, tangible expression on paper. Father is essence; Spirit is communication; Son is tangible. Another example is that objects consist of height, width, depth.

There Is a Glory
(Romans 8:18,21,28-30)

There is a glory – a Holy Glory,
Revealed in Jesus Christ the Lord.
All those who love him – who trust him solely,
Will to that glory be conformed.
(See 1 John 3:2)

For all things work together for good
To those who love the Lord.
All things work together for good
For those called by the Lord.

There is a Savior – a Holy Savior,
Fulfilled in Jesus Christ the Lord.
All who believe him -- all who receive him
Find grace, and peace with God restored.
(see John 1:12)

For all things work together for good
To those who love the Lord.
All things work together for good
For those called by the Lord.

There is a freedom – a holy freedom
Found in Jesus Christ the Lord.
Free to be near him, no longer fear him.
His light and truth our hearts transform.
(see John 8:32-36)

There is a city – a Holy City
Prepared by Jesus Christ the Lord.
Where all God's children, his reborn children,
Will live in glory with the Lord.
(see John 14:1-6).

For all things work together for good
To those who love the Lord.
All things work together for good

For those called by the Lord.

So, look up, so be encouraged.
There is hope in Jesus Christ the Lord.
For all things work together for good
To those who love the Lord.

This hope is an anchor in the rock,
This hope is a sure foundation,
For all things work together for good
To those who love the Lord.
For those called by the Lord.

(music for this song is in Music section)

The Enticement

Habitually sin in a secret place
Eventually sin most any place
Ultimately flaunt it every place

James 1: 13-15
When tempted, no one should say: I am tempted of God.
For God cannot be tempted with evil, nor does God tempt anyone.
Everyone is tempted when they are drawn away by their own lust, and
enticed. Then, when lust conceives, it produces sin; and sin, when it is
completed, ends in death. (paraphrased)

Seven of the Greatest Personal Prayers
to make my own, especially today:

"God, be merciful to me, a sinner."
The penitent prayer.

"God, grant me the serenity to accept the things
I cannot change, the courage to change the things
I can and should, and wisdom to know the difference."
Author: Reinhold Niebuhr

"Not my will but Thine be done."
As Jesus prayed.

"Lord, save me!" The Peter prayer.
The instantaneous prayer of Peter out walking the waves.
As he was approaching Jesus, the waves and thunder scared
the faith out of him, and he knew Jesus was his only hope.

"Lord, help my unbelief." Prayed by a man needing a miracle,
requesting the gift of more faith.

The reflex prayer.
The silent, instant, desperate, fearful prayer of Nehemiah
as he asked king Artaxerxes to help the Jews and Jerusalem.
Nehemiah 2:1-6. "Then I prayed to God and said to the king"
(v v4-5) We daily need reflex prayers.

My prayer of gratitude.
"God, our Heavenly Father, thank you for your salvation,
mercy, daily providential care, a loving family, and
opportunities to share with others your grace and blessings."

Inexhaustible God

When God gives, He is not diminished. God's ability to give is not lessened by his continual giving. God is the infinite, inexhaustible source of all that God is and of all that God created. Remember the small lunch that, in the hands of Jesus fed up to 15,000 people or more – and there were leftovers.

As a human example (that is beautiful yet paltry by comparison), when a new baby comes into a family, the family loves that new child, but does not love the previous children less. Love is not partitioned.

The love for the newborn does not take away from, or dilute, the love for the previously-born siblings.

Another inadequate example is that when you take a pail of water from the ocean and pour it on your brother asleep on the sand, you do not lower the sea level.

There is a song that says God owns the cattle on 1000 hills, the wealth in every mine…. While we understand the intent of those words, they are somewhat silly in any realistic comparison to God. God owns the entire universe — all of it. He spoke it into existence. He continues to own it all no matter what he gives to his creation, including what he gives to people. Whether tangible or intangible, God's resources cannot be diminished or diluted.

Truth is singular.
It is independent of opinion, belief or understanding.
Truth is not developed, it is discovered.
Line up with truth, and it will protect you.
Truth is not a respecter of persons.
Miss truth and it will crush you.
Consider carefully your appraisal of truth.

Jesus Knows

Through all kinds of circumstances,
Jesus reads the index of my mind.
Through all kinds of crucial stances,
Jesus knows the intents of my soul.
Through the grind of life enhancements,
Jesus works to see the gold refined.
Amidst well-bred, yet, lonely glances,
He melds the empty spaces to the whole.

Through the pangs of undanced dances,
Jesus is a friend who never fails.
Through faux smiles and joyless lapses,
Jesus proves a joy spring never dried.
Though we've failed in many labors,
Jesus is a friend who never quails.
Though we oft disrupt life's favors,
Jesus, faithful, stands strong by our side.

There's no set of circumstances
Jesus cannot bring peace to our soul.
In life's joys or hurtful crashes,
Jesus smiles or weeps to tend our needs.
His endless life, eternal joy,
Is the greatest hope, the highest goal.
We daily strive, without alloy,
To closely follow Jesus as he leads.

Difficult, the narrow way is — but
Easy going where the crowds run wild.
The allure of bright light fizzles
Once the price is spent, the music played.
Dissipation and frustration
Seep into our heart and work their guile.
Enticements turn to consternation.
Too late, we see the enemy arrayed.

Reality now jars our senses.
Different light now penetrates our mind.

233

Could it be that certain fences
Guide us where we truly wish to be?
Could it be that our Creator
Knows a better way than we might find?
A path that anyone would favor
If they saw the picture as God sees?

Walk away from lying wonders.
Walk into the way of hope and love.
Leave the life that blindly blunders
Chasing fleeting bubbles labeled fun.
Choose the life of God the Father:
Life on earth that's guided from above.
Here, we find there is no other
Life where certain vict'ry has been won.

Our eternal manufacturer,
Creator God, beyond all time and space;
Has not abandoned us, his creatures.
Gives prolific witness of his art.
The vast galactic symphony of stars.
The sensitive responses of our face.
The moral guilt we feel for unjust wars.
In the very longings of our heart.

Turn to Jesus, Lord and Savior.
Run from him no more in guilt or fear.
Reason says to turn and trust your
Everlasting soul to God, himself.
Jesus knows you: soul & heart & mind.
Still, he loves and seeks you year by year.
Turn from sin to Jesus where you'll find
True love, hope, joy: secure in God, himself.

In The Stable With Mary

Several days in the manger. It's a functional bed
To lay the Lord Jesus where the livestock were fed.

Brilliant stars fill the sky on a clear quiet night;
But the storm that blew through was a bit of a fright.

The cattle got anxious. Now the baby's awake.
He crying for changing his pants— goodness sake!

Today Joseph's working on a job to get by.
Baby Jesus is hungry. How loud he can cry!

I'll scatter fresh straw on the floor of our cave,
Knowing this Christ Child is the Savior God gave.

I love you, dear Jesus. You're my sweet baby boy.
When we move to a house, that will be a fresh joy.

The real Christmas story was no Hallmark dream.
Brutal reality was redemption's first scene.

The life of our Savior from birth to his death,
Though blessed with God's favor,
                          was reviled length and breadth.

The Great King of Heaven left his glory above.
The Creator of all, spurned by those whom he loved.

Born amidst squalor, he died cruelly for crime.
The crime not his own. He paid yours and mine.

Gift of God's Love
See Jesus

A long long time ago, 'Neath stars and moon aglow,
In far off Bethlehem the baby was born.
Angels came down, singing around, 'Tis Jesus Christ,
Gift of God's Love.

See Jesus, the way of truth. See Jesus, the way of life.
See Jesus Christ the Lord, King of kings.
 Leave his heavenly throne; Make earth his new home.
'Tis Jesus Christ, Gift of God's Love.

The blind he made to see. The lame to leap with glee.
All other ills were cured by the touch of his hand.
And even the dead to whom Jesus was led
Received new life when he spoke the command.

See Jesus, the way of truth. See Jesus, the way of life.
See Jesus Christ the Lord, King of kings.
Make everyone whole Who would give him control.
'Tis Jesus Christ, gift of God's Love.

But Jesus had come to die. The crowd cried crucify.
And on a cruel cross Jesus was hung.
Bearing our sin, the victory to win.
'Tis Jesus Christ, Gift of God's Love.

See Jesus, the way of truth. See Jesus, the way of life.
See Jesus Christ the Lord, King of kings.
Die on the tree. Pay sin's ransom for me.
'Tis Jesus Christ, Gift of God's Love.

The grave could not retain the body in it lain.
Jesus Christ arose just as he said.
The stone rolled away. He's living today,
And offers life to the living and dead.

See Jesus, the way of truth. See Jesus, the way of life.
See Jesus Christ the Lord, King of kings.

Alive evermore. To heaven the door.
'Tis Jesus Christ, Gift of God's Love.

Now, Jesus is coming soon – Morning, night, or noon.
In power to take his own to glory above.
Peace he will bring. Forever we'll sing,
'Tis Jesus Christ, Gift of God's Love.

See Jesus, the way of truth. See Jesus, the way of life.
See Jesus Christ the Lord, King of kings.
Coming again. The Hope of all men.
'Tis Jesus Christ, Gift of God's Love.

The soon-coming King. Forever we'll sing.
'Tis Jesus Christ, Gift of God's Love.

(can be sung to tune of Sloop John B)

*Leadership is like a **wagon** and a **curb**:*
You cannot push it up!
But you can pull it up,
***IF** YOU STEP UP FIRST.*

Gospel Dispersement

Sometimes our contribution is to drop a seed or pull a weed.
We don't see the fruit of our labor.
　　　　Not everyone works on the harvest team.
But there won't be a harvest without the dropped seed.
There won't be a harvest unless someone thwarts weeds.
There won't be a harvest if no one plows soil.
We each have a role in God's schedule of toil.

So, we drop a word here, a kind deed done there.
We offer a smile and intentional prayer.
We may never see the impact on a mind.
Or see the results of this or that kind.
Our satisfaction is merely in knowing
We obeyed God's nudge in our part of the sowing.

But we must DO our part in the process of sowing.
Each part is needed if the fruit will be showing.
Each part is integral to the Church on earth growing
And the work of the Spirit through Christ's body flowing.

Let's keep our eyes open, our ears keep alert.
So we don't miss the moment of our vital work.
Let's always be ready to react, or act first,
As God's Gospel message is freely dispersed.

Victory does not come by vowing to not sin.
Victory comes by relentlessly resisting the current enticement
while simultaneously obeying the quiet voice of the Holy Spirit.

TO FIX HUMPTY DUMPTY

When Sir Humpty Dumpty fell off the wall,
The king and his men could do nothing at all
To put him together again as before.
Some crashes are such they can't be restored.

We all fall in love and plan to stay in.
Like blue prints that fade, we fall out again.
We laugh and we smile as if wearing a mask.
We say, "Oh, I'm fine" when anyone asks.
But there's throbbing wounds beneath the veneer:
Regrets, empty feelings, and hidden tears.

Kids get new dads or else a new mom
To make a new family; but something seems wrong.
As if something's wedged in that doesn't belong,
Or something is missing that shouldn't be gone.
Like words we've forgotten to an old song,
You can't get them right, but the tune lingers on.

Broken hearts, broken families, never made whole
Though the hurts are concealed deep in the soul.
It wouldn't be right to try fixing the first
By breaking another, making sins worse.
The wisdom or power or cunning of men
Can never put Humpty together again.

But the Healer is coming, the Mender of souls,
Who makes hearts and hurts and homes again whole.
The Creator unbreaks, he remakes the broken.
Impossible possible, through his words spoken.
And throughout the eons where joys never end
His love will put Humpty together again.

RENEWING SHEEP

When the Shepherd went out in the dark and the cold,
    it wasn't in search of a wolf to convert.
He went to look for a sheep from his fold
    that strayed from him off the path, and was hurt.

The Shepherd, Creator, could rebuild a wolf
    remaking it into a genuine sheep.
The ninety and nine are delighted enough
    when a harvest of hungry wolves is reaped.

The converting of wolves reduces their pack
    making it safer for flocks as they sleep.
Converting fast wolves can fill up the lack
    created by missing, wandering sheep.

The ninety and nine have cause to rejoice
    each time an infamous wolf is reborn.
All singing in praise to the Lord in one voice
    when to Jesus a dangerous wolf is conformed.

But sometimes the ninety and nine can get callused
    over a lamb gone too often astray.
A sheepfold deserter is faced with malice
    who stubbornly choses to wander away.

And when he's brought back to the fold by the Lord,
    the ninety and nine can be judging and cold,
And show him less love than he found in the world
    while living in sin, lost from the fold.

But Jesus the Shepherd says, "Sing and be glad.
    I found my poor lamb at last, at great cost.
I seek to change wolves into sheep as I've planned,
    but I won't let a wayward sheep stay lost."

And still, we today show love that's intense
    when a sinner is saved – a wolf born again.
Let's also rejoice when a brother repents,
    forgive from the heart, and welcome back in.

Note: The below was / is a response to the previous poem.

WELCOMED BACK *

That sheep, welcomed back a long time ago,
Has proven contrition: I know it is so.
A friend like no other, he always has been,
Though he went off God's rails and fell into sin.

That sheep has repented, and God in His grace
Has forgiven his sin and removed his disgrace.
To his family and friends, he's become a model
Of a servant of God that sin couldn't hobble.

The wolf that he was when blinded by lust;
Transformed to a sheep, honest and just;
His God-given gifts, discernment and power,
Being used once again to make Satan cower.

The legacy he leaves for his family and friends,
Is of a servant restored and faithful again;
The sins of yore are permanently past,
The friendship we share will continually last.

God has been gracious to grant us long life,
And fellowship free from envy and strife.
It's said, "one person sharpens another."
That's how it's been, Jim, for you're like a brother.
(Prov. 27:17)

    * *by Dr. David R Nicholas, President*
    Shasta Bible College & Graduate School.
    We've been friends since our youth.

I'll Follow You Sometime

We sing: "Jesus, I love you, I know you are mine."
But live like that love is in frequent decline.
We'll follow our vow some convenient time.

We sing: "All the follies of sin I resign."
But sample the follies of sin on Prime Time,
Excusing the lust of our eyes after nine.

We sing: "Burn out the dross, my gold to refine."
But we don't bear the cross after church meeting time.
The meaning of gold seems to change as we dine.

We sing: "Not my will, but your will is mine."
Then live however our glands are inclined.
Vows overruled by sins flooding our mind.

Just now I'm convicted that favorite sins,
Stored here in my memory to replay again,
Too easily are called on, then, invited in.

So, once we arrive at that great Pearly Gate,
When the Judge has rewards for the fruit of the saints,
We'll be humbled by mercy when told what awaits.

It's only God's grace that any are saved.
I'm grateful, so grateful my pardon is paid.
Without the Great Savior my hope would be grave.

Satan, the Liar, says:

No one will ever know.

What happens in LV, or _____ , stays in LV.

I'm a government official here to help.

There is a free lunch.

It's only a temporary tax.

You will win gambling.

Calories don't count on Christmas, Thanksgiving,
    birthdays, anniversaries.

I can handle my alcohol.

That person would make me so happy.

Society owes you care & contentment.

There is no God except you yourself.

If it looks good, feels good, tastes good; then it is good.
    It feels so right, it can't be wrong.

You don't owe anybody anything.

Nothing plus time and chance equals everything
    without a cause.

You can do whatever your heart desires.

If you do what seems best to you, you can't go wrong.

Consequences are thrills without ills.

Truth & Reality say:

Temptation is deceitful, overstated fantasy where you
    cannot choose the outcome.

There will be an accounting.

Ecclesiastes 11:9. Live it up. Do anything your heart desires.
    Do whatever it takes to be happy. Live for the thrills.
    But know this: for all you say and do,
    God will bring you into judgment.
    (my paraphrase)

Proverbs 14:12. There is a life that seems right to many,
    but its destination is eternal death.
    (my paraphrase)

Life's Regrets come from believing, & acting upon, Satan's lies.

In infinite contrast, Jesus says:
John 14: 6. I am the way, the truth, the life.
No one comes to the Father except through me.
John 10:10. The lying thief comes to steal, to kill, to destroy.
I have come to bring life: a life that is more abundant.
John 3:16, 36. God loves the world (people) to such a degree
that he gave his only begotten son that whoever believes in him
will not perish in eternal death but will have eternal life.
One who believes on the son has everlasting life.
One who does not believe on the son shall not see eternal life,
but the judgment of God awaits him.
John 1:12. To all who receive him, he gives the power to
become children of God; yes, to those who believe on him.
       (my paraphrase)

Next time, I'll tell you the story of this nautical mission to Catalina Island, 26 miles across the sea from Long Beach, CA. The Old Timer and 25 of us. Probably, you could no longer find the story in the LA newspaper.

THE LEGACY OF JESUS

Before Jesus finished our atonement, he extended forgiveness to his executioners. All that he owned on earth, his clothing, went to Roman soldiers. He granted an immediate place in Paradise to the criminal crucified beside him. He assigned care of his mother to John.

Then, on that cross of execution, he took upon himself the sins and guilt of the world for whom he died. He became sin for us. As he paid the ultimate penalty for our sins, he was forsaken by God the Father. Forsaken, until he cried out in a loud voice: IT IS FINISHED, and gave up his life.

With the sin debt paid, redemption accomplished, he conveyed his spirit to his Father. "Into your hands I commit my spirit." He relinquished his body to Joseph of Arimathea and Nicodemus for burial before Sabbath day began, where his body awaited resurrection on Sunday.

In a different gifting to his disciples, and by extension to those who believe in Jesus through their testimony, he bequeathed his love, peace, presence, and the power to carry out the mission he assigned: preach the gospel to every creature. In addition, Jesus pledged to return to gather his own to himself for eternity.

Even Jesus took nothing material with him when he ascended into heaven. It is only people, humans, whom Jesus promises to take to the place he is preparing. Similarly, it is only persons, individuals, that we can, through Jesus, take with us to glory. That is where our intent should focus: people and paradise. Jesus is the only one who has Paradise and has the power to bring people there to himself. What is your relationship with Jesus? Have you received his gifts?

ABOUT GOD AND YOU

the fact

God loves you, wants you in His family, and can give you eternal life.

the problem

Sin has separated you from God, from God's love and from His purpose for your life.

the solution

Jesus paid the sin penalty. He can recuse you from condemnation, put you in God's family, and can give you God's life now on earth and forever in heaven.

the method

Faith secures the benefit from the solution. Believe in Jesus. Believe His death and resurrection resolved the sin problem. Believe He has eternal life for you starting right now. Believe He has a plan for your life. Fully trust Jesus as your only Savior and Lord.

the means

Right now, by faith, sincerely make this prayer your prayer to God: "God, I know I'm a sinner. I believe Jesus died for my sins, and is alive from death to give me eternal life. I receive Jesus as my personal savior, and as Lord of my new life. I believe that my sins are forgiven, that I have eternal life in Jesus, and that I am now a member of God's family, and that heaven is my eternal home. Thank You, God."

the follow-through

Read The Bible over and over. Begin with the Gospel of John; then read 1 John. Go regularly to a good church group that teaches the Bible.
Develop friendships with solid Christians. Pray often. Share your faith.

One Solitary Life

(author unknown, public domain)

Here is a man who was born in an obscure village, the child of a peasant woman. He grew up in a carpenter shop until He was thirty, and then for three years He was an itinerant preacher.

He never wrote a book, never held office, never owned a home, never went to college, never put His foot inside a big city, never traveled 200 miles from the place of His birth. He never did one of the things that usually accompany greatness, and had no credentials but Himself.

While He was still a young man, the tide of public opinion turned against Him. His friends ran away. He was turned over to His enemies and went through the mockery of a trial.

He was nailed to a cross between two thieves. While He was dying, His executioners gambled for the only piece of property He had on earth -- His coat. When He was dead, He was laid in a borrowed grave through the pity of a friend.

Twenty centuries have passed, and today He is the central figure of the human race and the leader of the column of progress. I am far within the mark when I say that, all the armies that ever marched, all the navies that ever sailed, all the parliaments that ever sat, and all the kings that have ever reigned, put together, have not affected the life of mankind upon this earth as has that One Solitary Life.

THE CONSEQUENCES OF BELIEVING THAT
FORGIVENESS IS NECESSARY

The idea of **forgiveness** inherently, by definition, **requires** that something **needs** to be forgiven.

For something (an act or a thought) **needing** to be forgiven requires that some **offense** was committed.

For such an act or thought to **require** forgiveness, **demands** that the one who ought to forgive was in a legal and moral sense **actually offended** or violated by the one to be forgiven.

For an **offense** to be committed, a **standard** or rule must be **in place** which is recognized by **both** parties involved.

Such a known rule **cannot be** merely an **opinion** or a preference, or no forgiveness would be necessary just because the other party had a differing opinion or preference. (No offense is committed requiring forgiveness just because I serve coffee and you prefer tea. Yet, if I serve tea as you prefer, but include cyanide, now I have offended whether or not you or anyone else catches me.)

That **violated standard or rule** must be **higher than** – above and controlling of – **both** parties involved. If it were not so, then the *offending* party would merely say "I didn't break any rule that I acknowledge" and / or the *offended* party would say "I was not offended."

Yet, it is **admitted** and stated that **forgiveness** is **necessary**. (Few deny forgiveness is often needed.)

Therefore, **there is such** a higher standard or rule in existence that both parties admit is there, and to which they acknowledge fealty and accountability.

Such a higher standard or rule must **come from a superior standard maker** or superior rule generator.

For such a higher authority to make such standards and rules, it must be **able to think** and **evaluate** and have **purpose**.

The only source of such things in our experience is a **mind** – a **superior mind** compared to parties involved in forgiveness issues.

The only such standard-setting-mind in our experience comes from a **personal being** – in this case a **superior** personal being. This superior being is God.

Taken to its logical conclusion, understanding **that forgiveness is necessary**, leads one to God.

Since God is the Ultimate Standard-Maker, He is the only one who can ultimately forgive. People who forgive offenses against them personally are only able to give their own personal, finite forgiveness.

The great news is that the Ultimate Standard-Maker is also the Ultimate Sin-bearer. God the Son became a man in order to be able to take upon himself the consequences of mankind's guilt; pay on our behalf the infinite penalty for our breaking His standard; come back to life in order to give His eternal life to those of us who will freely receive Him in faith, believe Him, and accept his forgiveness and grace and Lordship.
Bible record: Luke 5: 15-26

Those who work evil
    love darkness and hate light and truth.
Those who work good
    hate darkness and love light and truth.

COMING HOME

It was early nineteen hundreds, before trans-ocean flights.
Teddy Roosevelt, from hunting, was sailing home this night.
After two weeks on safari, killing African wild beasts,
He's on board a luxury liner with music, wine and feasts.

On the same trans-ocean liner, but several decks below,
Stood a missionary couple list'ning to the fog horn blow.
Thirty years they gave in service, taking health and hope abroad.
As a doctor and a nurse, they had pledged their lives to God.

As the ship docked New York Harbor, there arose a happy cheer
From the several thousand people come to greet the liner here.
Throngs of celebrating fans were shouting Roosevelt's acclaim.
None were there to greet the medics. No one even knew their name.

As they held each other closely to fight the chill and damp,
The man turned to his wife, cleared his throat, and softly asked,
"How is it that the President, just home from two weeks hunting,
Is given such a welcome, while none cheers our arriving?

"We've sacrificed careers to helping needy people live.
We left our home and families -- gave all there is to give.
But there's no one here to meet us – no one here that cares.
They celebrate the hunter, but not the ones who shared."

Said his wife, "I have the answer. These cheers are his reward.
But ours is living people. Our praise is from the Lord.
We can't be disappointed. Of course, we're here alone.
In this world we are just travelers. We are not yet home."

TWO EXIT PATHS

For a child of God, two Paths exit the dark valley of the shadow of death—the valley of Psalm 23. One is an earthly exit; one is a heavenly exit. For those who are not in God's family, there is a third exit: an exit to separation from God and his love forever. That exit leads to the "second death". That exit is not under discussion here except for this caution and encouragement: join the family of God now to avoid this third exit.

The Valley of the Shadow of Death is real, is dismal, and is experienced several times on earth. However, there is always an exit. When a person is a sheep of God's flock, both paths that emerge from below the shadow of death are traversed in the appointed time under the leading of the Good Shepherd. Both paths lead out of the grayness, discomfort, and questioning which is the shadow. Both paths lead to confidence, blessing, and peace. Both paths are on the ascent.

One Familiar trail leads God's sheep up out of the valley to meadows where there are green pastures, and paths of righteousness, and a welcomed refuge to lie down in rest. Where there are still waters and an overflowing cup. Where there is a table prepared, and oil for anointing one's wounds. Where tested, questioning souls are restored. Where the shepherd's rod and staff bring rescue and comfort from danger and evil lurking in earthly environs. Many sheep walk this trail several times, each of varied intensity.

One Unfamiliar trail leads out of the valley into the scenes of heaven. Into the presence of the glory of the Great Creator, God the Son, the eternal Shepherd. A sheep traverses this trail only once, but to a sheep in the flock of the Lord it is safely traveled with divine, loving companionship. At the destination of this path there is no further evil, no pain, no more shadow, separation, sorrow or death. There is reunion with the other sheep who previously walked this paradise trail. There is delight in the glory of the Lord. It is a destination of eternal joy.

Yes, for the Christian, there are two paths that emerge from the valley of the shadow of death. One that leads direct to heaven, and one that remains on earth for a while. For the child of God through Jesus Christ, there is comfort, companionship and consolation along both pathways.

Weaver of Light

There's a man we know as Jesus who works light upon a loom.
It's the very same man, Jesus, who arose from out the tomb.
He's sewing seams with glowing threads as he weaves and tailors light,
Making glistening Gowns of Glory, making robes of brilliant white.
He will cloth us in his glory when we reach our heavenly home.
He'll prepare us for his presence as we gather 'round His Throne.

Jesus was transfigured before them, and his face shown as the sun, and his garment became white as the light.   Matthew 17:2

Believers, now we are the children of God. We don't know what we shall be. But we know that, when he appears, we will be like him, for we shall see him as he is. 1 John 3:2

The Apostle John reports in Revelation 1: 12-18: I saw Jesus, clothed in a garment and wearing a golden belt. His head and hair were white as wool, as white as snow. His eyes were like a flame of fire. His feet were like fine brass, brilliant as if refined in a furnace. His voice was as the sound of many waters. In his right hand he held seven stars. His speech was as a sharp double-edged sword. His face was as the sun shining in full strength. As I saw him, I fell at his feet as dead. But he took me by his right hand, saying: "Do not be afraid. I am the first and the last. I am he who lives, who was dead, and am alive forevermore. I have authority over death.

In John 17 (read the entire chapter to get the context), Jesus says of those who believe in him: I give to them my glory.
(the above scriptures are paraphrased)

BUILDING MANSIONS SIDE BY SIDE

My daddy was a carpenter and built a lot of homes.
At night he liked to play guitar: put music to his poems.
He taught me to be happy and to make of life a quest,
To always be a Christian and always do my best.

Daddy took me by the arm and led me down the aisle.
The people and the preacher saw daddy's tears and smile.
He told me and my husband we'd never be alone
With marriage blessed by Jesus as we built a Christian home.

Daddy took me by the hand and he began to cry.
Said that he was mighty sick and prob'ly soon would die.
He said that he would miss me, and that he loved me so,
That 'till we all would join him, he'd watch the grandkids grow.

He said Jesus was a carpenter and promised us a home.
That Jesus must be busy getting all the building done.
With the millions of believers needing mansions up above
He'd ask if he could help construct those houses made of love.

My daddy said that he would ask if he could build our place.
I imagine dad and Jesus would make it some show place.
Dad said he wasn't worthy, but it fills my heart with pride
To imagine dad and Jesus building mansions side by side.

Working side by side with Jesus, building mansions in the sky.
My daddy got promoted, he really didn't die.

My daddy was a carpenter and build a lot of homes.
At night he liked to play guitar: put music to his poems.
He taught me to be happy and to make of life a quest,
To always be a Christian and always do my best.

Christ Tapped Me on the Shoulder

Bob Phillips, a college friend, whom I have not seen or talked to in about 30 years since visiting together at Hume Lake Christian Camp in CA where Bob was a past Director. In college, Bob gave me a powerful book by Vance Havner, which I still have, and have read more than once. Bob also gave his testimony in meetings in which we were both involved, and because of that, he has spoken to my heart through the years, though he is totally unaware. Bob is one reason I like to put ideas into rhyme, for poetry helps my recall. Bob gave a poem in his testimony which I have never written down until now, but which clings to my soul. He said it was his life story, but in some belated ways, it is also mine. Thanks Bob. I hope you don't mind my sharing your poem as best I can remember it.

Christ tapped me on the shoulder once when I was young and free.
All He said was, "Son, you'd better follow after me."
I knew I should but I had plans to strike out on my own.
I felt that I could travel best if I went on alone.

Christ tapped me on the shoulder next in 1958.
All He said was, "Better come, the hour's getting late."
But I was young and, in my glance, I knew that He could see
a look that said, "I have no need to follow after Thee."
There were many reasons He might have simply passed me by.
Instead He smiled and I could see compassion in His eye.

Christ tapped me on the shoulder next when all my dreams were gone.
There was but kindness in His voice, He simply said, "Come on."

Christ taps me on the shoulder now a hundred times a day.
Again, He's proved the joy that comes to those who walk His way.
To all these things I testify that all who hear may know
how glad I am when once He called I had the sense to go.

BE FOUND FAITHFUL
Encouraging Each Other

May we be found faithful as the children of the Lord.
Pleasing God as family, all nudged in one accord.
Encouraging each other in our stressful daily lives.
More and more as evil days impose deceitful lies.

God, help us to be faithful when convenient or ill-timed.
When faithfulness is popular or constantly maligned.
Whether it is lucrative or a financial loss.
Whether done with pleasure or a duty-hoisted cross.

May we support each other in the service of the King.
By living and by telling, the gospel message bring.
May our favored hymns express our prayers and heart-felt goals.
May the peace of God within us be a guardian of our souls.

When God's family is together — a gathering of his church —
Delighting in his presence, we taste of heaven on earth.
The lifting of our spirit as we gaze on God above
Revealed in Jesus Christ the Lord and his undying love.

"May we be Found Faithful" is our theme in daily living.
The underlying message of our reading and our singing.
The overlying love we share, the spirit in our hearts,
To buoy us through the tides of life the days we are apart.

We can only be found faithful by the strength of God within
As we look upon his promises above the lure of sin.
Trusting in his guidance and his peace within our heart,
Faithfulness will be our theme to treasure and impart.

SECTION FIVE

5 MUSIC

EIGHT SONGS WITH SHEET MUSIC

There Is a Glory

Today You'll Be in Paradise

My Confession

May Her Day be Beautiful

A Baby's Lullaby

There Is One God

Beautiful Angel

Poor Child's Christmas Prayer

About the Author

There Is a Glory

J Joy

1- There is a glo - ry, a ho - ly glo - ry, re - vealed in Je - sus Christ the
2- sa - vior, a ho - ly sa - vior, ful - filled in Je - sus Christ the

Lord. And all God's child-ren, who trust him sole-ly, will to that glo - ry be con-
Lord. All who re - ceive him, all who be - lieve him find grace and peace with God re -

-formed. For, all things work to - geth - er for good to those who love the Lord. Yes,
-stored.

all things work to-geth-er for good to those called by th-e Lord. There is a | Lord. There is a

free-dom, a ho - ly free - dom, found in Je - sus Christ the Lo-rd.

There is a ci - ty, a ho - ly ci - ty, pre - pared by Je - sus Christ the

James E Foy

Today In Paradise

-giv-en and your par-don has been read. So, you'll be with me in heav - en, no mat-ter
-giv-en and your par-don has been read. So, you'll be with me in heav - en, no mat-ter

what the mock-ers said. You can't be held by Ro-man spikes, no more fear and no more
what the doubt-ers said. You can't be held by cancelled vice, no more fear and no more

dread. To-day you'll be with me in par-a-dise be-fore the guards con-firm you're dead. To-day you'll
dread. One-day you'll be with me in par-a-dise. Keep trust-ing what my prom-ise said. One-day you'll

be with me in par-a-dise be-fore the guards con-firm you're dead.
be with me in par-a-dise. Keep trust-ing what my prom-ise said.

2

May Her Day Be Beautiful

1- When I wake up in the morn-ing and see her ly-ing there, her eyes still closed a-gainst the light of dawn. Al-though I would-n't wake her, I light-ly touch her hair And watch the rise and fall of lace that she has on. Lord, keep her sweet breath com-ing, her pure heart beat-ing strong, pro-tect her from all ev-il and from ev-'ry kind of harm. And may her day be beau-ti-ful as mine will be for me, be-cause I held her close this morn-ing in my arms.

2- When I walk each day be-side her, I'm hap-py I'm not free. She has a ra-diant beau-ty in the sun. I've seen the hid-den splen-der, and know the ec-sta-sy. The web we wove and held to-geth-er glist-ens on. Lord, keep her sweet breath com-ing, her pure heart beat-ing strong, pro-tect her from all ev-il and from ev-'ry kind of harm. And may her way be beau-ti-ful as mine will be for me, be-cause she walks to-day be-side me arm in arm.

3- When I lay down in the ev'-ning, I know things are al-right, be-cause we'll be to-geth-er through the night. When moon-beams through the win-dow cast ha-los 'round her face, I know God loaned to me an an-gel in this place. Lord, keep her sweet breath com-ing, her pure heart beat-ing strong, pro-tect her from all ev-il and from ev-'ry kind of harm. And may her rest be beau-ti-ful as mine will be for me, be-cause I held her sleep-ing safe-ly in my arms.

There Is One God

J Foy

1- There is one God, and he is right - ous. There is one God, and he is
2- There is one God, and he is ho - ly. There is one God, and he is
3- There is one God. He is all - know - ing. There is one God, and he is
4- There is one God, and he is lov - ing. There is one God, and we be-

jus- tice. We praise your name that you have paid our ran - som. Oh, just and
mer-cy. We praise your name that we have been for - giv - en. Oh, ho - ly,
with us. We praise your name, your pow -er, and your wis - dom. Oh, wise and
-lieve him. We praise your name, we have a home in hea - ven. Oh, lov - ing

par - d'ning God, we come to you as child - ren.
mi - ghty God, we come to you as child - ren.
pre- sent God, we come to you as child - ren.
Fa - ther God, we come to you as child - ren.

Beautiful Angel
(Two Dreams Together)

Jim Foy

1- He said: "I'm no an- gel.   I'm on-ly a man.   I on-ly can give you the
2- said: "It's a plea-sure   just see-ing your smile. But there's no way to mea-sure what I
3- said: "We both real- ize   there's no end-less bliss. There's no per-fect day dream -- life as

best that I am.   I could ne-ver be per-fect,   but would al-ways be true. And
find all the while   that I'm try-ing to please you --   to give you first place -- the
one end-less kiss.   But in life as it takes us,   when we're up, when we're down, I will

al-ways be grate-ful   for an an-gel like you."
fab-u-lous trea-sure   that I see in your face."
try to be wor-thy   of the an-gel I've found."

female solo

"I've been called an an-gel   by oth-ers", she said. "But I hope that the say-ing has-n't
"You do bring me plea-sure   and hap-pi-ness, too. But my real last-ing trea-sure is just
"I'm not think-ing of 'wor-thy',   I'm think-ing of gifts. As we both go on giv-ing our

gone to my head.   If I could be an an-gel,   if good dreams come true; I'd
be-ing with you.   You say I'm a an-gel.   In the life we'll ex-plore, what you'll
hearts just like this.   I will give all I am, and   you give all to me. As we

give all my heart, Love.   to a man such as you."
get from this an-gel,   is for-e-ver-more."
live for each oth-er,   the dream comes to be.

DUET

Then, this beau-ti-ful an-gel   and this hea-ven blest man. Such re-gu-lar peo-ple.
Then, this beau-ti-ful an-gel   and this hea-ven blest man. Such re-gu-lar peo-ple.
Then, this beau-ti-ful an-gel   and this hea-ven blest man. Such re-gu-lar peo-

1

Poor Child's Christmas Prayer

cost of things so out of touch, Please, if there's a way would you help him. find a

gift that is-n't too much. And, Lord, help mom-my and dad-dy to know how

much they are loved. And, I'll need help to feel real-ly I don't need a gift more than

love. And thank you for par-ents who've shown me that though we've been

poor here on earth, we've a man-sion with you up in hea-ven

'cause of Christ-mas and our Sav-ior's birth

James E Foy

ABOUT THE AUTHOR

JIM FOY has three daughters, fifteen grandkids, more than that greats and still more by the time this book is in your hand. He was third born in a family of eight children. A believer, a voter, an American, a writer, a speaker, and somewhat shy. Jim believes the Bible, enjoys philosophy, likes pickleball, appreciates beauty and travel. He was quite active in Toastmasters in the 1990s, and earned the right to be one out of nine speakers chosen worldwide to speak at the International Convention. Some of the material herein is taken from speeches made back then. He also has spoken primarily to youth in the 1960s at such venues as Youth for Christ and Young Life.

Jim has made more than enough mistakes in life, and, hopefully, learned from them. Jim is grateful for genuine forgiveness. He believes in eternal truth, and that it is our responsibility to discover and honor truth. He has written songs not included in this book and has written other books.

Jim is a survivor of being kicked squarely in the chest by the two hoofs of a horse he tried to mount vaulting upon from behind as seen in old Western movies. Had his wife, Nancy, not been there to beat the air back into his lungs, this book would not be in your hands. He also, forty years later, survived an upper aortic aneurysm discovered accidentally when physicians scanned the scar tissue from that old chest injury. At that time, four clogged arteries were also discovered which required four bypasses. So, he's grateful for that horse's kick.

Jim says: "My daughters have heard and read my thoughts their entire lives. If you know my daughters, and if what they heard from me had any impact upon them and their children, then it's not dangerous to read this book. The lives of my children indicate it could be beneficial. You will probably find it entertaining, stretching, and interesting. You'll almost certainly find some fresh approaches to life, romance, and real religion. You might be stimulated to discuss thoughts herein with others. There is true love, true religion, and true truth. I trust this book is a prism to unveil new ways to discover truth – beautiful ways. It is old truth seen from a different angle, focused on different facets, and, I hope, expressed enjoyably."

James E Foy

Made in the USA
Coppell, TX
04 December 2022

87848603R10164